Blind
Shady
Bend

Blind Shady Bend

a novel by

Adina Sara

REGENT PRESS

Berkeley, California

Copyright © 2015 by Adina Sara

[paperback]
ISBN 13: 978-1-58790-328-1
ISBN 10: 1-58790-328-8

[e-book]
ISBN 13: 978-1-58790-329-8
ISBN 10: 1-58790-329-6

Library of Congress Catalog Number: 2015942448

Manufactured in the U.S.A.
REGENT PRESS
Berkeley, California
www.regentpress.net

in memory of Arlene,
who once took me down a dusty old road
called Blind Shady

Fall

1.

I CAN'T SAY HOW LONG I'd been sitting there, plopped in the middle of my front room floor and wedged between too many damned throw pillows, when I heard the knock. My tea had become cold, I know that much. My morning ritual, sipping a steaming cup of Lapsang Souchong, black smoky leaves brewed to death, gives me the kick I need to start my day. I like to take it over to the armchair where I get a decent view of the goings on around the neighborhood, meager as they are.

But I was tripped up that particular morning on my way to opening the front curtains. I think it must have happened when I leaned over to pick up a pillow, that maroon and gold one, made in India with glassy beads that were quite lovely until Amos discovered he could paw them loose and swat them around like shiny dead bees. What used to be iridescent flaps of shine were now a mangled bunch of loose hanging threads.

Mother always had this ridiculous penchant for throw pillows and I hated them back then, hated having to push them aside every time I sat down and then prop them back up in fluffed up groups of three, she insisted on three. How I came to replicate that frivolous decorating twitch I will never know.

I think what I did was set the mug down to pick the pillow up, and next thing I knew I was on the floor, legs splayed wide like a school kid, noticing all kinds of things you usually can't see when upright. Dust balls beneath the sofa, that dark green hooked rug (another one of Mother's specials), looking more like chartreuse with the field of yellow cat hairs covering it. I could see water stains beneath the flowerpots proving I did tend to them every once in a while. How did I ever end up with so many God-damned African Violets?

At first I didn't think it was a knock. Sounded more like the wind hitting the fuchsia limb against the side of the house. But no, there it was again, louder this time and I supposed I'd better hoist myself up.

"Coming," I called, but I really had no desire to move. My age has been gaining on me lately, occasionally edging out in front. Next year this time I'll be hitting 70. Now how the hell did that happen? It's just a number, people say, at least the old ones do, but I just as soon not think about it. Anyhow, I kind of liked it down there on the floor. From that vantage point, I was able to notice a thin slip of morning light cross the room, landing first on a spider web suspended between the curtain rod and door frame, then moving down to spark the silver buttons of my slipper toes, finally catching the satiny blue edge of my tablecloth. I was having a fine time really, nowhere particular to go today and no great reason to raise myself up to standing.

Just then I became aware of Amos's litter box, stationed at a particularly unfortunate angle, kitty-corner as it were, from my mid-floor position. Some brief movement of air must have carried its putrid aroma directly my way.

"Coming" I yelled again, grabbing the leg of the sofa for leverage, pulling myself to where I could gather the strength to stand. My sweater had slipped off somewhere during the mid-morning slump and a thin string of spittle had slid down the side of my mouth, moistening the inside of my ear. I don't want to think about what I looked like.

It was the Fed Ex man, holding out a registered letter like it carried something contagious. With finger pointed, he instructed me to sign at the X. I pulled my sweater back over my housecoat but his eyes never left the envelope. I could have been wearing nothing for all he cared. I signed where indicated and before I could so much as say thank you, he was already back in his truck, gears grinding and off he went.

I moved slowly to the kitchen table. Who sends me registered letters? I didn't even get much in the way of regular mail. Bills, catalogues, more bills, the church bulletin. I've asked them to take me off their list but it does no good. People don't come by here much, other than the meter reader, Wilbur every other week to trim the hedges, and Haley across the street whenever she's locked herself out. I keep her extra key, that's all. And once in a while I pour her a cup of tea because when she locks herself out it usually means she's been fighting with her husband and needs to talk. I don't mind Haley's chatter because she doesn't go on too long, just needs to air a few sharp words about him, reminding me again that I was better off without one.

I kept fingering the envelope, felt its thickness, not wanting to open it. I decided that a letter of this nature called for Pa's ivory handled letter opener, the one with foreign lettering on the side, Arabic or Chinese maybe. I didn't keep many of his things but for some reason I couldn't throw this one out. I vaguely remember that it was connected with one of his war stories. That and his ivory carved pipe, shaped like a skull with the lip broken off, were about all I had left of him, which was more than enough.

The envelope opened in one slick slice. A flurry of business cards spilled out first—a realty office, Department of County Records, an attorney. I had to pull on the thick document to get it free.

"In re the Estate of Raymond Edmond Blackwell...." I read the title once, then again, and on the third time, my hands began to shake so hard I had to set the paper down to steady myself.

It was a simple, straightforward legal document. "Raymond Edmond Blackwell hereby bequeaths his entire estate to his only sister, Hannah Mavis Blackwell. Said estate consists of five acres of real property, Parcel 671386, located in an unincorporated area of Nevada County, State of California."

I reread the pages, about five in all, lots of legal jargon I couldn't make out, mainly because wet splotches from my eyes smudged all the words into nonsense. I read from top to bottom, the law firm title, the court, case number 02673B, I read Ray's name and then read it again aloud because I hadn't heard it spoken for so long, because for so long I had avoided the mere sound of it.

I turned back to page one again, read "In re the Estate of…" out loud, slower this time, thinking it might help slow down my heart a bit, breathing hard, I closed my eyes to try and picture him, with his crazy hair flopped over his eyes, my baby brother gone, this time for good.

The doors to Hanover Combs and Greer were heavy, and I wasn't too eager to enter, so I waited outside the front door until someone on the inside pushed through, allowing me to scoot inside. I kept my hands clasped tightly on my handbag, but that didn't stop the whiff of mothballs and spearmint from breaking loose. It was a stupid little accessory, designed to hold a lipstick and hankie and not much else. Picked it up for cheap at the church bazaar because someone told me they came in handy. Never needed it until now. I just toss my things into a zippered knapsack and go on my way. But the embossed stationery seemed to call for the navy blue suit and gold clasped handbag and I rose to the occasion. Why on earth I kept the navy blue suit I'll never know. I bought it for Ned's funeral and it still fits, believe it or not. That blue suit and a strand of pearls (not real pearls but pearls enough) and this silly handbag made me feel like someone who belonged in a fancy waiting room like Hanover Combs and Greer LLP. I even used the occasion to swipe on a streak of Radiant Rose, what was left in the tube, careful not to draw it over my lip like I see on so many old women who are too nearsighted to aim right.

Ernest Combs was close to my age, which calmed me somewhat, but not quite up to my height or girth. To think that silver embossed stationery and those snazzy waiting room chairs announced this sprite of a man. I tried not to chuckle, but it came out anyway, disguised as a weak re-arrangement of throat phlegm. He didn't seem to notice.

"Have a seat," he offered, and so I did, on the far side of a greatly oversized desk that made the man appear even smaller.

"I trust you understand the terms of this document," Mr. Combs began, wasting no time.

"Ray died." It was a foolish obvious thing to say but it was all I could think of. "Do you know how it happened?"

"I was informed that he had been in a motorcycle accident on Highway 49. According to the report, he ran into a truck. The police traced him to our firm. I never met your brother but his file was in our office, along with your name as beneficiary. I am sorry to be the one to tell you. I assumed you were aware of the cause of your brother's death."

"Kleenex?" offered Mr. Combs, pushing a box of tissues toward me.

"I didn't know" was all I could say, "I just didn't know."

Mr. Combs handed me his business card along with

a thicket of papers decorated with yellow flags flapping "sign here, sign here." He handed me a packet of business cards—realtors, appraisers, bank managers—all of whom I would need to contact "ASAP," he instructed, like I was in some kind of trouble.

Maybe it was because I was still crying, or maybe the business part was over, but Mr. Combs' voice had changed. He walked over to my chair and laid a hand on my shoulder.

"These affairs take some time to sort through," he said, so softly I almost couldn't hear him.

I reached around the chair for my coat but was incapable of finding the sleeve of my jacket, poking my arm wildly into the open air and missing the garment altogether. I took one last noisy blow into the tissue and was glad to let him help me out of the chair and escort me to the door.

Somehow I made it back to my car, clutching the proof of my brother's death against my chest. I barely recall the drive home. As soon as I walked into my house, I started pulling out desk drawers, rifling through book shelves, looking for something, I couldn't say what. I found papers I didn't know I had, piles of old documents tucked deep inside the old metal file cabinet in the garage, stuff Pa told me to hold on to. Faded bank statements and wadded up wet Kleenexes slid off the table and Amos shredded them like we were having a party. I felt a burning in my chest, brewed myself some chamomile but it didn't help a bit. Shock, I think is what people call it.

Maybe I ought to just go see the place. Take a look around this unincorporated area of Nevada County, wherever that is, a ways past Lake Wildwood, where we used to go on vacations, not so far. All these years, I figured Ray for India or some south sea island or dead, long past dead, not living just up the highway. Why didn't he call? Why didn't he just call?

Those questions fell heavy and thick and required another long loud sip of chamomile. Don't think about him, I kept saying to myself. You just came into a piece of land. Think about that.

A few of the business cards the lawyer gave me had landed among the papers on the floor. A bright yellow one with thick black lettering lay just scant inches from Amos's paw. I wiped away a clump of wet kibble that covered the name. *Lucky Lundale Realty — I can make your dreams come true.* Fat chance of that. I couldn't remember the last time I'd had a decent dream.

2.

NOBODY KNEW REAL ESTATE along San Juan Ridge like George Lundale. He opened Lucky Realty back in the seventies, when just about anyone could afford the flat prices. The Ridge was one of the least populated stretches in an area of sinewy terrain edged by tributaries and streams skirting the great Sierra Nevada mountain range. Thick with history from the gold rush days, even now, over a hundred years later, occasional flashes of gold specks found their way into the few tourist shops that lined what was left of Main Street.

The flower children who had grazed these hills back in the sixties had all but gone to seed, moving on to more realistic pursuits. The new generation was not so enamored of twisted old roads, contaminated wells and busted propane tanks. People had recently begun to migrate to neighboring valleys where brand new highway exits spilled onto asphalt-glazed strip malls and rectangles of houses in lusterless neutral shades sprouted clean and dull on either side of the highway. People wanted flat surfaces, quick, clean and ready-made.

By the mid-90's property values had sunk, jobs were nowhere to be found, and San Juan Ridge settled into a kind of dull ash, having long ago lost its place in history.

Real estate on the Ridge slogged along one death or divorce at a time, and fine old houses, empty for decades, rotted back to the ground. George had grown accustomed to sitting around reading racing forms, maybe half his calls turning out to be wrong numbers. But George was a patient man. You had to be in real estate.

Then something started to happen in the last few years. Lots of money flying around from those computer guys and mortgage rates so low any idiot that could sign his name straight could qualify. Wide-eyed city folk started coming around looking for unusual places to invest extra cash, maybe take on an adventure, brag to their friends about a real estate killing. Like that pre-fab monstrosity across from Pete's place. George got a sweet deal for not much effort. He was living off it still. Of course that guy who bought it, that sprinkler salesman, went ahead and ripped out a magnificent grove of madrones to make room for an asphalt driveway wide enough to drive a train through. He put up one hell of a satellite dish on the roof, too. Stuck out like a sore thumb.

It was a good sign, that deal. Even on slow days now, George could feel the shake of possibilities stirring. Like today, when George got the call.

In the seconds before the phone rang, George had been balancing back in his chair, a move he had just about perfected, at that exact fulcrum where one inch farther he'd flip over altogether, and one inch forward he might as well be working. He teetered soundlessly in this relaxed, almost weightless position, amusing himself over that honeysuckle old Ida Flynn planted along her fence. George had predicted those vines would eventually cause problems for her neighbor, Isaac Price, and sure enough last week it took his fence right down, creating a tortuous sweet smelling disaster that blocked the entrance to Blind Shady altogether. More fuel for the folks who wondered whether Ida had any business living on her own any more.

The ring startled him backwards and he had to grab the leg of his desk so he wouldn't fall over. Got to the receiver at the third ring.

"I need an appointment to see some property off of Highway 49. The address is 14747 Blind Shady Bend. I was hoping I could set a time to meet you next week to take a look at it."

"Excuse me" George interrupted, like the salesman he was, even half-asleep, "did I get your name?"

"You didn't get my name because I didn't give it. I'm calling because I understand you handle property in this area and I've just come into a piece, it belonged to my brother and he's left it to me. I need to take a look before I decide whether to sell."

"Sell" was all George needed to hear. He rocked forward and grabbed his pen and pad. "What's that address now?" as he spun around to the book of county records, listing all properties by parcel number. Who died up there? He was trying to think but nobody came to mind.

14747 Blind Shady, Parcel 671386, his fingers traced veins of roads that came off Highway 49, Tyler Foote Crossing, Murphy Road, Lost River Road, Wits End, lines too small to read, there it is, Blind Shady Bend.

"I'll be damned!" he hoped she didn't hear, the property adjacent to Pete's, where Blind Shady makes a sharp left, levels out, then dies altogether at the end of a dusty half-mile stretch.

The locals pretty much thought of that parcel as Pete's place, since he made a decent living for himself digging through the old culvert that ran down the middle of the property. Long ago dredged of gold, the culvert had been a prime spot for the miners who populated the area over a hundred years earlier, as gold washed down from the Yuba River, settling into the hundreds of tributaries and ravines that pushed their way through the mountains. George had vague recollections of a pot farm getting busted out that way a couple of years back, and wasn't that the place? One thing for sure. Nothing grew on that land any more except Pete's imagination. And wasn't his luck about to change, George chuckled silently to himself.

"I see it now, Raymond Blackwell" oh my God this is going to be good, he realized, having almost forgotten the woman was still on the phone.

"That would be the one," she confirmed.

"I know that parcel very well and I'd be happy to show it to you," the salesman in him recovered from the shock without so much as a hiccup. "I could get a good price for you. Properties are hot in that part of town, hot." Pete would give his eyetooth, assuming he still had one left, to buy that place. George was already imagining the bidding wars.

"Hot" he repeated but the word had lost some flame in the retelling and still he heard nothing on her end, no sound at all.

"Are you still there ma'am?"

A throat cleared, once and loudly. "I'm not so sure you understand. I told you I just want to see it, that's all I said. We'll talk about selling when I'm ready to talk about selling. You need to show it to me first."

With that, she granted him her name, and confirmed she would arrive Monday of next week, at ten am sharp.

"Did she name a price?"

George didn't bother to look up before grunting a reply. He knew who it was. He could smell the breath.

"You'll be the first to know," he said, then got up and walked back to the water cooler for no reason other than to indicate he wasn't in the mood for Pete's company.

Pete had a habit of dropping in on George at irregular times, the realty company being two doors down from The Nugget. George had noticed Pete come in while he was on the phone, tried to keep his voice down in an unsuccessful attempt to muffle the substance of the phone call.

"Oh come on, you've got to know something." Pete was persistent when his livelihood was at stake, which is how he perceived any interference with his precious next-door treasure chest.

"I don't. She said she wanted to see the place, that's

all. The property's not yours anyway so pipe down."
George had returned to his desk where Pete had already
made himself comfortable, having moved a sheaf of papers off to the side to make some sitting room.

"Get your ass off my desk. I'm not talking to you
about this."

Pete leaned in close, perfuming George's workspace
with an acrid blend of Chesterfield lights and tuna fish.

"C'mon Lundale. What's she planning on doing with
it?"

"Nothing. I told her I'd help her sell and she told me
she didn't know if she was planning on selling and somehow I neglected to bring you into the picture. Maybe because the last thing that woman needs to know is she
might end up with you as a neighbor."

Pete didn't blink, expecting the insults and even wel-
coming them. They reassured him that that he held a
place in the landscape, recognized and secure.

"Tell her the place is worthless. Tell her it would take
a ton of money to make it livable and the guy next door
is a drunk."

"Tells me what you know about real estate. She's
from Roseville. She's Blackwell's sister. This isn't what I'd
call a regular customer. She didn't make a sound when
I told her it would bring a good price. If I were you, I'd
start digging fast as I can because the place never was
yours to begin with. Or did you forget that little detail?"

Pete couldn't understand how city people landed in these remote places. They kept creeping in, driving their little sedans into ditches, organizing town hall meetings to get electric poles installed, changing zoning laws so they could build bigger houses for their bigger cars that broke down like bludgeoned buffalo trying to maneuver the crooked mountain turns. He spent his life trying to avoid them.

Pete had purchased his land when even paupers could own a piece. What attracted him to his two-acre dust-bin was its proximity to the old county dumping ground along Blind Shady Creek that had long ago been pit stop central on an old gold mining trail. He'd grown up in nearby Grass Valley and had known about the area as a child, made his way in search of what just about everyone with a brain had given up on, the prospect of mining gold in his own back yard. Though pretty much mined of gold by now, the property on Blind Shady still offered plenty of treasures for Pete to sell at his flea market stall, as well as to loosely labeled 'antique' shops in the area that attracted weekend tourists. There wasn't a day that Pete didn't brag to someone about what he had lifted out of the ravine: an 1863 dime, a jackknife (thick with rust but still sharp enough to do some damage), sea green opium bottles, even a bit of lace he swore was a hundred years old and no one cared enough to argue with him.

Since Ray got busted the first time—that was back in the early 90's—Pete had pretty much helped himself to whatever showed up in the culvert next door. It was abandoned after all, he told himself. When he was sure nobody was around, which was most all the time, Pete would saunter across the property line to see what kind of treasure might turn up. He would bring a pick or not, blessed with two thick hands. Practically every try he'd unearth a tin toy, hatpin, picture frame framed in mud. The uncovering of a wooden sewing thimble, traces of turquoise paint still on, served to reinforce his smugness. And he wasn't above making a couple of slight enhancements, to draw a better price. Like carving a date, say "1886," into a plain piece of doorframe. It worked.

Pete prided himself on his reputation. When the old Meriwether place was torn down, a bunch of locals followed him out there to watch him extricate stuff not even fit for the garbage. Deft and deliberate, he chipped away at a decomposing Ford pickup that the wilderness was slowly swallowing. The steering column had sprouted acorns; the tires had turned to mulch. He picked away at the rubber treads, extricating a swatch of denim, frayed beyond recognition, but denim nonetheless. A poor sucker's favorite pair of Levi's and there would be some fool out there wanting to buy it.

Stories gathered and grew about how Pete got $50 for old lady Groman's hairpins, $100 for Jess King's beat up rocker. For some reason, people in the city enjoyed dusting up their whitewalls to get their hands on rusted objects that just may have been touched by a real gold miner at one point in time. Their stupidity was a mystery that gave Pete a great deal of pleasure.

"Did she sound like she had money? Tell me something dammit!" Pete was pleading this time. George was doing his best to ignore him, fumbling through receipts and such as though he had real work to do. "Will you talk to me George?"

"All right I'll tell you." George straightened up in his chair, clearing his throat to keep the smirk from breaking through. "It's privileged information and she swore me to secrecy but I'll tell you and you got to promise not to breathe a word. She murdered her husband some thirty years back, claimed it was self-defense, and just got released from prison. Out on good behavior she assured me, and said she's looking to get married again. I gave her your number."

"Fuck you Lundale," he said, by way of goodbye.

3.

"GIRL, WHAT'S GOING ON?" Darlene was practically screaming into my message machine after I missed my second hair appointment. The first time, the day after I got my big news, I overslept, plain and simple. And then again the next week, I was headed to her but stopped off first at the hardware store, just for the hell of it, and got caught up in the drip irrigation department. It's one of those little things I still do for myself, fiddle between overhead sprays and quarter inch drips. The guy there knows me already; when he sees me coming he goes the opposite direction. I don't care. It's something I can do, something I enjoy doing, rearranging my drip lines. For some reason, the news of Ray's land got me thinking about irrigation. There I was, so busy pricing things I don't even need, that I missed another appointment with Darlene. Worse things have happened.

My hair's getting a bit frazzled, the grey beginning to peek through but it's not so bad, really. I shake my head and feel a new weight of curl on my neck. I can grab handfuls, softer now that I've washed out all the gunk she sprays on to keep it neat. Darlene has been trying unsuccessfully to smooth out my hair for twenty years at least, thick, painful, ugly rollers, stinky liquids that stung my skin and one that made my nose bleed.

Darlene was never one for innovation, though she has

provided a fair share of comfort, year after year, in the form of thick soft hands and endless chatter. Her ex-husband's new girlfriend, her neighbor's new twins, her son-in-law, oh that son-in-law, and I would close my eyes, let the hot water, soft finger tips and gentle pull of scalp lull me into a sense of being genuinely cared for.

"You're going to look like a banshee," she advised, when I told her I was sick of getting color. Darlene cares about me, she does. She came by to visit when my back went out last year, brought muffins and a pot of soup she claims she made but I don't believe it. Tasted canned.

I raked my fingers through the dried-out tufts, weighing it against that tortuous two-and-a-half hour procedure resulting in an itchy nose and blue streaks down my neck. Left to its own devices, my hair was really a mat of weeds. They say vanity is one of the last things to go and I was beginning to feel it, finally, waving goodbye.

"Let me know if you're coming next Tuesday," Darlene's voice screamed. "I've got you down for 10:00. Girl, I hope you're gonna show up this time."

Darlene called everybody girl, even Harry. Harry has the 9:30, right before me. He liked to stick around and talk to her while she spread the purple gunk in my hair. He made me nervous.

"Goodbye Harry" were the only words I'd ever spoken to him. I didn't like him seeing me undone like that, but it wasn't me he was looking at anyhow. I could see his reflection in the mirror, standing behind Darlene, eyeing her backside like he was about to bite into a steak sandwich.

"How do you stand him?" I have asked her but Darlene just ignored me, already busy pulling at my curls, intent on her next masterpiece. For all the attention she has given me over the years, nothing ever changed. Same mousy brown curls, short on the neck, and that one wave over my left earlobe, dipped and fussed over with her two fingers, tenderly, like she was dropping one last dollop of icing on a cake. Sometimes I imagined myself flat in a coffin, eyes sealed shut, skin sallow, but that soft mousy brown wave dipped over my ear, unfazed by the change in my circumstance. Darlene's signature.

Darlene's about the closest thing I have to family, sad to say. I started going to her right around the time Mother got sick. Darlene listened to every gory detail. She could have shaved me bald and I would have kept coming. Saw me through the whole mess of it and a long mess it was.

The first stroke left Mother shaky and the next one left her frozen up and down one side so all she could do was clasp one hand to her chest and look halfway up, her right cheek and eyebrow raised toward that God of hers, who was still not listening. Four years of that, Pa acting like nothing had changed, just plodding along like he always did, stopping from time to time to fluff her pillows or move a straw closer to her lips so she wouldn't have to strain so hard to suck. He called that helping. I did the dirty work but that's what daughters do.

Going to Darlene helped me take my mind off nursing Mother. Other than my regular weekly hair appointments, my days were filled with picking up prescriptions, Digitoxin, Zestril, Pepto Bismol, Heparin, Diflucan which didn't help Pa's ringworm one bit, then over to Anderson's for All Bran, fudge bars (they really perked her up), snail pellets, Raisinettes (my meager addiction), and sugar-free tapioca for Mother, all of which I could do with my eyes practically closed.

And then it was just me and Pa. He lived on past her for more years than I'd like to remember. Like a couple of robot ghosts passing through antiseptic hallways, we shouted innocuous instructions "remember to pull out the recycling, it's Friday," "remember to pick up your Zestril its almost empty," "why don't you do it long as you're going out" and so I would. He did all right for himself. Made it to 89. His heart finished him off finally. I could hear the breathing during the night, louder and louder, though he never complained. His heaving kept me awake sometimes and I'd lie awake wondering how many more years of this do I have?

There isn't much to say about my life. When I look around at what little there is, only the leggy, lovely fuchsia, sprawled alongside my front doorway, seems to keep my interest, only because it refuses to die. Each year it grows bigger and bolder, shooting red firecracker flowers out between dried winter limbs. Splaying itself over its tame background, it is the singular feature of my entire surroundings that holds any possibility of surprise.

"Honey, is everything all right? Look here, you've got some gray coming in." She said it like it's a disease.

"I've decided to go grey," I blurted out.

"You're what?"

"And maybe grow it out a little longer, not so short in back."

"Are you all right?" she asked again, her voice straining to understand.

"I'm sorry about not calling. Time just gets away from me."

Darlene tapped my shin, "Uncross your legs," she reminded me and I obeyed. What choice did I have with the scissors pointed at my brow? I could tell she wasn't happy with me.

A curve of brown fell into my palm. My real color hadn't been brown, but the kind of black that turned reddish in the sunlight. And so thick. No hair clip was wide enough to hold it all up. Even when I fastened it with heavy elastic bands, I was always having to blow stray strands away from my mouth.

I was never what anyone would call a beauty, but now and again a strange woman would stop me in the market, pick up a handful of my hair like she was considering taking it with her. "What I wouldn't give," she'd whisper. It happened more than once.

While Darlene snipped and fussed, I finally opened up and told her about my latest news, how it got me to thinking about Ray again. She had heard bits and pieces about him over the years, what little I cared to tell. She

22

knew about all the investigating I had done to find him, driving up and down and around the area searching for him, placing ads, calling what friends he had but no one turned up and no one knew a thing. Pa told me not to bother, it was good riddance for him. And Mother did the only thing she was good at, shaking her head slow from side to side then looking up to the sky, like she was trying to listen to something God might be telling her. But He knew about as much as we did.

Darlene kept pushing me not to give up. Twenty years was nothing. She watched those TV shows and told me how on Cold Case Files, a woman found her missing husband working on a road crew twenty-five years after he had run off. Twenty years was nothing.

But I had put in my time. It had taken me a good decade before I stopped looking through the mail for any sign, a parking ticket, something from the draft board, something that might trace me to him. Some of his motorcycle buddies came knocking after the first few years and they knew a whole lot of nothing.

Once Connie Mulligan, who knew Ray in high school, said she was sure she saw him on a TV game show but Connie had been losing her mind bit by bit and no one flinched at the possibility. Still, I wrote the TV station, sent them a picture, but never heard back. It was futile all around.

No, I was done searching.

Then, about ten years ago, Ray would have been nearing fifty, a letter came in the mail, addressed to me.

That didn't stop Pa from ripping it open.

"Looks like your brother's surfaced" he said with a mouth full of cheese sandwich, tossing the wrinkled letter to me like it was a used Kleenex. That was Pa. Once he crossed a line it stayed crossed. He had wanted no part of his pot-smoking draft-dodging son, no part of his memory. It fell on me to do all the grieving there was to grieve.

The note didn't say much but I did keep it in my nightstand for some years to come. Put it in one of those plastic sheets to prevent it from yellowing. The plastic sheet protector was worth more than the note, really. Just said "H. Some day you will understand. I wish I could have taken you with me. R."

"Take you with me where?" I shouted at the sorry piece of paper, not even a nice little note card just some worthless sheet of yellow lined paper he pulled from a three-ring binder with the frayed nubby edges where it tore loose from the spiral bind. Week after week I'd pull another nub off until the side was smooth. That's how he faded, one nub at a time.

"Hannah, you're making a big mistake. This is going to add 20 years on you." Darlene was talking about the gray again. I'm not even sure she heard the part about getting my brother's land.

"It may be the best 20 years yet," I say, slipping an extra five in her apron pocket. "I'll be back in two weeks.

No color next time. Just a trim."

"I'm telling you. You're making a big mistake."

Darlene cared about me. She really did care.

4.

WINSTON BACKED HIS TRUCK down the driveway onto Blind Shady Bend and became aware of a new groaning sound, a painful metallic gasp as he shifted gears, heading toward the first bend in the road. The truck had one hell of a time bumping over the potholes that came at regular intervals from the edge of his property down past the old fill site, and only barely pshutted its way down the hairpin turn at the defunct water tower. He couldn't recall the last oil change, and figured it was overdue for new rotors. He sighed at the very thought of it.

Winston didn't feel like waving this morning. Lately, he'd been getting lazier with his waves and today he had no interest at all. There were fewer and fewer folks around that he recognized and none of the new ones bothered to wave back. The Henleys gone to a nursing home somewhere in Cornville. He'd meant to pay a visit but time got away from him and they were likely dead by now anyway. Mrs. Heilsbrun after the second turn and before the car cemetery, she and him had a wave going on some twenty years now. Phil Heilsbrun used to come into the store, stocking up on roofing nails in late autumn, hose attachments in late winter, always ahead of the game that guy was. But he stopped coming around some years back and sure enough, heart attack had got him. With Vera it was the cancer. In her breasts. Winston sometimes thought it was his fault, that if he'd only touched her more, he might have noticed the lump before it was too late.

But since their spouses passed, it seemed like he and Mrs. Heilsbrun had grown shyer, their waves more timid. Used to be one of them would sing over the motor of his car, "Looks like we're in for a warm streak," or "Hope you had better luck with your huckleberries. Mine just fell rotten." Something cheery and short while he slowed down to make the curve. These last few years it was just half a wave, neither wanting the other to make too much of the friendliness.

He had one hand on the steering wheel and his waving hand poised and ready, just in case, when Pete came running out into the road. Winston slammed on his brakes which brought out yet another new sound, a more troubling one, high pitched and haunting, like it came from the dead.

"Hey, did you hear?" called Pete, breathless and still in his pajamas.

"Hear what?"

"Lundale got a call from some old lady asking about my land" pointing to the vacant site adjacent to his. "Can you beat that?"

"It's not your land, Pete" Winston reminded him, then wished he hadn't. Last thing he wanted was to engage Pete in this kind of half-baked gossip that spread like wildfires in these parts and died down just as quickly.

"Heard it from the source. Turns out Blackwell left

the land to his sister. Can you beat that?"

The idea of someone coming in to claim this property, maybe clean it up a bit, did capture Winston's interest. Against his better judgment, he pulled up the emergency brake, resigned to getting the whole story.

"Lundale says she sounded strange but wouldn't say much more than that. Wonder if she's anything like her brother?"

Winston never knew the man but remembered the rash of motorcycle noise that roared through the trees back when Vera was bedridden. In those days he was exhausted all the time, with Vera needing constant tending, keeping up the hardware store, trying to cook himself and the boy a decent dinner. Last thing he needed was to be awakened by roaring engines in the middle of the night. But he didn't inquire, figured other neighbors would complain if it got too bad.

"That was a long time ago, Pete. I'd guess 15 years at least." His son Robin was grown, a father himself now, so it had to be a decade, at least, maybe more. At the time, Winston had worried about his son getting into trouble over there but the trouble went away on its own. Once every few months or so, a lone motorcycle would ride up and Winston figured it to be the owner, came to recognize the harmonica wailing through the madrones in the late night air. There'd be that sweet skunky smell mixing with honeysuckle in late September but by and large the place was quiet. Apparently this mystery neighbor wanted no trouble, caused no trouble, and deserved his tranquility as much as the next man.

Winston didn't dare open his mouth, but he did recall reading something a few months back about a motorcycle crash on Highway 49 that killed the Blackwell fellow. It happened all the time. Bikers thinking they could make it across the 4-lane stretch, trying to outrun the semis that came barreling down the winding highway. This time the motorcyclist had lost out to a produce truck heading north. Newspaper said the guy lived on Blind Shady Bend, which is why he'd taken notice.

"Don't get yourself riled up," was all he said to Pete. "The property's been a dump for years. Might be a good thing for all of us if someone cleaned it up."

With that, he raised his hand, giving Pete a full-on no-nonsense wave, and headed on down Blind Shady Bend and into town.

Winston held the title of General Manager of Highway Hardware, complete with his own office (a huge closet really), two tall metal file cabinets (bottom drawers stuck shut), and a sense of stature and significance that no one thing before in his life had come close to providing. He'd started as a stock boy almost thirty-seven years before, and he still felt just a little more upright when he walked through the front door, past Joyce and Gladys at the registers, quick nod to Roger in Paint, Gil in Electric, and Frank, too old to fire, Frank who barely fit between the aisles but knew plumbing like nobody else.

Winston took pleasure in shaking out his heavy metal spray of keys, the longest of which unlocked the metal door marked "W. TILL – MANAGER." He'd automatically take a quick shy glance behind before entering. Even at this point in life, when doubts and fatigue and burgeoning confusion interrupted him at unexpected intervals, the certainty of his relationship to that one small place kept him from feeling that his life was all but past.

Most customers preferred to stand around and wait for him before asking anyone else which spot remover to buy. They even waited for him to cut new keys, as if the other employees didn't know how to work the machine properly. Customers were more than happy to line up outside his door and wait, so intent they were on his sound and patient advice. Whatever time it took would be less time than buying the wrong thing and then having to drive all the way back to return. They knew that when Winston said, "Howdy, may I help you" he really meant it.

But today Winston had to keep his office door shut—not even a crack to allow in the shuffling sounds of customers wandering the aisles. He had screwed up an order last week. Six cartons of three-penny nails, enough to build a new hardware store, when he only meant to order six boxes. He'd been making other mistakes lately, little ones that no one noticed (he hoped), and that he managed to fix before anyone from accounting found out. This mistake was going to take some time to clear up, and the kids were due home by 3, (was it 3 or 2?) because Robin mentioned something about working late over in Sierraville. Today there would be no time to help customers find overhead sprinklers, no exchanging inside hinges for out. All the things he loved to do. Today there would be none of that.

He couldn't locate the order book and the key to the inventory file cabinet had jammed in the lock. The only locksmith within reach was recovering from hip surgery.

He sighed, and just like that his mind turned, as it constantly did nowadays, to his son Robin. Robin with his marriage shaken loose, the kids with no mother, and Timothy's nose running a yellowish green snot. Maybe he ought to call a doctor. What if something happened to that child, then what? Robin was in too much of a hurry to be any kind of father to those kids. Dropping them off like baggage at school, pushing them into the truck, out of the truck, they might as well be sacks of laundry. Sweaters twisted inside out, broken toy parts, mismatched shoes, all tossed in the back seat where they'd get sandwiched between screwdrivers and wrenches. Fast food wrappers, wrinkled attempts at artwork, their small lives were already turning into a cluttered heap.

"It's just a cold, dad. Kids get colds." Robin didn't seem in the least bit concerned about his son's dripping nose. Maybe that was a good sign. Maybe grandfathers were too old to know the difference between simple colds and early stage diphtheria. But the green stuff had been coming steady and it couldn't be right.

How was he supposed to help with the kids—a man who couldn't figure out how to open a jammed inventory cabinet. A man who left the key to the safe in his trousers on top of the washing machine and today he desperately needed to find that nail order so he could get a full return. It might have to wait until Monday but it's a holiday Monday he thinks, Memorial or Veteran's or maybe that was last week. Winston's mind was racing now, bedraggled grandchildren, stuck file cabinets, and now he started to wonder whether he remembered to turn off the humidifier in the kids' room.

At this last, overwhelming possibility, Winston lay his head down on the soft wad of accounting books splayed across his desk, flopped his arms out flat across the table in exhausted supplication, and allowed his tired body to convulse in three heaving, excruciating sobs.

No tears came. He wished they would, imagined they might cool down the hotness that burned in his throat, bathe him in some interior kind of way. This life had become all too much for an old man to sort through. He shuddered with the enormity of his existence. How was it that life led so desperately downward?

"Mr. Till, are you still there?" Lindsay's gentle knock informed him that it was 2:30, time for him to end his day, finally.

"Yes, dear, I'm just finishing up" he answered, collecting his coat, his lunch bag that hadn't been touched, some horse stickers for Timothy and princess stickers for Grace (hadn't he given them the same ones last week?)

and said his goodbyes to the staff.

He hadn't accomplished nearly what he needed to but for some reason, Winston found himself looking forward to the drive home. Robin had hinted that he might leave the kids for the whole weekend. He had landed a great job in Peardale, twenty miles south, a deck with built-in spa, whatever that meant. Winston tried to picture folks lying naked outside in full view of their neighbors and got stuck on the thought.

What would he do with the kids all weekend, maybe take them to the hardware store again. They seemed to enjoy playing up and down the aisles, Lindsay treating them to the mints behind the counter, Len giving them sandpaper samples and address numbers and Elmer's glue. Or maybe they'd just stay home. He liked being home with them, even with nothing to do. There was noise in the house now, noise that he didn't need to generate. He was glad he had offered to let Robin and the kids move in. It made him feel like a father, made him drive faster than usual to beat them home.

5.

THE ROAD FROM SCHOOL to home ambled along a seven-mile stretch of highway, which usually put both kids to sleep. The hard right onto Route 49 usually stirred them awake, then past the boarded up vegetable stand, the brand new health food store, the field of cows and horses that no longer held their interest. But the smell of livestock woke them fully, preparing them for what was coming up at the next bend, Highway Hardware, and by now they were craning their necks to see.

"There's Grandpa's store," Timothy announced at the juncture, then checking off the next few landmarks, Ervin's Gas and Oil Change, the Chinese restaurant, the old Lutheran church that seemed to have more weeds than worshippers, and finally the field of buried automobiles that sprouted clover in the winter and wild iris in the spring.

Maybe ten feet past the car cemetery, the truck swerved hard and left onto an unpaved, unmarked stretch of road, milepost 4.8, and before the steering wheel had a chance to straighten came the next hairpin, to the right this time, causing the kids to sway back and forth across the seat. "Whoa!" they called out every single time, one of the highlights of the long trip home. Not many people ever made that second hairpin turn. The faded wooden sign marked Blind Shady Bend was known to only a few residents, and they liked it that way. "Make a sharp left just after the car cemetery" was all anyone said, should directions be called for. They rarely were.

As usual, Robin had been the last to pick the kids up from school. The teacher never said anything, she didn't have to, she just sat at her desk, art supplies and tinker toys and books all stacked neatly on the shelves, so quiet you could hear the scratching of her pen as she finished up the details of her day. Blackboards washed down with a thoroughness that suggested he was later than his usual late this time, and her eyes confirmed it when at last she acknowledged his presence.

"Today is teacher training day. Did Grace give you the notice? School ended at 2:00."

He didn't recall reading any notice, but it was most likely his oversight and not Grace's. She was the one who remembered to put the fruit rolls in their lunchboxes.

"Sorry. I never saw it."

"They are in the library. You'd better hurry, it closes in 15 minutes."

Well it wasn't Miss Larner's fault either. She was paid to teach, not babysit the children of frazzled parents.

He heard Timothy crying before he opened the library door. The way Grace explained it, he had kicked her when she was leaning down to pick up her pencil, so she grabbed his shoe and threw it across the aisle to teach him a lesson.

"Gimme back my shoe" Timothy screamed, "I want my shoe."

"Knock it off" Robin yelled not at his bossy daughter, but at the crying, shoeless little boy.

"Stop acting like a baby," he shouted to the little boy who still sucked juice out of Batman cups with nippled lids, still kept his frayed blanket tucked safe on the bottom of his backpack, rubbed its silky edge against his lips when he thought his dad wasn't looking.

"Get up, get your things, we gotta go." He gave his son a quick propelling pat on the rear that only made the crying worse.

Robin grabbed the shoe, holding the crying boy in his other arm. By the time they managed to get to his truck, Grace was already stationed in the middle, in the place right next to Daddy's, seat belt locked, hand on the emergency brake, ready for his signal to push in the button and let it down. She was nothing like her brother who preferred to curl into the window seat, thumb in mouth, staring out at nothing.

Robin lifted the boy into his seat, helped him with his belt, and tossed the loose shoe in the back of the truck, together with their backpacks.

"Where's your shoe?" Grace demanded, as though the health and safety of her brother's feet really mattered to her.

"In the back."

"You have to put it on." She sounded just like a mother.

"No I don't. I like wearing one shoe."

Robin backed down the path of the school driveway, turned up his music station to where "ashes of love, cold as ice" overwhelmed the endless drone of "No I don't, yes you do."

"That's stupid, you can't wear just one shoe. Daddy, Timothy is only wearing one shoe."

"Daddy threw it in the back so mind your own business."

Robin heard his name registered in shrill, high tones, blasting over Kelly Clarkson's latest. Sometimes, the back and forth of their diatribes rocked them into a kind of submission, an exhausting lullaby, and all it took was turning up the radio a decibel or two to quiet them down.

None of this was his idea, not the marriage, not the pregnancy, and then the second one, also her idea. Every child should have a sibling, Cynthia had insisted. He knew only one thing: if she wanted to leave her children because some guy tells her she has 'healing hands' she could go to hell.

"You said a bad word Daddy."

Grace had been listening to him. She surprised him that way more and more lately, seeming more like an adult than a kid.

"Sorry honey. Guess I'm thinking out loud again."

"What's thinking out loud?"

She was starting to annoy him. Asking questions Robin didn't have the energy to answer.

"Just when you have words in your head and you say

them out loud even when you don't mean to."

"Like when you dream in the middle of the day?" Grace ventured.

The girl's too smart for me, he thought, careful to keep it to himself this time. He ruffled her hair with his free hand, let his fingers get caught up in her soft brown waves. She smiled up at him, clearly loving how the two of them understood things that Timothy didn't. They sat knee to knee, and at the stoplight, Robin bent down to smell the sweet shampoo of her hair. "You're my big girl," he whispered, as if that made up for having a mother who didn't gave a shit about her.

"How many mailboxes to Grandpa's?"

"Seven" said Grace, it was the same number every time and this game was getting too easy for her. But she still enjoyed winning, enjoyed how Timothy still wasn't fast enough to say seven first.

"Seven," said Timothy in automatic echo, and Grace rolled her eyes up toward her dad's, and he recognized briefly the smug self-assurance of his ex.

"Let's count, to see if you're right."

The counting game united them for the short distance ahead. Mailbox number one said Livingston, marked by a sheet metal gray box riddled with bird droppings. The Livingstons may or may not have inhabited the place any time during the past century. The mailbox was always empty, the name barely distinguishable from the bird blotches surrounding it. There were no other life traces, but it was hard to know with the long and twisted driveways and weed covered asphalt.

Up a ways and to the left was the newest mailbox — huge circled letters announcing The Daschle Family, twinkling with moons and stars and nonsensical stickers that they must have bought on sale at Highway Hardware. What kinds of people decorate their damned mailboxes, Robin wondered. The fancy mailbox wasn't the worst of it. The new neighbors had installed a lawn and white picket fence that made the place look like a tornado had picked the house up from some suburban housing development and dropped it mercilessly in the middle of this godforsaken stretch of road. Poor suckers. Robin and his Dad were convinced that Lundale had sold the new owners a bill of goods. "An up and coming neighborhood," Robin imagined Lundale telling them.

After the Daschles, the road narrowed a bit, branches of sweet birch and scrub oak slapping at the sides of the truck. Grace reached across her brother to roll up the window so the branches wouldn't scratch his arms. Next came the mailbox series, three in a row, utterly abandoned, the likely remains of a cluster of mobile homes that had dropped there in the late '60's and dissipated over time. Timothy kept track on his hand, number 3, number 4, number 5 this came to, one of his hands was now finished and he set his other hand on his lap to prepare his last two fingers to reach number 7.

Pete's mailbox, to the right about 200 yards further

on, was over-sized regulation green. P.S. was scribbled on the outside of the mailbox as an afterthought, its wide throat slung open like a hungry bird that perpetually retched out catalogues, envelopes, wrinkled wads of mail. Come spring the mailbox would be mercifully hidden by a dramatic display of day lilies, iris, and columbine. But in early November, only a mass of prickly thorns jutted out from the thick mulch of junk that heaped higher year by year at the mailbox's base. Pete the garbage collector. You didn't have to know Pete to know him just the same.

One more to go, they were bracing themselves for the scream SEVEN! Grace bounced up in her seat, readying herself for another win, but Timothy saw it first, across from Grandpa's, just past where the magazine man lived.

"Look Daddy, there's someone in the bushes."

Robin stopped the truck a few yards shy of his father's driveway, cranked his head up over the two little heads, and saw sure enough, a sign of life. The property across the road from them hadn't been inhabited for years, not since he was a kid. The idea that life was stirring again on Ray's old place caught him off guard.

The place had been deserted for so long, it was as though none of those years had happened. Every once in a while Robin would think about snooping around to see if any of Ray's old owl carvings were still around.

Timothy was right. Robin could see what looked to be mounds of dark fresh dirt scattered across the gravel driveway. He leaned across the kids, rolled the window down, strained to see if anyone was in the bushes but saw no one. He thought about getting out to take a look, but not with the kids, not now.

"Daddy, I think I saw a baby stroller."

"No you didn't," he refused her, putting the truck back in gear, jerking forward toward his father's place.

6.

THE TERRIBLE SOUND of Winston's brakes announced his arrival, but no kids came running to greet him, like they often did. They must be out back somewhere, he could hear their voices through the trees.

He found Robin sitting at the kitchen table, his head in his hands. Pale. The gray pall of age settling around his son's eyes, taking the years away too soon. Not a boy any more yet not quite a man, he was coming up on thirty. Vera gone already fifteen years. While she was ailing, the boy was just starting to break free of her hold, finding the legs to stand on his own. Of course Winston didn't pay much attention to the boy in those terrible months, but he seemed to be fine, going his own way. And then teetering over, crashing at the loss. Winston could almost put his finger on the boy's problems, started early but sealed when his mother passed. And maybe he could have done something different. Been a better father. But how?

No use figuring it out anymore. What was done was done. Robin was a father himself now, saddled with the two kids and still a kid himself, that scraggly hair of his still in his eyes. Look at him, Winston thought, studying the figure slumped at his kitchen table, wearing a man's hard boots, tool belt spread across the table top, no woman around to object.

"Tired, son?"

Robin was too tired to answer, but nodded. Winston knew. He saw plenty from the sidelines. If it were up to him, he'd have insisted the mother take her share of raising the kids but Robin didn't even know where the woman was. Off to Denver last anyone heard with her guru, laying her healing hands all over the place while her own children screamed for a mother's touch.

Winston wanted to touch his boy who was now a man, sitting in front of him, the big strapping hunk of him, wrap his arms around him and squeeze his troubles away. But it was too late for that.

"Anything you want son?"

"Something cold. Screaming headache."

Winston poured a glass of orange soda and put it in a tall glass with ice cubes. It was always Robin's favorite. Vera wouldn't let him have it with all that sugar, but after her death, Winston stocked up on it, bought it in cases, along with those jerky sticks filled with nitrites. Sometimes for no reason, he'd toss the boy a jerky stick or some of that sweet soda and they'd share a wordless smile, a "she should only see us now" kind of secret. Some good things had come from the years without her.

"Thanks Dad," and as he reached for the glass, both sets of their fingers interlocked around the cold wet shape, and they felt the warmth seep through the cold.

Robin took a sip and the cold and sweet shook him out of his slump. He started talking, offering more details than his father was accustomed to hearing. Turns out the Peardale job fell through. All he really had to do this weekend was a few hours finishing sanding the Sampson's porch railing, and then over to the Jaekel's to set the fence posts. It was turning out to be one of the few short Saturdays he'd had in months, and with his dad already committed to taking the kids for the weekend, maybe he could take some time for himself, maybe drive out to Sterling lake, take a rowboat out past the weekend fishermen, past the kids in their rubber tubes, past the smart asses with their drop lines and homemade worms no rainbow trout would take a second look at. He'd go past them all, drop the oars down, where the loons and marsh birds nest, and lie there, naked to his shorts, shaded by the whip grass, let the boat snag up in the thicket and not give a damn if it ever broke free.

"Wasn't Peardale that big spa job?"

"Contractor said they might be getting divorced. Holding off on the hot tub deck remodel for now. It was going to be a lot of work. I was counting on the money, but I could really use a day to myself."

"Well this might cheer you up. I got some news about the place across the road. Remember that motorcycle guy who lived there when you were a kid? He's the one who was killed in that motorcycle crash a few months back. Turns out he left that old abandoned place to his sister. At least that's what Pete told me. Says he got it straight from Lundale. The place is a dump. Got me to thinking she might need some help fixing it up. Year's worth of work at that place, easy."

"Daaaad" the sound that came out of Robin's mouth was more of a bleat than a word. "I told you not to go making plans for me without asking me first."

The boy had a lazy streak in him. Here was an opportunity you'd think he'd jump at. But Winston could never tell his son anything. Vera had done every this and that for him, told him he was special when he wasn't, really. Content to sit around and whittle with that old pocketknife with the carved elk head handle, he had found it at Pete's, or came by it on his own somehow, and claimed it with a vengeance.

"What does he like to do?" Winston would ask Vera, as if only she knew the answer to their son's mind. "Likes to whittle is all I can see, and nothing ever comes of it either."

But that was not true. Robin had finished an owl's head while still in grade school, and it actually looked like an owl, with softly curved feathers and one eye that seemed to stare back. Also a raven carved from manzanita, the deep red bark giving it life if you held it under a translucent moon. There may have been others. Winston kept them in a box in the toolshed. He couldn't bring himself to throw them away.

"I didn't make any plans for you, just saying it might happen, that's all. Wouldn't it be something? Right across the road?"

"Right across the road" it sounded like Robin was saying, hard to be sure since he talked with his hands over his mouth. Still, Winston took it as a sign to keep talking.

"Think about it. Whoever gets that place will need to do something with it, can't imagine they'd just leave it to rot. I'm just telling you, there might be something there. You should call Lundale, look into it. You have to take the lead on these kinds of things, son." And just as the words came out, Winston knew he had gone too far.

Robin stood up, righted his chair, it seemed that the headache was gone, or temporarily pushed aside, it was hard for his father to tell.

"I'm going for a walk," he announced, without so much as looking back.

7.

CALLIE WAS EAGER to head back across the road. There were threats of rain and she had all these seed packets that needed to go in soon. Ralph had hung around this morning longer than she wanted, said he had some business to take care of on the computer. She wished she knew how to use the thing so she could find out what he was plotting. It seemed like plotting, how he never told her anything specific, and next thing she knew, he had her and the baby moved into this place where there was absolutely nothing for her to do. He installed the big TV satellite dish 'to keep her occupied' is what he said, that's how little he knew her.

If she hadn't discovered that wonderland across the road she'd be going crazy here. Callie knew she was supposed to thank him for buying them this great deal of an investment, at a steal he reminded her, and she did thank him. But she didn't mean it. Not a word.

Callie waited until Ralph pulled out, waited until the last rumble of gravel echoed its way down their driveway, making sure there were no sounds left, no chance he might have decided to flip into reverse and wheel back again, maybe he forgot a phone number, his notebook, a chance to snag another kiss, grab her ass which he managed to do any excuse he could get.

She put Daphne in the stroller and off they went to

47

that empty plot of land across the road that she discovered not long after they moved in. The dilapidated shack at the end of the driveway looked abandoned, no trace of anyone living in it, the floors littered with dust and broken glass, no signs of life.

But she had only poked her head in. She was much more interested in the spaces along the edges of the driveway that bent every which way, interrupted by snags of wild roses and juniper bushes and that horrid wild weed that nicked her legs and got caught up inside the stroller wheels. Really nothing on this land but a gnarl of undergrowth. But for the penstemon that grew wild and thick, waiving their red and purple shoots, and occasional bursts of golden honeysuckle, there wasn't much in the way of color.

That ground cover drove her crazy. Shoots ripped through the delicate mat of thyme that she had carefully planted last spring but this ground cover was ruining all her plans. So much for the soft aromatic carpet she imagined trailing along the driveway. Even if the thyme grew, it would be overpowered by the acrid smell of the ground cover, something like skunk but not quite as horrid. It reminded her of her dad—that mixture of Aqua Velva and vomit that suffused the laundry basket because he just threw his shirts in there as though no one would notice.

Well maybe that's where she learned her sloppy ways. Her grandpa used to tell her she was impossible to teach, but he said it with a smile so she didn't care. She used to follow him around his garden every chance she got. He taught her the names of plants and let her use his tools, even the sharp ones, and never cared how dirty she got. It was the best way she knew to stay out of her house and not get in trouble.

The woman at the plant store had told Callie all about the rough ground cover that permeated the surface of the landscape. The Miwok who used to live on the western slopes of the Sierra Nevada range called it Kit-kit-dizze. According to the woman, it grew nowhere else in the world. The pungent aroma of this prickly mountain weed reminded her of nothing she could name, but when the sun and breeze hit it just right, the bitterness dissolved into something deliriously sweet, as though someone covered it over with a crust of pure sugar. The locals called it Mountain Misery and in a few months of trying to extricate its roots to make room for seedbeds, Callie figured out why. She tried washing her clothes with bleach but the smell stuck. She needed to allow time, before Ralph came home, to rinse off the smell.

It wasn't like she didn't have her own garden to work in. Ralph had installed a perfect rectangular lawn and had laid the water lines for flower boxes designed to disguise the sprinkler heads he had installed. "You can plant whatever you'd like" he allowed her, "just nothing messy. It wrecks the system."

But Callie wasn't a neat gardener and begonias in pots reminded her of sick people, her great-aunt Daphne stuck in a hospital bed surrounded by thick dark green waxy leaf plants that seemed to thrive on fever and the smell of decay.

It's not as if Ralph would care that she was gardening across the road. He had bought her all those garden tools. He remembered all the things she told him about her grandpa and he was thoughtful that way. Ralph tried to get her interested in his little projects, and he even brought plants home for her once in a while, boring pansies and daisies that she left to wither. Callie sometimes wondered if he even cared what she did all day, as long as she was happy to see him when he came home.

And she enjoyed the secrecy, the feeling that she had a life without him, even if it was something as silly as poking around in an old abandoned pile of weeds. The place was all hers as long as he didn't know about it. That's what mattered.

Callie had worked things out pretty well for herself, she was proud to acknowledge. Her ears were well tuned to the smooth sound of Ralph's engine making the hard turn at the end of the road. By the time he approached their driveway, she always managed to meet him out front, like she was just coming in from a walk, and it was a lot like the old days, him honking, her whirling into his car and off they'd go to nowhere in particular. She used to love those days back in high school, and this was as close as they came lately, meeting him outside their house with the baby in the late afternoon. She still felt the thrill of his truck hitting its brakes when he'd pick her up, so she could lift her skirt high and hoist herself in, swinging her legs around, her hair a bit tousled from the jump. She could still do that, even with a baby in her arms.

The thought of tonight's pot roast dissolving in to-matoes with sprigs of thyme she collected and dried from across the road made her feel pretty damned good about herself. She gathered up the baby's pacifier and quilt with one arm, strutting about like someone with somewhere to go. She was wearing her bright pink polka dot t-shirt, the one that was too tight across her breasts so even with the thickness of her nursing bra, her bold nipples announced themselves through the fabric. The lavender shampoo had flavored the skin around her neck and shoulders and she felt proud of those huge, shameless nipples. The morning shower had done her a world of good.

"Come on pumpkin, we're going for a walk," she told the baby, and the two of them headed out, stroller wheels bumping along the gravel path, causing the baby's head to bobble and bounce, while Callie's hips swerved and turned to the beat of her own satisfaction. Callie didn't much care about Ralph's garden plans with this private field all to herself. The place was aching for her touch. She grabbed packets of nierembergia and phlox, they came free with either the twenty-five anemone bulbs or ibex-gloxinia mixture and she bought them both, un-able to resist the colors in the catalogue. Ralph and his stupid lawn.

Today Callie planned to cut back more of the spindly ground cover and transplant (carefully) what green there was of the scented thyme bed over to more compatible ground. It would be an iffy job and depended on the baby sleeping. She remembered to bring the trowel this time, and the loppers, and a big plastic bag to store any stray seeds or other potential survivors. She even remembered the coping saw in case the madrone limbs were too thick for her loppers, and felt proud of herself, though there was nobody she could brag to. It was a private kind of pride. Something she was starting to get used to.

New circles of color surprised her every day in and around the scrub oaks and rock beds and tumbleweeds. The mixed seed packets should start opening by early spring if she got them in soon enough, and if the sunflowers ever opened, it seemed like this place would be more hers than the place she lived in. She spread her tools around, splayed her legs out so her skin absorbed every single scent and prickle of ground, and started clipping.

The Queen Anne's lace came apart in her hand. She blew on the remaining tufts and made a wish. White dust flew wild into the air and a few droplets landed on Daphne's head, seeping into her hairless fuzz.

"Let's take a bunch of these," she whispered to Daphne, who was reaching out with chubby hands to the free-floating pollen. Callie snapped off another stalk, then another. She stuffed them beneath the stroller on top of the extra blankets and plastic baby toys. She knew she was being silly, hiding them like she was afraid of getting caught. But that was part of the fun. She'd never seen another soul along this dusty stretch of road and who would miss a few sprays anyway? Besides, even if she was trespassing, the flowers were hers, she was the one who had scattered the seeds.

The stroller wheel crunched over a dead patch of columbine, one of her favorites. She wondered if they'd return next spring. So mysterious, what came up and what didn't. Farther down the driveway, the path seemed to pull the wheels without her guidance, down into a clump of rocks and brush, at the porch steps now, farther than she usually strayed, trespassing now, no question about it. She had great plans for the coffins of planter boxes that were precariously balanced on the broken porch. Last year's weeds had all but dissolved into a dust of dead leaves and she inspected them carefully, hoping to recognize them. Every day, either intentionally or by the whim of a wheel from Daphne's stroller, some new green thing would announce its life, giving her more reasons to return.

Callie tested the porch steps carefully, glad the baby wasn't old enough yet to move around. What would she do then, with splinters and rocks and rose thorns everywhere? She found the shaded front porch of the shack to be a perfect spot for nursing. She set down her tools, feeling at home in this abandoned refuge. The air was so sweet it made her close her eyes and breathe deep, in time with the squeaking satisfaction of Daphne suckling at her breast.

Ralph would definitely have a fit if he ever found

her like this. He had made a point of warning her about this place. He said it used to belong to a dope dealer, the guy was supposedly in prison, but he could get out any time. Be careful, he had warned her, stay away. But Callie didn't pay him any attention. There were all kinds of rumors about the abandoned property, not just from Ralph, but also at the market, the hardware store, people around here talked. The rumors came out in whispers mostly, about the drug guy and his friends. The motorcycles. But as far as she was concerned, that was so long ago it didn't matter any more. You just had to look around to see nobody had been here forever. For her the land was a private paradise. Let them all talk.

It was the Realtor who told Ralph about the guy who got busted. Callie never trusted that Realtor, never trusted this fancy house he sold them in the middle of nowhere would amount to anything. He got them in for practically no money down. Some kind of low interest loan and property values were starting to go through the roof he said. Ralph showed her all the numbers, practically guaranteed to make them rich by the time they spruced it up a bit to sell. The lawn was the Realtor's idea, come to think of it. He assured them they'd be long gone by the time the interest rates changed, with enough profit to buy something really big.

Daphne was sleeping quietly. This promised to be a productive afternoon. Callie snapped a few seeds from the Queen Anne's lace and then noticed how the dirt was soft at the base. Using her five fingers as a trowel, she whittled away at the edge of the root ball, extricating a nice little hunk. She had no idea how it would take the transplant but decided to put it near the lavender. Something to surprise her when and if it decided to bloom.

Callie backed the stroller out of the dirt, thought she heard some footsteps off in the distance. The stroller was heavy, weighted down with Queen Anne's lace plopping out from the side, and now the penstemon, heaped gingerly over a couple of salvia branches she had broken off a ways back. Bring peat pots, she reminded herself for next time, and maybe a bag of fertilizer.

Better get out of here, she decided, as she backed the stroller up toward the road, feeling guilty and giddy all at once. Hurrying up the hill she got snagged once again when the front stroller wheel slipped into a patch of soft earth, nearly tipping it on its side.

The man surprised her just as she managed to lift the wheels out of the dirt and back on to the road again.

"Are you OK?" he said, running toward her, "are you OK?" he called again.

Callie froze where she was, first from the sound of someone's voice, and then with the shock of recognition.

"Robin? Robin Till?"

"How do you know my name?"

"Robin Till" she said again, not a question this time, because she absolutely knew the answer.

"Do I know you?" he asked and she took off her sun

hat, pulled at her skirt. No time to check her t-shirt for milk stains so she leaned into the stroller for cover, and waited for him to approach.

"Mr. Murray's homeroom. Miss Hayne's history. Just about every class in tenth grade. Thorpe and Till. I always sat in front of you. Remember now?

"Callie? Callie Thorpe?"

He was looking straight at her now and his eyes were bluer than she remembered. Robin's egg blue, she was thinking, almost translucent with the light shining into them.

He hadn't changed much. Still looked like he looked in tenth grade, except for a shaggy beard, more like he forgot to shave, like he really didn't care what he looked like. But he was cute, carried his cuteness like an innocent, like he had no idea. He hadn't grown any. She didn't think he was more than 5'8". She tried to picture him back in their homeroom, always quiet, off to himself most of the time. No one she'd ever remember but somehow she remembered him anyway. He was a soft-spoken, shy kid, the kind that might have gotten bullied except no one noticed him enough to bother. Back then he didn't have any muscles to speak of. That much certainly had changed.

"What in God's name are you doing on this property?"

"Just picking some flowers. I live over there" and she pointed to the house across the road with the flowered mailbox and satellite dish and doublewide driveway.

"YOU live there?" and she could see he was fighting back laughter. "How long you been living there and I

56

didn't know it?"

"My husband bought it last year, right before the baby. I've been inside mostly, caring for her, but I started taking walks after we moved in, the air does her some good, and it does me too. What about you? What are you doing here?"

"I live just over there, at the end of the road, last house down, with my dad. He's lived there forever."

"Well, small world I guess."

"You probably shouldn't be trampling around on this place."

"That's what my husband tells me, but I don't see why. Nothing here but a lot of weeds and quiet. Keeps me entertained since I'm home all day with the baby. It's a great place to practice my gardening skills."

"You can't make a mistake, that's for sure," he said, grabbing at a stray branch that nicked his fingers, drawing a dot of blood.

"Maybe you're the one that should be careful around here," Callie quipped, prying the beginning of a smile out of him. "And what brings you on to this land?"

"I thought I saw some activity when I drove home, fresh dirt in the driveway. I heard there might be a new owner here so I wanted to check things out."

A new owner. Callie didn't like the sound of that at all.

"Well it was just me. Making a mess. No intruders."

"Just wanted to be sure" he said, starting to turn back up the road, just like that, when she would have wanted him to stay a little longer.

"Maybe we'll bump into each other again." Her words came out flirty, she could hear it, the singsong, and she bet he heard it too. "I'm home all the time" she added, like a dollop of spice, she just couldn't help herself.

Callie hurried now towards her house, the shakings of a million seeds stuck to her skin and clothes. The stink of Mountain Misery filled her shoes and the baby's hair was shrouded in Queen Anne's lace. She shook herself and the baby off on the porch, then swept all traces of her secret garden into Ralph's neat little empty flower boxes, where they would be swallowed into the dark earth.

8.

SECOND FRIDAY OF THE MONTH again. That meant Wilbur would be coming, late as usual, only three hours of good light left. Wilbur, master rose pruner, according to him anyway.

"Did they teach you this at your master rose pruning class?" I'd ask him, pointing to those molehills of cigarette butts he tucked around the bedding plants.

"They're loaded with nitrogen. The plants love them" he'd shoot back. Wilbur liked to play with me and I had to admit I liked playing right back.

Wilbur had kept my hedges razor straight and my twelve prim and proper roses fed for more years than I could remember. "Needs more iron," he would drone in his flat voice, peppered by a thin hint of disdain, "needs more iron," as though that was my fault. I've never cared much for roses, too much trouble, and I would remind him that the roses were his idea. Not to mention the wisteria he had trained and trellised into almost gothic proportion. "Quality, not quantity," he squawked, always having the last word.

Wilbur and I had developed a well-worn flirtation, grounded more by our common love of absurdity than anything resembling attraction. He'd set his pruners down but kept the burning cigarette dangling from his mouth. "Coming, Madame Blackwell" whenever I called out for help lifting something or other. "Whatever your little heart desires," he'd tease me but I ignored him.

Goodness, I had ten years on the man, but smoke and drink and a lifetime of working in dirt had deepened his pores and made him look older than me. If you didn't know better, you'd think we were a married couple, me barking orders "When's the last time you fed the azaleas?" and him sniggering through the smoke of another unfiltered tip, "Last time you reminded me is when."

I looked forward to Wilbur's visits. I'd offer him a glass of lemonade or tea which he always rejected, "thanks, got my own," he'd tell me, unscrewing a thermos of rum and whatever he decided to mix in with it. Together we'd sit on the top step of my porch, after the sun finished the best of it's beating, him chugging from his thermos, me sipping tepid lemonade, and we would discuss next month's agenda.

"I'm sick of the buddleia," I'd belt out of nowhere. "I'm sick of it scratching the car when I drive up the driveway. What can you do with it?" He'd take a long swig, shake his head, "Whatever you want me to do with it" and I loved the sound of it, loved the way I could almost guess what wisecrack he'd come back with. After Ned, I never had much interest in men, and no regrets there. But sitting with Wilbur on the stoop of my house grousing about what was wrong with everything, felt like a kind of love to me.

That letter from the lawyer came the day after Wilbur's last visit, a month gone already, I remember because he'd left his trowel on the door step which he never does, and

I noticed it when I opened the door for the FedEx man. Four long weeks and I found myself waiting on the doorstep when he arrived, like an anxious teenager, and without a word I led him to the back of the garage, where the remains of whatever Ray had left behind were stored.

I'd forgotten about those boxes over the years but ever since I got the letter, I started thinking maybe there was a clue there, maybe Pa put some of Ray's things away that he didn't want me to see.

"Is there something wrong, Madame B?" Wilbur could read my face, and I wondered just how well he did know me. Maybe better than I knew myself.

"Wilbur, can you help me with these?" He reached for the boxes. They were too far back so he went for the tall ladder, barely snagging them with his fingertips and the bottom one slid out, light and fast, slipping past his certain grasp. Bits of balsa wood, some carved, shapes of wings, broken bird beak shapes, all mixed up with sea shells, hundreds of them, broken into sand, spilled all over the garage floor.

"Where do you want these?" he quipped but I stood as if frozen in the doorway, my hands over my mouth, a look of terror in my eyes.

"Stay there Madame B. I'll get every last one up for you." And he did, one carved sliver at a time, returned them to the old box, along with a yellowed paper with drawings of birds, carefully measured and detailed, feathers, claws, beaks, labeled and dated in Ray's immaculate script.

I knelt on the floor to scoop up the broken bits of our childhood, not a single shard worth keeping. "Better toss them out" I said but my voice must have been cracking because Wilbur, tough old Wilbur, put aside his glasses and came over to me and in a way I can only describe as kind, held me in his sweaty arms as I cried and cried like a baby until I ran out of tears.

And that's what finally got me to make the call. I had picked up the Realtor's business card several times over the past few weeks but that bright smiling picture of him, with a name Lucky Lundale no less, was just too cheery for my taste. I wasn't ready to get sucked into anything. It can wait, I told myself, but the holidays were coming, busy season at the church, and acquiring this five acre piece of land seemed like a present of sorts. At least I needed to open it and see what was inside.

The ride up to Nevada County took some wind out of me. This old Corolla isn't used to gravel roads. Makes me miss driving Ned's Dodge Dart with that classic Slant Six engine. They only made it for a few years and according to Ned, there was never a better engine made. We named it Dotty back when it was brand new and every now and then I think about how he used to gloat over how quiet her engine ran, even when he pushed her second gear up hills.

Ned loved to baby that car. On the weekends he'd come over, he and Pa would take turns shimmying under the chassis while I talked to the ends of their legs. Guys from Pa's work, from around the corner, would drop over, stick their heads under the hood, cursing praises, softly touching and admiring every gorgeous inch of her turquoise body.

Dotty is still parked in the garage, I keep her covered with a plastic tarp that time has begun to eat through. No telling what she looks like. I don't have the heart to investigate. It was Mr. Harrington, Ned's father, who finally got me to crank her up after Ned died. He and Pa shared a bond as though they'd been in battle together. The loss of sons gave them something to talk about. So they drank, not much, just what the facts called for. Some months went by before they approached the car, like they might offend Ned if they so much as nicked it. She hummed like a kitten when they started her up, next thing I knew they were changing the oil, taking her out on the interstate, a couple of overgrown teenaged boys, and the car was happy to be back in gear.

It took me some months to get in, change the seat so I could reach the pedals, clean out the glove compartment. I threw out every scrap of paper in the garbage and didn't so much as look. I reached under the seat and found one of Ned's leather gloves, the left hand, one he'd been looking for. I slipped it back under the seat where it still is and always will be, as long as I'm around.

People whispered when I drove it, I could sense it, like trails of road dust, whooshed up behind me. I could sense their pity, eyes following the young widow, though we never did get around to marrying. After the doctors gave him the death sentence all our wedding plans got steamrolled. It all happened so fast. We talked about taking our vows at his bedside. But he went from bad to worse before there was time to think about anything other than holding hands, praying together (which I only did to please him, believe me, prayer didn't help the situation one bit), and saying goodbyes to his family and buddies. Sometimes I regret not taking our vows. I loved the sound of Hannah Harrington. Used to practice writing it on napkins, with oversized H's for flourish. But no sense thinking about that anymore.

Every once in a while when I'm driving a long distance, I find myself thinking about Dotty, picturing Ned behind the steering wheel with that fancy leather cover he paid extra for. Tapping on the shiny turquoise dashboard along with whatever tune was playing on the radio. Thin slips of yellow hair falling into his eyes, I'd whisk his hair away so he could see the road and he'd grab my hand, kiss it, bring it down to his thigh if the light turned red. We had some good times in Dotty. I think that's why she kept on running for so long, a good ten years past Ned at least. You can't find parts for the Slant Six engine anymore, something that would have made him furious.

San Juan Ridge is about sixty miles north of Roseville, crossing through a series of winding mountain roads that up until now I've made a point of avoiding.

But once I got the hang of the highway, once I figured out it was just roads leading to more roads, I kept my speed at a sensible 40 mph. Everyone passed me, which was fine with me. Going slow, I noticed how concrete big box shopping plazas disappeared into scruffy looking strip malls, and occasional gas stations eventually faded into open pasture land. Then the pines and maples and oak trees started, thickening at each turn of the wheel, interrupted by roads, marked, unmarked, then marked again. Highway 49 came up large and clear, like the map said, and just as large, a sign reading *Lucky Realty—Own A Piece of Paradise*—reared up a few miles past the turn-off to Nevada City. It was located in a claptrap of a building, making me glad I didn't bother to dress for the occasion. The building also housed a used clothing store, a palm reader (Sister Matilda), and a windowless establishment with neon lights flashing *The Nugget*, even in the middle of the day. I turned off the ignition, amazed and relieved to have come the distance without incident.

"Seven-acre parcels are going like hotcakes around here," the Realtor must have said to me at least ten times. I could see right away that this Mr. Lundale had big designs on my business. All I wanted to do was see the place. I may have come off as rude, well so what if I did. This was Ray's place we were talking about, not some commission for him to write up on his chalkboard.

"Let's just go up there Mr. Lundale. I don't have much

time to waste here."

And so we did.

I couldn't see out the windshield for the dust, could barely hear his ranting on with all those gravel bits pocking the road, fighting with the tires.

"The place needs some work but even as is, you'd be surprised what folks will pay around here to get country property."

I was holding hard on to the strap of Mr. Lundale's monstrous truck, felt like I was being bucked by a horse. My stomach was not as it should be, and I was worried about what I might do to his leather dashboard.

"Please slow down," I tried to say, but he was lost in his own spit-shined reveries.

"Yessirree, we'll get you a good price for this" was his answer. I rolled the window down, took in a loud rush of air to keep the contents of my stomach at bay.

Just then, the truck hit a pothole, bouncing us both up and out of our seats. He downshifted with a broad sweep of his muscular arm, then resumed his excessive speed. "Almost there" he winked, maneuvering his mountain monster past a sign that read Blind Shady Bend.

At the end of a winding rock-strewn stretch, he stopped the truck, set the brake and reached over to open my door.

"This is it. Let me come around to help you down."

I had to step high over the logs, careful not to snag my ankles on the underbrush. Here and there I noticed signs that somebody had been digging in the dirt, but for the most part, it was nothing but broken tree limbs and weeds everywhere. People around here certainly didn't believe in grooming their hedges. I have to say I was pleased Mr. Lundale wasn't treating me like an old woman, trying to protect me from the roughness of the landscape. He didn't bother to guide me through the thicket, just let me wander around on my own. I was grateful for that.

"I've got the name of a good tree man," he offered, as though I had asked him. "Spend a couple hundred on clearing will make you many thousands more. People like to see what they're buying. Of course, that's all up to you."

"Of course," I answered, and then moved on. He finally stopped talking and let me be for a few quiet minutes while I stepped deeper into the brush, scratching my pant legs against the undergrowth that released unfamiliar though not unpleasant smells. I leaned over to pick what looked to be mimula, but of a purplish-red tone I'd never before seen.

Broken chicken wire fencing, weeds raging their way across the landscape, so this is where my runaway brother lived. Or didn't live. It was hard to know, hard to imagine anyone living in a place like this. Everywhere I turned, a spindly rough ground shrub and dwarf wild roses bit my ankles. Gnarled twists of manzanita scattered every which way, like an antelope's graveyard.

So many years gone, there's no way to know if Ray came straight here after he ran away. I always figured he'd come home eventually. So often I'd stood at the living room window, pulling back the curtains, stretching the dainty lace circles of fabric until I could fit my fist through them. Ray and Pa screaming insults in the driveway, and Mother crying in the kitchen. I remember how he mounted that Harley of his, remember how the shine of his belt buckle caught the sun like he was sending signals to me. Signals I couldn't read. He never even looked at the window, never even knew I was there. He just beat at the dust with his heavy foot, like a bronco about to rush the gates. I tried calling to him but my words couldn't make their way through the roar of Ray's Harley starting up in the driveway.

"Don't go," I pleaded with him the time that turned out to be the last time. But, stubborn selfish brat that he was, he had already pulled up his bootstraps and cranked the gears. He wouldn't have heard my voice even if I had been screaming, which I was.

"Will you smell that air?" Mr. Lundale bellowed, as we made our way down the driveway. A gully ran down the middle of the property, littered with logs, automobile tires, God knows what else. "This air will keep you alive way past your time," I heard him call out.

After about fifty feet of rocky driveway, the house finally came into view. It looked like it was being held up by weeds and rocks, like a mild breeze would send the rafters flying. Lundale caught up with me, despite my best efforts to stay out of his way. I hoisted myself onto the grand wrap-around porch that was sprouting a second tier, as fallen logs from years past thickened its surface. Young trees had forced themselves through the floorboards and seemed to be contributing to its structural support.

"Don't worry about the house. Mostly cosmetic," Mr. Lundale puffed, out of breath from trying to follow me. "The neighbor's son across the road is handy with a hammer. Fine young man. His father runs the local hardware store. Just say the word, he can help you fix it up good as new."

Brittle and broken and covered in what looked to be decades of dust, the porch appeared concave in parts, with monstrous tree roots rendering it convex in others. I had to step carefully to avoid nicking myself on rusted nails. A rotted out wicker chair leaned against the house, looking like it might have been painted white at one time, but that time had long since passed. A pool of pine needles had collected on the threshold and I grabbed a fistful, sniffed in the spicy smell.

"Careful, now" he warned me, but I was already inside. Not hard to do seeing how the front door was missing half its hinges. The floor was strewn with rodent droppings, thorny branches, aluminum cans, unidentifiable refuse burned brittle by the years. Bees hovered dangerously close.

But even in this dilapidated state, there was a kind of charm about the place that I couldn't refute. A simple living room with two small windows facing up to the road, an essentials-only kitchen, one narrow countertop for the sink and a few cupboards, an alcove for the filth-encrusted refrigerator and stove, and a small pantry filled with rat droppings and who knows, maybe some baby rats in there too. And through the pantry, probably built on as an afterthought, an ample bedroom with a wall of windows that opened to generous views of green and space and sky. I was surprised by the size of the room—bigger by a third than the living room. Bent nails and bits of wood hung loose from the wall, remains of what must have been a built-in platform bed. I tried to picture Ray lying there, feet up on the wall like he did as a kid. Nobody screaming "Get your goddamned feet off the wall" at him.

"Did you happen to know my brother?"

"Can't say as I did, ma'am. This place has been empty for as long as I can remember. Just needs a little TLC. We can go back to my office and check the comps. Depending on your time frame, I think you'll be happy with the sum this baby brings. Like I said, plenty of fools out there will pay a pretty penny for a site like this."

"Don't be in such a hurry Mr. Lundale. I'm not yet sure what I'm going to do. I just wanted to see it, if you'll recall."

He got very quiet after that. I walked around the back, looking for traces of what, I couldn't say. Found a filthy whiskbroom on the back porch, some petrified match books in the kitchen drawer. A rusted spoon on the sill above the sink.

On the drive back, neither of us spoke a word, just

listened to gears shifting, the hiss of cicadas and honeybees splitting the air. I didn't give him much room for goodbyes, just took the slick packet of brochures and a stack of business cards he insisted on handing me, the Lucky Lundale Realty card right on top with his picture staring at me, in case I might forget that smarmy smile.

9.

A FAINT BEEP WENT OFF somewhere in the kitchen, the microwave timer stuck with fifteen seconds left, an irritation like a fly buzzing in the next room. Daphne was finally asleep in the stroller but she needed to be changed. Later, Callie decided. Ralph would be starved when he got home and she just remembered to add the turnips to the stew, they were still rock hard and he liked them mushy. She turned the heat up and hoped he wouldn't get home just yet, hungry as she was. Daphne finally asleep after all those fitful minutes of steady rocking, and Callie's arms were still tingling from the task of keeping the child moving and still, moving and still, moving and still.

She wheeled the stroller into the bedroom, very carefully closed the door just enough so that noises would not enter but cries could still be heard. She beeped off the microwave and took a deep breath, soaking in the silence. It hadn't exactly been her idea to have a baby but it did seem like the next thing to do.

Ralph's business was doing well, better than expected. Automatic sprinkler systems guaranteeing evergreen lawns, how could it not succeed? New subdivisions were getting approved every week in the valley and the people looking to live in them were the kinds who were attracted to bright green lawns. Ralph had insisted on expensive high-gloss pamphlets, he was that kind of visionary. "Put the money in," he liked to say, "and it will come back doubled."

Ralph was gone a lot, of course. He had to be. There was no one in the company that believed in the product as much as he did. Sure he loved the money. But he seemed to love the thrill even more. It was the beginning of a new time along San Juan Ridge. Funky old properties dotted with doublewide trailers and crumbling geezer shacks were on their way out. People were plopping pre-fabricated houses onto cheap land, rolling out perfect lawns and a couple of azaleas or whatever the ladies liked, rocking on their decks to the sound of their money growing.

And those houses required sprinkler systems. Simple as that. A young generation was buying up country acreage and they wanted lawns so their kids wouldn't track mud across the wall-to-wall carpets. The gold had been mined out of these parts long ago, but there was a new kind of gold popping up above ground, and Ralph Daschle had pick in hand.

This week he was talking to some builders over on the east side of Lookout Mountain, closer to Riverdale. "I'll probably be a couple of hours late tonight, maybe more" he called to her that morning, "It's all flat land out there, honey. What I call lawn country!" but she was bending over to pick up Daphne's bottle, now covered with crumbs, and only heard "maybe more."

"We're gonna be rich, baby" he yelled too loudly, honking all the way down the driveway, and sometimes she just wanted to kill him.

She remembered now that he said he'd be late, and

relaxed into the late afternoon. The baby down, turnips and pot roast cooking, Callie sat on the window seat, let her shoulders sag into their sockets, and listened for the rumble of gravel. The road was quiet. Dead quiet, but for the soft snap of lacewings and finches, darting through the wind. Whatever few minutes Callie had until Ralph got home, or Daphne woke up, she reveled in this precious fleeting quiet. She walked barefoot to her room and faced the mirror like it was a confessor. Looked deep but could only see the surface tracings of her tired old lines.

Callie removed her blouse, unhooked her bra, and sighed. Look at them, she almost cried. Drawn and puckered now, not at all like a young woman's breasts should be. The baby had done something to her nipples, thickened them with all that pulling and yearning, so they looked like discarded bits of leather hardened in the sun. And the shape, once round and tight, had gone slack. You'd think all that milk would have filled them out more but they did the opposite. Drained them. She had read somewhere in a woman's magazine that breast feeding enhanced the size, "breast feeding's not just for the baby. It will give your man a lot more to love…" or something along those lines. Nothing but lies. Hers were drawn and tired and flopped shapeless against her freckled skin.

Callie tugged at her jeans. Size 4, she used to wear a 2, but these were still too tight. She pulled hard and slowly stretched them over and around her belly, ugly belly, lined with blue zigzag reminders of those last few horrid months. The aching back, peeing all the time, she figured out early on, watching other expectant mothers prancing around all pink-cheeked with their bright clean maternity clothes, she knew early on she wasn't cut out for this.

The baby made a gurgling sound. She stopped still in front of the mirror and prayed. Sometimes the gurgle preceded a full out scream, and sometimes it faded mysteriously back into silence. Shit, not yet. Don't fucking wake up yet. Please God, please.

Callie turned back to herself, her ugly misshapen blue-lined self, and touched it. Not on the skin, but on the mirror, feeling the cold hard glass against her fingertips. Touch me, her body called but she wouldn't dare. It had betrayed her and did not deserve her tenderness.

And now the shower, full force, just what she needed and she let out a guttural sigh that sounded like it came from far away. The sound, no it was the baby, crying now, cries getting louder, so she turned the water on higher, turned the nozzle to pulse so the water beat down hard on her back, her neck, the sticky creases between her breasts, her ears, loud water rushed over her so she could not hear, even if she wanted to, the baby awake and screaming from somewhere across the other side of her life.

Ralph got home late, like he said he would, the turnips dissolved completely just the way he loved them. It really didn't take much to make him happy.

Even the baby was happy now, having completed a

good long sleep after that earlier fit that brought Callie's shower to a premature halt. The house smelled delicious and she had even managed to clip a few mimulas for the table, a scraggly spray of forget-me-nots, one sprig of thyme that managed to put out a nice smell despite its pathetic appearance. Sauce and flowers and newly polished toenails, all on account of a few lucky little naps that had scattered themselves mercifully, like jewels, across her day. This is a mother's life and it's not so bad really, she decided, stroking the baby's head, the fuzzy fine fur, too sparse for color, thin and pale and mostly bald. She traced the tender spot that offered scant protection to the tiny unfinished brain and nuzzled her lips into the overwhelming softness. Sucked it in.

"You're looking pretty" he greeted her with a pat on the ass and a quick nuzzle to the baby who was starting to make cooing sounds which Ralph insisted was Daddy. Grabbed a beer first and then his wife, eager pecks on the mouth and "dinner smells good baby." He was a good man, he was. She pulled her blouse down, it had wrinkled in their embrace, and she noticed a stray flower stem tucked into her waistband. Whisked it away. Ralph was right, she was pretty.

Later that night, he took her, hard. It had been a great day and this was his way of celebrating. Thirty-six homes were going up near Riverdale and guess what, every last one of them was going to need a sprinkler system.

"I told you baby, I told you, I told you," he grunted as he bore his way inside her, smacking his hips full throttle against her. Sometimes Ralph could be gentle, even sweet, but those times usually coincided with some vulnerability, a lost sale, some deal gone sour, and she would nurture his smallness in her deft hands, make him feel like a man again. But this time she wasn't expecting much in the way of tenderness. This time he rode her like a bull, so wild he was with pleasure.

"Honey," he said, wiping the sweat from his eyes as she rolled out of his grip and on to her side, facing out to the small patch of sky outside their bedroom window, "honey, this is the deal we've been waiting for. Once the developer agrees to buy my systems for this Riverdale project, the rest of the valley will hear about it. He knows the mayor, Callie. He knows the fucking mayor. Over on the other side of Lookout Mountain they're starting to bulldoze. Do you know what that means?"

"Sprinklers!" she laughed, wiggling his soggy cock back and forth like a garden hose. What was left of his juice splattered against the sheet and she rubbed it all over his belly squealing "sprinklers, more sprinklers." They squealed and grabbed and rolled into each other one more juicy time, with the glee of the soon-to-be-wealthy, the glee of those who think they can see the backlit edge of their wildest dreams creeping into view.

Ralph had always been a dreamer, but the good kind. He didn't just lie back all starry-eyed and certain, no, he worked on those dreams. Ralph could sell anything, even back in high school, he pushed a cart up and down the aisles of the football stadium selling nothing but crushed ice from his parent's doublewide freezer. No overhead, he figured wisely, but for the cost of small paper cups, and the sweaty hot kids in the stands gladly gave him fifty cents for a cool swab of freezing slush to wipe their foreheads, sneak down their girlfriend's blouses, scrunch between their teeth when the ball was out of play. It was a genius plan and Ralph raked in more money than the soda and pretzel vendors combined. Something cheap and cold was really all anyone needed and that's exactly what he delivered. Back then, as now, Ralph was not ashamed to admit he was damned proud of himself.

She saw his pride and confidence from the stands as he called up and down the stadium aisles "ieeeeece chips ice cold ieeeece chips" and she saw it when he took her to the movies in his spit-polished truck. She saw all that pride and confidence and couldn't get enough of it. She sidled up to him hoping some of it would rub off, like crushed ice against hot skin.

Here it was six years later and it still felt that way, though he had moved from ice chips to refrigerator magnets to car alarms to automatic sprinkler systems, while she, she was still Callie, the girl in the stands, looking for an arm to hook into, looking for someone to lean on.

"Night baby" he mumbled, turning into her, "I love you, baby" he whispered into the sticky pillow.

Callie turned her eyes toward the night. Ralph's arm wrapped around her, she didn't dare move, afraid to wake him. She stroked the dark hairs on his arm, soft in one direction, bristly in the other, and found herself thinking about Robin again. It usually only happened at times like this, quiet, in the dark, when dreams and what was really happening got mixed up into indecipherable whirls. She hadn't run into him since that first time, several weeks back, maybe more, she wished she could remember exactly. She tried picturing him but Ralph shifted slightly, and the coarse hairs on his arm tickled her neck. Callie couldn't help but wonder if Robin had as much hair on his arms. She didn't think he did.

10.

ON THE WAY HOME from Ray's place I missed the turn-off and headed clear to Lake Wildwood before I figured it out. Then I had a hell of a time finding my way back to Exit 28. It shook me up a bit. I had to pull over and then decided it best to stay away from the super highway. Instead I worked my way along the old route 60, dead-end town after dead-end town, all victims of the interstate—folks walking slowly through the streets as though they had no place in particular to go.

And then there I was back home, turning on to Mead-owbrook Lane, and sure enough, the first thing I saw was the floozy across the street, up on her ladder again, trying out a peacock blue this time. She's been sampling colors for years, it's what she does. She bought the house the year before Pa died and we hoped it was a sign the neighborhood was going to spruce up. She turned out to be just another crazy who managed to scrape togeth-er enough to afford a two-bed one-bath blip in this tired neighborhood. She had hoisted her ladder in front of the house the week she moved in, and ever since she's been slathering on stripes of blues, grays, golds, even tried a sickening pinkish peach once, then back to blues again (which was a relief) forcing the neighborhood, and me in particular since I'm directly across the street, to bear wit-ness to her endless color whims from one month to the next. I turn my head away whenever she's out front, don't want so much as eye contact.

And down the block I spotted the idiots with the beat-up Ford flat bed, always loaded down with an ever-changing burden of car parts, sheet rock leftovers, paint-stained 2x4's that precluded any possibility of future use. Whenever the wife hurled herself into the driver's seat and started the monster up, a cloud of exhaust left a trail of fumes in her wake, like a giant fart. Her departures set all the neighborhood dogs to howling and sometimes, in the night, I imagined myself sneaking across the road to slash holes in all of their tires. I still could.

Next door had become a rental after Ruth died, 'dear old Ruth' as mother used to call her. She and Mother were pretty good friends in the beginning. Ruth loved to tell us how she bought the place in the forties for just under two thousand, could have bought the whole block but Horace wouldn't hear of it. Horace was a good bit older than her and by the time Ray was born, Ruth was already widowed.

"Poor Ruth" my mother often sighed, but Ruth didn't seem so poor to me. Pushed her lawn mower every Saturday morning up and back over an uneven yard and kept her roses blooming way past their season. As a child I remember thinking it wasn't Ruth who was poor, it was my mother, though I couldn't have said why.

Here I am talking about my crummy neighbors and look at me. I only planned to move back in with my folks for a few months after Mother got her stroke, back in 1964.

Ned had been gone almost a year and the apartment we shared never felt right after he died. Technically he lived with his roommate, Frank something or other, I never really knew the man. Frank kept Ned's mail and some of his furniture so people wouldn't think the wrong thing like they did back in those days, if a man and woman lived together out of wedlock. Makes me feel old just thinking about it. But it was our apartment, married or not, and I needed to get away from the memories. I was always listening for his key in the lock. I couldn't get off to sleep. So when the folks needed my help, I figured moving back in with them would be a good transition until I figured out what I wanted to do next.

Well I figured wrong. Just like that a few months turned into 43 years. Here I am still living in my parents' house, with both of them long dead and who can say why fate snags you back to where you started?

I dropped my keys in the square turquoise glass ashtray that I kept on the end table next to the door. Why ever did I choose that ugly thing to hold my keys? It was something mother picked up at what she liked to call vintage shops. She managed to convince us it was valuable. Piece of crap is what it is.

I took a good long look around my living room. Square windows, square tables, square pictures on the wall. All I could see were the squares.

I kicked off my suddenly aching shoes and one of them tumbled sideways against the ceramic vase covered with seashells, of all things, that served as a doorstop next to the front door. The shoe tipped the vase onto the tile entryway and the thing split into three neat pieces. I was thrilled to see it come apart. I couldn't for the life of me remember which family vacation that came from. All those souvenirs looked so bright and fresh when we first brought them home, only to reveal themselves soon after as useless, unattractive, and frivolous. Pieces of my mother. And why was I still holding on to them?

I stumbled into my kitchen, hot and thirsty and filthy. My hands were cut up in places where I must have accidentally rubbed against the wild rose thorns and that stinking ground cover. The sweat under my armpits had come and gone, leaving behind an acrid scent of dust and excess. I went to the sink, watched the mud break loose from my fingers, and bent over to let the water cool the top of my head, run down along the sides of my neck, my road map of creases. I was tired, but a different kind of tired than I was used to, the kind of tired that made me feel alive.

I wandered from room to room, closed my eyes and counted eight steps to my kitchen counter, didn't even nick my hip on the chair on the way over, and decided that I had been living most of my life as if blind-folded. Now the blindfolds were off, and the bright light stunned me silent.

Don't ask me why I never sold this place. I had a chance after Pa died. That was thirteen years ago and new condo developments with built-in everythings were going up over in Trinity Pines, while interest rates were going down. I had the chance.

But it was easier to stay. Darlene is only five minutes away, Merle's produce market closer than that. Landscape supply yard is practically walking distance, though lately Wilbur's been taking care of that sort of thing.

The church is practically around the corner. I still walk there from time to time, when one of the kids is getting confirmed or married even (they do grow up fast) or they need me to show another new girl how things are done in the office. So many years my life revolved around that church. I must say I still take pleasure in hearing the noon bells and off-key sounds of choir practice. I loved my little office, a closet really, but with clerestory windows that opened out to a tidy garden. The smell of cut grass on Tuesdays and Fridays, the lilt of Sister Agatha's good morning, lifted me out of my life quite nicely, Catholic or not.

The hallways smelled of warm bananas and peanut butter. Sounds of locker doors clanking and high voices humming were the background of my days and it was a good job by all accounts, easy walk from home, pleasant though never thought-provoking conversations. I was comforted daily by the clacking of untied shoelaces along stairwells, the soft chalky finger tracings up and down the walls. The Sisters were kind and never appeared to care which way or even if I prayed. They knew what I had lost. Had the decency never to mention it. I was happy for that.

When the school day began, it was up to me to air out the rooms, let the light in, and at the end of the day, flick off the lights, stand in the stillness as my office turned silent, like a tomb, shut tight by the shades. No parents, kiddies, nuns or tidy bits of paper followed me home and I wouldn't have wanted them to.

Sometimes the mothers would give me their babies to hold while they tied shoelaces or signed forms. Gave me an excuse to leave my desk, walk around the halls, pretend a little. I loved the babies but loved giving them back just as much. Probably best I never had any of my own. Still, it was the part of the job I knew I'd miss the most.

Sister Marguerite hasn't yet given up trying to get me to come back. Since I retired eight years ago they haven't found a single person to handle the office like I used to. One of the girls couldn't manage to get payroll out in time. None of them can spell worth a damn. They even offered to pay me to train the new ones but I was done with all that.

I do have a hard time finding reasons to get out of the house sometimes. It feels like I've started to fossilize, along with all the junk I've been digging out of my closets. By the time I got that special delivery knock on my door, I had pretty much stopped thinking about my brother, much less any possibility of changing my life.

I overslept Tuesday morning and missed my 10:00 with Darlene. This time she called and woke me up. Said she could squeeze me in at 2:00. Sure why not. She made such a deal of it.

"Why couldn't you call to cancel?"

"Because I was asleep."

She's been mad ever since I told her to stop putting all that crap in my hair.

So I went ahead and told her why I'd overslept. She wouldn't just take the headlines, she needed the why. I told her about going up to see my brother's land, about the Realtor. "He had one rocket in his pocket, wanting to make a sale," I said, but she didn't seem to find it funny.

"Don't tell me you're moving out there," she barked. "Do you really think you could manage all that land by yourself?" and on and on like that, like it was her sorry life, not mine, this was happening to.

It's all too much to think about. Right now I'm out of milk, Amos is mewing up a fit since I was gone all day yesterday. He knocked over one of the African Violets just to show me who's boss. Dirt all over the floor, and Wilbur isn't due here again for two more weeks. I forgot to remind him to pick up more bone meal and something else, I can't remember now.

I set the envelope of papers the Lundale fellow handed me down on the one square side table that didn't hold an African violet or one of Mother's glass doodads. More business cards, one from Highway Hardware—that's the guy who lives right across the road. Good guy to know, the Realtor kept reminding me. Also his son with the girl's name, the one who knows something about building. His business card simple enough—Robin Till—Handyman. A couple of tree guys, in case I wanted to do some clearing. And of course Lucky Lundale Realty, like I could ever forget him.

I looked around my living room, the pillows, the faded furniture, framed watercolors of birds on frozen ponds, dirty dishes on the counter. Even my reflection in the hallway mirror repelled me, sagging skin around my eyes, and since when did my earlobes grow longer? I counted six stray whiskers sprouting every which way tucked under my chin, like they were trying to hide from me, like I'd never notice.

I was tired from yesterday's drive, my head ached from the ranting real estate chatter, the bunions on my feet screaming from all that tramping around over logs and uneven ground. I opened the pantry, hoping to find something to soothe me. That old apricot liquor festering on the bottom shelf looked pretty good and I took a long, slow sip. What was it, the dust of the drive, or the idea that Ray was back in my life, made me take an extra swig.

I paced around the house and found myself in the kitchen, peering into the refrigerator. Such a dull display of choices. My meager food budget gives me enough for the good kinds of bread, with thick crusts, and lately they've been selling those fancy spreads with garlic, lemony dill, red pepper, seems like every day another flavor hits the shelf. A couple of dollars worth of spreads and breads and pieces of fruit lasts me a week, throw in a radish for some crunch.

But now I was confronted with an almost empty V-8

juice bottle, bloated blueberries drowning in clumps of cream left over from Sunday's little brunch at the church. The fancy garlic spread had something blue growing on top and the dark bread was too hard to cut into. Nothing but soggy fruit and stale almonds that I buy because they're supposed to be good for you, don't ask me why. I craved a cold glass of beer, or rocky road ice cream floating in a frosted beaker of ginger ale or maybe a thick hunk of rare meat with Worcestershire dressing. Something Ray might have gone for.

I found the bathroom comforting. I sat on the toilet though I didn't have to go, just sat there thinking. How much money could I get for that place? Who would ever buy it? I wondered what the inside would look like painted, might not be so bad. All those wild roses scattered around the property. Those gorgeous madrones. And was that a patch of pansies growing in the middle of nowhere? And that smell. Goldenrod? Tansy? And what are the neighbors like? Questions large and looming without answers kept spilling out of me and I tried hard to pee but nothing came.

I picked up the handyman's business card and walked into the bedroom, intending to make a call. Had to start somewhere. Winter was on its way, every day getting a little bit cooler. I started to dial but then thought better. No sense rushing. Let the idea of it settle in. Let the rains come.

Next thing I knew I had fallen on to the bed, scared the crap out of Amos who was bundled under the blanket where he knows he's not allowed. Amos sidled up to me, wove himself like a thick wad of wool beneath my arm and chin and settled there. I wrapped my arm around him so the room would stop swaying and fell into a sleep so hard it felt like death.

Winter

11.

"I'M HUNGRY."

"You had breakfast an hour ago. There are bananas in the basket on the kitchen counter. Grace, reach the bananas for him."

"I don't wanna banana, I want spaghetti." Besides, Timothy could reach the bananas for himself. He was tall enough.

"Gracie, get him something, please, just get him anything." From the living room, they could hear Grandpa's chair squeak, like he might be getting up. Timothy walked over to the doorway but Grandpa was still in his chair. He lowered his voice this time.

"Why can't I have spaghetti?"

"There isn't any spaghetti" Grandpa muttered.

"Yes there is. It's in the tall thing with the tomatoes painted on it, right next to the toaster."

"You can't just eat spaghetti. You have to cook it first."

"I can cook it Grandpa, let me cook it." Grace chimed in, eager to get in the middle of it all.

"Have some cereal. There's fruit bars. Grandpa's trying to rest."

It seemed like Grandpa was always resting. Sometimes they could hear his snoring through the walls while they played alone in the living room.

Timothy had managed, without Grandpa hearing, to climb up on the counter and pull out a piece of spaghetti from the ceramic canister, and was chewing on the raw strand slowly.

"Grandpa, Timothy's eating the spaghetti."

"No I'm not." But now they could hear his chair slide back, his newspaper fall to the floor—they had finally gone too far.

Grandpa walked into the kitchen, his hair all funny and sticking out around his ears. It looked like his pants button was open but Timothy didn't want to stare. Grandpa walked over and took the soggy stick out of his hand.

"Its really not spaghetti 'cause its not covered with tomato sauce."

"Then what exactly is it?" Grandpa asked, his voice about as loud as his voice ever got, which wasn't much. Usually when he was mad his words just slowed down a lot, and got even quieter. Way different than Daddy's kind of mad.

"Its just plain noodles" Timothy explained, "You didn't say we couldn't eat plain noodles."

Timothy could feel himself getting smarter than Grandpa, saying things he knew weren't exactly true and Grandpa just gave up so fast.

"It isn't good for you if it isn't cooked. It'll give you a stomachache."

But Timothy loved nibbling off the hard, crunchy bits, feeling them dissolve into a gooey paste inside his mouth. It never gave him a stomachache.

"Teach us how to cook it Grandpa. We can cook it ourselves. Just this one time, please?"

Maybe it was that extra 'please', but there he was, filling up a pot with water, adding salt, telling them to keep away from the flame because a flame is dangerous, (Grandpa made everything sound dangerous), showing them how to slowly add oil then listen for the noisy water and then add the noodles, slowly slowly, (this could also be dangerous) dropping them so that splats of scalding water didn't bounce onto their skin. Timothy and Grace were sitting now, Grandpa standing over the stove, describing in detail some of the horrible things hot oil can do to skin. And the hardest part, (Grandpa made everything sound so hard), was lifting the noodles with a fork to test for doneness.

"Can we go outside and build a fort now?"

They had been inside for two long wet months. Most of their puzzle pieces had slid somewhere underneath the sofa and there wasn't anything on TV in the middle of the day. Outside was calling them loud.

"Its cold outside, Gracie, be sure Timmy has his jacket" which really made Timothy mad. But at least they could go. You never knew with Grandpa. Sometimes he didn't let you do anything, just made you sit and draw pictures with those broken pieces of crayon he kept in a wooden box. But today they could go outside and Grandpa didn't even ask where they were going.

Timothy raced to keep up with his sister who was already on her way out the door. They had become very interested in forts ever since Grace started drawing them for some school project. She let Timothy help color in her drawings. She got to use the orange and red and gold crayons for the flowers, but she let him use the green and brown ones to color in the ground and trees.

Now that they were outside again they were going to do a lot more than draw. They'd been waiting forever for the chance to go back across the road and work on their real fort some more, dig deeper under the moat, see what treasures they could find. On a day like this the ground would be filled with mud from all the rain and it would be easy to carve a riverbed just with their fingers.

Timothy followed his sister into the blank space of land across the road from Grandpa's, over broken sticks and pieces of wood and metal, jagged and menacing. But there was his sister, almost out of sight already, up around the hill of trees that met the road below, hunting, poking her long stick into secret places and he never was sure what she was looking for.

"Wait for me Gracie!" He tripped and grabbed his way along the path she had already opened. When he turned back to see how far they'd gone, Grandpa's house was harder to see, hidden by tree stumps and wood piles and not even looking like Grandpa's house from this new distance.

"Gracie, wait," he called out, but she was side stepping logs and holding her arms out wide, like flags. It looked as though the wind was carrying her.

Grace landed on the far side of a felled tree, in a clearing that dipped low beyond the road and from this new place there was no sight of Grandpa's house, no mailboxes to count, no familiar shapes or structures to recognize.

"T, over here," she shouted from behind a log, waving her arms hard so Timothy caught sight of her yellow sleeve and raced right to it. Scared, but not too scared, just the right amount, his heart tight and giddy, so glad his big sister was there to lead him, so glad she was far enough ahead that he could pretend he was all by himself, but not really.

"This is going to make a perfect moat," she told him.

"Wowee Gracie, this is neato."

"Yeah, this is neato, but you can't tell anybody, not anybody, not even Daddy. Do you promise T? Or I won't take you anywhere ever."

"I promise." His hand went up, vow-position, he pledged her allegiance with an eager heart. His sister, brave and fearless and certain. He could never have found this place without her.

They needed rocks. Not too big, just big enough to hold up the dirt and keep the sticks in place. Timothy had appointed himself scout with no objections from his sister who was busy gathering up twigs and making dirt mounds for the moat walls. Walking with his head down so as not to miss the perfect rock, he carefully picked up and discarded bunches of plain brown ones that didn't have any special markings or colors. He had to go slowly to find a good one and sure enough, there was one with blue and green lines, and another smaller one that sparkled when he held it up to the sun. He pushed them deep into his back pocket, not sure if he was even going to show them to Grace.

He had been walking this way for a while when a sound coming from behind a grove of trees made him stop and look up. Placing one quiet foot in front of the other, he edged forward, then again, stepping farther away from his sister, forgetting now about the rocks and listening instead to the unfamiliar sound, like a grunt an animal would make, maybe a possum, they usually only came out at night and he knew they couldn't hurt you. But this was daytime and the grunt suddenly changed into singing, and now Timothy felt himself propelled magnetically forward, not noticing that the dirt below his feet turned into a pathway of white rocks, a driveway, not his driveway, but whose?

Timothy stopped still. He looked back to see if he could find Grandpa's house—was it back that way, or the other way? He had turned himself around and was completely lost. Grace was not behind him. He called her name but quietly, so as not to scare the animal or whatever it was. That stinky bush scratched his arms and clumps of rose bushes stung his ankles.

He picked up one foot very very slowly, held his

breath, took another step, let the air out, and in this way, edged closer to where he could squarely see an old woman sitting among a pile of rocks, rocks tucked up around her pant legs, rocks in her lap. She was holding them up, examining them against the light, brushing dirt off their sides, spitting them clean.

Timothy couldn't see her very well through the bushes. He moved a little to the left, but his foot disturbed a mound of pebbles that scattered loose, then he tripped trying to quiet their clinkety sounds. He wanted to hide but too late because already the woman had stood up and was looking straight in his direction.

"Who's there?"

Timothy couldn't speak. He managed to grab onto the nearest pine bough for support, but the needles stung his hands. Everything itched, his hands and feet felt hot and all he wanted to do was run, right now, back to Grace, to Grandpa, safe inside.

"Do you have a name?" While he was searching around to find his way back, the woman had walked over and was now crouched down to meet Timothy's eyes. He would have been scared to death except that one of those sticky weeds that grew everywhere had caught in her hair and was sticking up like an antenna behind her ear. And there was a dark patch of dirt on her cheek so she looked kind of like something you'd see on Halloween. Only funny, not scary. And now she was smiling at him.

"Timothy," he said, barely a whisper.

"Timothy. Wonderful, strong name. Timothy, do you

live in those trees?"

He shook his head.

"Did you fall down from the sky?"

"No," he said, wanting to add "silly," but stopping short.

"Well how did you get to be standing here in the middle of these pine trees? Are you lost?"

Timothy kind of remembered Daddy and Grandpa talking about some lady moving in and maybe this was her. She had a smell on her that he liked, kind of like the trees, but then she was all covered in dirt. The woman liked rocks, he could see that, and wished he could go over and examine the ones in her pile. But wouldn't dare ask.

"You must tell me if you are lost so I can help you."

"I live over there with my grandpa and dad" pointing a dirty finger in an uncertain, upward direction.

"And what's your daddy's name?"

"Robin Till."

"And does he know where you are?"

"Yes" he said, a full blown, immediate and unrehearsed lie.

"Well why won't we walk back to the road and see if your daddy is looking for you."

Timothy had never been in big trouble with Grandpa. Once when he spilled cereal on the floor a little but not big trouble, just the kind a broom could fix. This trouble was getting bigger every step, with Grace probably looking for him and getting him in even more trouble.

"I can make it back myself" he said, and then turned squarely in the wrong direction, heading toward the place with the junky mailbox, dragging his feet.

He felt her take his hand and let her lead him slowly back around and up her rambling driveway until finally he could see the letters on Grandpa's mailbox.

"Do you know the story of Hansel and Gretel?" she asked, pulling a rock out of her shirt pocket.

"Yes" Timothy answered, but he wasn't sure if he did. Still, he took the rock, careful not to look at it. He would save that for later when he was safe inside.

"Next time you wander off, take a fistful of rocks, the white ones are best, and drop them along the way, so you can find your way back home."

They crossed the road together but she didn't go farther than the gate, watching him walk up to the house by himself. He was relieved she didn't follow him in. When he got inside Grace was playing checkers with Grandpa who was bent over the board, looking more like he was asleep than playing a game. Neither of them said anything about Timothy being late.

Grandpa finally made his move, looked up for a second and asked, "How's the fort coming?" Timothy didn't even bother with an answer.

"When's Daddy coming home?"

"You two will probably be in bed, but I'll have him tuck you in just the same." Always the same promises.

They slept together in the same bed Grandpa had shared with Grandma. They had never met her, only knew she got sick and died way before they were born. There was a picture of her on the dresser with Grandpa. She looked a little like Daddy only fat and with a white wig. They were glad they hadn't met her. She didn't look like she'd be much fun.

Grandpa let them sleep in his old bed because the other room was too small for them to share. But they were getting too big for it, at least that's what Grandpa said, and Daddy slept on the sofa in the living room so there was no place else for them to go. Usually the bed was big enough for both of them, but not now, with Timothy's legs flopping over to Grace's side, and the steady groan that meant he was having another one of his nightmares.

"Timothy, stop kicking!" Grace hissed, and she kicked right back but he didn't feel a thing.

Wake up T!" She shook him, shook him hard, "wake UP," and this time the jolt was too strong, his saliva let loose, the pillow wet and cold on his cheek, eyes still closed, he fought his way into this rude return, sat up into the hazy light. "Move over," his sister's voice too loud in his soggy ear.

Timothy sat up, rubbed his eyes. The room, dark still from the shadows of sleep, looked like the forest. Except it wasn't a forest, and now he could see his sister's arm, the window shade, the fuzzy flannel of his pajamas soft against his chest.

"I saw her."

"Saw who?"

"The lady. The lady in the forest."

"Timothy you were dreaming. And kicking me. Move over."

Timothy knew he had not been dreaming. He knew he had met the lady in the forest with the rough hands, eyes like animal eyes, small and sharp, that looked right through him. He knew he didn't dream that. And there was the rock, the rock the lady handed him, safely tucked inside his underwear drawer, he'd pull it out later to prove to Grace that the old woman had been there, been real, real as Grace is now, only much bigger. He rolled over, as far from his sister as he could possibly roll without falling over the edge.

"I saw the lady." Timothy's words came out muffled, wet with saliva. But she understood them.

"What lady?" Grace shouted. "What lady are you talking about?" She tried shaking him, but the boy had already fallen back into a deep and noisy sleep.

12.

A DAY DIDN'T PASS when I didn't think about that place, trying to remember how wide the porch was, whether the kitchen had shelves. I had taken to drawing pictures from memory and every week the place grew bigger, more beautiful, the mess of it fading into background. Last time I drove up there, I was struck by the greenness of it all. Here it is winter, nothing blooming but acacia, but on Ray's land, all those pines and manzanitas and madrones, like the darkest teas brewed all at once, dripping their essences on to every wet surface. I found rocks I've never seen the likes of, turquoise streaked rocks, and I can only imagine Ray noticed them too.

I think I must have scared the living daylights out of the little boy across the way. At least I finally learned where the hardware store owner lives, and his son, a carpenter, right across the road for heaven's sake. It seemed like everything was just falling into my lap.

Not that I had come up with any plans mind you. Just noticing how it felt to drive up there, spend a couple of hours. Just poking. Not a bad drive either. Took me less than two hours, most of it quite pleasant.

But I must be talking about it more than I intend to. Last week, sitting under the hair dryer, I could see the lips moving, heads turning toward me then quickly away, as if I couldn't tell I was this week's subject of gossip.

Darlene is outright furious. "You can't be serious," she hissed, yanking too hard on the curler. "It's dangerous for a woman your age to be living out there in the wilderness. What happens if you fall? Do they even have phone service out there?"

It's nice that she seems to care about my welfare but she's more likely worried about losing my business.

"How about if we keep meeting alongside the highway every couple of weeks. You can do my hair in the back of my car, forget about the curlers. It's not that far. I'll pay you double."

She didn't think that was a bit funny. Pulled hard on a wad of curl while she gave me one of her looks.

"Who's going to know if you've gone missing out on some wilderness road, with no electricity," yelling at me as if the hair dryer were still on.

"Good God, the house across the road has a TV antenna the size of a spaceship, and I counted three beauty shops about fifteen minutes away on Main Street, if that's what you're worried about."

She didn't like that one bit. Took out the rest of my curlers without a word. I let her yank and pull without complaining, even shook out my own plastic apron after she had finished whisking away the last stray hairs from my shoulders.

Harry, on the other hand, seemed to think the whole idea was pretty good, said it would perk up my life a bit, though I think he's wishing he could perk up his own. Harry's at that stage of life where he reminisces far more than anyone cares to listen but for once since all the years we've been switching places at Darlene's hair cutting station, I was almost interested in what he had to say.

"My brother-in-law bought a place a few years back out your way" Harry said, as though I'd already moved. "Did well by it, prices keep going up and up. Wish I'd have had the foresight. Boy if it was me," and by now I was the only one listening, everyone around us back to their magazines and chit chat, "I'd fix the place up to the nines, is what I'd do."

At home I found myself rifling through old drawers, closets, shelves. Something about seeing Ray's land put me in a state of upheaval. I couldn't sit still, pulled every drawer open, discovering things I hadn't seen for years.

Just the other day I turned up a few pieces of Mother's good china: the gravy boat, pitcher and a couple of chipped plates, the English tea rose pattern that really is lovely, broken or not.

And those turquoise Melmac monstrosities I thought I had tossed out after Mother died—there they were under the paint cabinet, packed for shipping. It looked like Pa's work, secured so tight you'd think he was packing explosives. He got busy after she died sorting and packing but then he'd walk away in the middle, leaving wrinkled newspapers on the floor for me to clean up. Well that Melmac just might serve me fine in that old dust heap of a kitchen. The shade of turquoise might even match the color of the mildewed windowsills.

Momentum moved me in a way I hadn't felt since, well, maybe the days when Ray and I used to ride our bikes through the fields. I was a grand old twelve, he was just seven, with those plastic streamers flying on the handlebars of our two-wheelers, we'd ride up behind what's now a labyrinth of outsized stucco claptraps but what was then fields that led to more fields and fields beyond. We'd try to get lost but the land was so flat, we just rode and rode until our legs hurt or until we heard mom's blood-curdling "Hannah-Rayeeeee, Hannah-Rayaeeee" startling us back to the kitchen where she greeted us with melted cheese sandwiches and sprigs of sour grass that she added for crunch.

Piles started building in every corner of my house. I created games with myself (Ray would have laughed) seeing if I could toss a glass from the sink into the garbage by the back door without breaking it. I was giddy and reckless and hoped no one could see me through my windows. Sure enough I broke two glasses, including the one that Pa used to store his dentures, and the other was already cracked at the base, so it didn't count. Otherwise I have to say my aim was pretty darn good.

Found some old ashtrays carved with my initials, and those salt and pepper shakers from Ray's woodworking classes, all things he made me from summer camp. I found yet another box filled with bits and pieces of his bird carvings, early stages, nothing like the beauty that I remembered seeing on his porch railing out on Blind

Shady Bend.

As I shuffled out to the garage carrying everything I was sick of looking at, I almost tripped over Amos who was constantly underfoot and anxious. Don't tell me cats aren't aware of what people are thinking. He knows something's up. Been clawing at me in the morning a little harder than usual, not his regular soft nudge to get me out of bed. But I wasn't about to be slowed down by a cat. I kept going. Framed photographs of places I can't remember visiting, my college diploma hung to cover a patch in the stucco, Mother's paint-by-number cat-stuck-in-a-tree fiasco. I tossed them all.

13.

"TIME TO GET UP IN THERE." They recognized his gravelly voice. "Get those waffles while they're hot!"

Dad must be gone already. Grandpa only made waffles when Dad wasn't home. So many signals they read and understood without a word.

"Can Daddy come in here and wake us up?" Timothy yelled out, just in case.

"Time to get up! Breakfast is ready." Their grandfather's disembodied voice coming through the closed door was not at all the way they hoped to start another day.

Timothy took off his soggy sleep-worn pajama top and put on his hooded sweatshirt, pulling on what was left of the neck string too hard so it came out altogether. Grace didn't say a thing about it, just put on her new bathrobe that Daddy bought her because he said big girls don't wear nightgowns at the breakfast table. They stumbled through the morning routine they had all but mastered, brushing teeth, washing, wiping, putting down the toilet seat, even rinsing all the foam down the drain, and made their way down the hall to what already felt like a bleak beginning to another Sunday without their dad.

The sound of butter snapping hot on the griddle and the sweet smell of cinnamon propelled them to double-jump the two steps down to the living room.

"Grandpa, what's for breakfast?" they called out,

though they knew the answer. It was just something they always did when Grandpa made his famous Waffles Supreme-O with the powdery puff sugar and baby raisins and almond slivers ("That's what makes them 'Supreme-O'," he told them). He let them drop the raisins and almonds one by one into the batter, if they didn't eat them all first.

Every surface of the kitchen was covered with canisters and bowls, practically the entire refrigerator emptied, while Grandpa, cloaked in Bisquick dust, stirred a thick wad of molasses into his secret concoction.

"Anyone hungry for waffles?" He asked it every time, and every time they ran to him, each grabbing one of his legs, trying to lift themselves up like baby chimps, so that he had to set the spoon down finally, reach down and attempt to lift them up in one incredible squeeze.

"You're getting way too big for me" he groaned, which made them laugh, not because it was so funny, but because he said it every single time. They grabbed on to his shoulders, clinging to him with their legs, and his sticky molasses fingers got caught in their uncombed morning hair.

"Who wants peaches? Who wants strawberry syrup?"

"Me, me!" they screeched.

"Who wants chocolate?"

"Me, me, me, me, me!" By this point Grandpa was screaming along with them, sounding like another five-year-old in a crooked, overgrown frame. This was the best that mornings could be, getting sticky rich waffles, seeing his face all splattered with flour, the kitchen a playing field. Most mornings it was cereal, cold, Cheerios or Chex, a slice of apple with the skin on, and quick rush out the door. "Time to go, time to finish, clear your dishes, let's go," their dad always in a hurry to get them off.

But this was a morning that promised to spill over into day, hanging out with sloppy clothes that turned sweet with cinnamon, and nothing to hurry about.

"Your dad decided to take the boat out after all. He should be home by dinner." The kids were too busy licking syrup off their fingers to listen to the excuse.

When the first batch of waffles was flipped and stacked high, Grace carried her plate from the stove to the table, each step carefully measured. One time Timothy dropped his plate and it took forever to get the sticky syrup out of the rug. That would never happen to Grace.

"Careful T!" she yelled to her brother, "don't drop the plate" but Timothy was able to hold the hot stack steady all the way to the table. "Good job!" said Grandpa, but his reassuring voice was drowned out by Grace warning loudly, "Look out T, don't drop it again."

The telephone rang at the worst possible of times. Cold waffles. Don't answer it, Grace begged, but Grandpa reminded them, "It could be your daddy," which got Timothy out of his seat and straight to the phone.

"Daddy?"

But it wasn't his dad calling. It was a woman's voice, asking for Robin Till.

"My daddy isn't home right now. Do you want to talk to my big sister?"

"No" the voice on the other end so loud they could all hear it. Timothy dropped the phone, ran back to the table.

"I don't know who it is."

But Winston was already up and halfway to the phone, wondering himself who would call if it wasn't Robin.

"Hello? Who is this?"

Winston was having a terrible time making out her words.

"My name's Hah" he thought he heard. "Help" and "live across the road" came out loud and clear.

The woman's words spilled out fast and shrill and there was a disturbing amount of static which may have been in the phone line itself, or in the background, possibly wind or water, he was trying to figure all this out but her voice interrupted his thinking.

"Please, can you help me?"

"Slow down Ma'am. This is Winston here. I think you want my son but he's not here today. I'm not sure when he'll be back but is there something I can do for you?"

"You know how to fix broken pipes? My pipe is broken, sheered off at the wall and water is gushing all over the floor."

"Now ma'am, calm yourself down, first of all. Nothing will get settled while you're in this state. Now, do you have a wrench?"

"That's how I broke the damn thing. With a wrench."

Ah hah, he now understood. Her own doing. "Now let's see," he said, clearing his throat to buy a little bit of time, then rearranged the words again, "let's see now, did you try flipping the generator switch? It's over by the pump, should be a red switch somewhere on the generator. It will turn off the well pump, stop the flow while you call an emergency plumber."

He gave her a couple of numbers to call, told her to call back if it didn't work. Scratched his head trying to picture some old woman trying to make order out of that rat hole across the road. So Pete had been right about her moving into the old house after all.

He returned to the table, the children laughing at him, "What's so funny?" but he knew what was funny, aware he had flour dust all over his cheeks and head.

"You look like a clown Grandpa" and sure enough, eyeing himself through the reflection in the window, he could see he had inadvertently smeared some flour on his face while he was talking on the phone.

"So I do" he said, and clapped his hands in front of their faces so that excess flour flew into the air, bringing more waves of laughter. He was glad he had them all to himself, no Robin around to interfere with his clumsy way of doing things.

"Who was on the phone?" Grace wanted to know, and so he told them about this lady who moved into the crazy old house across the road. She had busted her own water pipe with a wrench and didn't even know she had a generator switch to turn the water off!

Grace and Timothy knew all about generator switches. Winston had showed them where theirs was and even let them flip it on and off to learn where their water came from. He let Grace write ON and OFF on the metal panel when she learned her letters. Winston could tell it made them feel good to know they were smarter than some grown up woman.

"Is she coming over here?" Timothy asked, wondering if she was the same woman who had given him the rock, but Grandpa was piling their plates with peaches and boysenberry syrup, the phone call forgotten by everyone, it would seem, but Timothy.

Not two bites into their second serving of waffles, a loud knock on the front door disturbed their lazy morning once again.

Timothy ran to see who it was, and sure enough, it was her. He ran back to the kitchen, afraid that she might tell Grandpa he had crossed the road, wishing he could hide somewhere, but where?

"Who's at the door?" but the boy squeezed himself behind his grandfather's legs, whispered, "I don't know."

"For goodness sake, boy." Grandpa sounded angry as he scooted back his chair and went to the door. They watched him look through the side window to see a woman, that woman, had to be. He took a deep breath, not quite sure what to do next but her face was pressed against the glass, she was waving so he had no choice whatsoever but to open the door and welcome her in.

"Hello, Mr. Till is it? I just wanted to come over and thank you." Her foot already across the threshold, holding out a hand to offer a small bouquet of wildflowers, some already wilting. "These are my way of saying thank you. It's the best I've got, not much blooming over there, but you really saved me."

"Come in, come in," he said, though she already had. "Is everything under control over there?"

"You were right about that red valve. Stopped the water right away. It's a wet mess over there, but I got the generator turned off. Just dropped by to say thank you."

"Oh you didn't have to" he said, taking the flowers, not so much flowers as blooming weeds that were already dropping brittle leaves all over his carpet. "Come on in, we were just finishing breakfast" he gestured, but she had already walked passed him, the smell of waffles seeming to draw her into the kitchen.

"Something sure smells good in here."

"Why don't you have some waffles with us? We can't finish them all."

Yes was all she said, yes I think I'll do that, she said it lots of times, as though she was speaking to herself and not to him.

Grace had seated herself up on the counter, clacking her feet against the cupboard, and Timothy tried but failed to squeeze himself invisible between the cabinets and his sister's legs.

The woman looked down at him, gave him that same smile he remembered from last time, but luckily didn't say a word.

"What are you cooking?" she asked Grace, edging her way closer to the stove.

"Grandpa's Waffles Supreme-O. We get to put the raisins in but only I get to stir it because Timothy might spill." Grace slipped off the counter and began to demonstrate her stirring skills, dribbling a sticky handful of raisins into the bowl.

"I can too stir," the boy objected, but Winston had anticipated the controversy and handed Timothy another table setting.

"Timothy, please set the table for our guest."

Grace immediately lost interest in her bowl stirring advantage, and ran over to where the woman had joined her brother at the table.

"Bet you don't know my name?"

"I bet you're right."

"It rhymes with face."

"Its Grace," Timothy blurted out, not wanting to play this game.

"My name rhymes with banana," the woman offered. "And what does your name rhyme with?" she asked, turning to the boy with a wink that was meant only for him.

"Timothy rhymes with…" but he was at a distinct disadvantage. His was not an easy name to rhyme.

"He doesn't know how to rhyme yet," Grace informed her.

"Yes I do!" whined Timothy, causing the woman to put her fork down, and place her hand on the boy's shoulder, pat it lightly.

"You're right. Timothy is a hard name to rhyme. But what about finding a word to rhyme with "Tim?"

"Him" he yelled. Grace shrugged in disapproval.

"So is everything OK over there?" Winston asked, returning to the kitchen after setting the bunch of weeds in a vase. He was having a hard time believing this was the same woman who had been screaming over the phone just a few minutes earlier.

With most of her waffle left on the plate, the woman stood up and started to walk around the living room, fingers fawning over the woodwork. "My my," she said, "looks like someone here has a knack for fine detail."

"This was my father's home and my grandfather's before that. Four generations back and all of them builders," he told her, "until me."

"I'm sure you had a hand in some of these lovely shelves." She seemed to be wiping dust off of every surface, picking up photographs, and then setting them back down again.

"No, I am not by nature a builder." And then he stopped, surprised to be saying something so personal to this stranger. "Now I am familiar with building terms, yes, and then of course, my son, Robin, he has the builder blood in him. But me, I prefer the clean feel of paperwork to the mess of saws and drills."

"Well it certainly is a comfy place," she remarked, to

which he added, "Comfy sounds like one of those words Realtor's use instead of run-down." Her interest in his house was making him feel unusually playful. It wasn't often Winston had visitors.

"Oh, I know about Realtors all right. I've got one trying to get me to sell my place across the road," she started but quickly stopped as the kids jumped up to clear their plates, asking and granted permission to play outside. He watched her walk over to a photograph of Robin as a little boy that had been on the bookshelf for as long as he could remember. She was holding the photograph up to the window as though that might help identify him.

"And how long have you worked at the hardware store?"

The next thing Winston knew, he was retelling stories he had long since forgotten.

"Vera and I were married in this very room, nothing fancy. My wife never wanted people to make a fuss over her."

Hannah fingered the lace curtains, more holes than lace. "Vera made those," he offered. "I suppose I should replace them but they serve their purpose still."

"What happened to your wife?" she pushed on.

"She's been gone coming on fifteen years. It was cancer." He couldn't bring himself to say the word breast. "She used to take such good care of this house. Back when she was alive, you wouldn't ever see smudged handprints, or flour on the floor," he said, swishing away some of the morning's mess with his foot.

"I'm so sorry" she said.

"No," he said, "it's been too many years to feel sad about. The place used to be so neat, but I have to admit, my Vera erred a bit on the side of fussy."

"So how old is your son?"

"Robin's coming close to thirty now, only fifteen when his mother passed."

"Robin." She repeated the name, as though she wasn't quite sure she'd heard it right.

"Yes, Robin," he confirmed, remembering now how Vera went into labor on a spring day, the apple tree outside the hospital room window teeming with birds.

"I always thought it was a girl's name, even suggested Robert. But Vera reminded me it was her body bringing him, her pain getting him out into the world, and she always did have the tighter grip."

I've gone on too long, thought Winston, but Hannah Blackwell had seated herself squarely on the sofa, without being asked, holding up a picture of Robin and the children. "Nice looking boy," she offered.

"He was supposed to be home but I told him to take the weekend off. He's got a boat over on Fordyce Lake, small fishing boat, he doesn't get to it nearly often enough. The boy works too hard. No time for himself."

"Well you tell him that I'm very interested in having him work for me. I've been leaving him messages but he may not be getting them for all I know. Anyhow, I haven't been able to stop thinking about the place so I started coming up every couple of weeks, thinking that one of these times I'll figure out what I want to do with it. From a distance, it seems so quaint. I tend to forget what a mess it is, and once I get here, I start breaking pipes, making matters worse."

She had made her way to the door by now, ready to leave it would seem, but he had a slew of questions he wanted to ask her, the most pressing being how much work she had for his son. And whether or not she was planning to actually move into that mess of a place and become his new full-time neighbor. There were more questions pushing behind those obvious ones, but all this visiting was more than Winston was used to. He needed to lie down.

"I'll let him know you stopped by" was all he could muster by way of goodbye.

14.

IT TOOK ROBIN another three weeks to finally get back to Hannah Blackwell. He was half-hoping she'd give up on him and call Lundale for the name of any number of guys around here who could do whatever work she had. There had been lots of messages from her over the past few months, and every time she ended the message with "no hurry," but still he couldn't bring himself to call her back.

It wasn't like he didn't need the work. His father had gone easy on him since he and the kids moved in, desperate when Cynthia disappeared on them. But his promise of "just until I can find us a place to live" turned into close to five years now, and Robin could feel the old man growing tired.

"There's a year's worth of work over there," his father had reminded him again last week, and then he walked real fast out of the room, leaving Robin alone to ponder the inescapable truth of it.

He didn't know what he was afraid of. Maybe she'd ask too many questions. It was a long time ago and he didn't have to tell her anything. He hadn't stepped foot in Ray's old place since whenever it was that Ray finally left for the last time. Had to be at least ten years.

He'd never forget that first time he laid eyes on Ray, sitting on that rotting front porch. It was one of many long Sunday afternoons during the time his mother was sick. His dad was focusing his full attention on her, wiping her forehead, checking her medicines, cranking up pillows high then low, as though if he made just the right move, she'd be well again. His mother too weak by then to talk to her son, just sending him looks and he couldn't say if she was smiling or crying. Her looks made him want to look away, was all he knew for sure. Though his dad never said it in so many words, Robin knew it was better for everybody if he just stayed away from the house.

"Don't be gone too long," his dad instructed, but Robin knew he meant stay away as long as you can. Fine with him. Less time to have to think of something to say to his dying mother.

And so he'd wandered onto Ray's place, probably looking to score some of that white oak for carving, not expecting to meet up with anyone. And suddenly there was this guy, asleep in a rickety wicker chair on that shaky porch, a guy with a shaved head, tattoos ribboned down his neck, red and blue snakes wrapped around thick seams of veins. Even fast asleep in a chair, he was the kind of guy who would scare the shit out of anybody. Robin had stopped dead in his tracks, figuring on a way to turn around and split but the man had already spotted him.

"Hey you!" he boomed, and for a split second Robin felt like an animal caught in a trap, too scared to cry, too frozen to run.

Robin tried to imagine a sister of Ray's, maybe some

kind of biker chick all in leather, even though she'd be old by now. Since the weather started clearing, her messages had started to come more frequently. That first time she called back in October, he didn't put her together with the property across the road and even if he had, he was pretty swamped finishing up projects that people wanted done before winter. He thought he told her to call back in the spring, but it didn't stop her. Not even that miserably wet December stopped her, no, she kept calling, every few weeks, saying she wasn't in a hurry, she just wanted his opinion, could he at least meet her and give her a general assessment. She was a funny one, seeming so anxious to meet with him, but then saying there was no hurry. It was like she didn't know what she wanted, like she was fishing for someone to tell her.

It was his father who finally broke him down with the truth of the matter. There could be months of steady income in this. Ray's old place was a teardown, but if she was interested in paying him to fix it up, it just might be his ticket out of there.

And now here he was, finally, making his way down Ray's old driveway. He could feel the woman watching him as he walked up the curved path, saw her standing on the porch, arms akimbo, almost rude he thought, no wave or gesture of recognition, just an unmoving stare, and he had nowhere to go but forward. He wondered if he was late but no, wristwatch confirmed 10:00 am and that's what her message said.

She seemed to be measuring him, clocking his paces, memorizing him. He speeded up his stride but then thought different, slowed back to a saunter, wasn't about to twist himself into a dither just because an old woman was facing him straight on, looking like if she had a rifle she'd be taking aim. Robin intended to get this over with, a favor to his dad to whom he owed so many favors, and so set his mind to tell her whatever she wanted to hear as quickly and cleanly as possible. And be done.

"So, you must be the handyman." the woman called out as soon as he came within voice's reach.

"Yes ma'am." He slowed to a stop and put his hand out to shake. She took it with both of her hands. She was a strong one, had a grip like a man.

"I apologize for taking so much time. Been busy finishing up other projects and you did say you weren't in a hurry."

She did not answer, just stared, instead, at his hands, at his shoulders. He quickly moved out of her gaze, and turned toward the house.

"How long have you been living with your father?"

"Not too long," he cut her short, walking ahead of her but she quickly caught up.

"And where did you live before that?" she continued, her stares now softened, all smiles and curiosity. So he started talking.

"I used to live in one of those planned family communities over by Lake of the Pines. Even the lake was planned. No sooner we made the down payment than my wife took off, left me with a baby and three year old girl."

"How old are they now?"

"Grace is eight, Timothy turned five last week, January 12."

"You don't look nearly old enough to have an eight year old. You look barely old enough to drive," she laughed the way older people laugh at younger people, like they know everything, even when they don't. But she was right about him being a young father. Grace was born two days shy of Robin's twenty-first birthday. Back then he thought he knew everything, sliding his cigarettes up on his dashboard so he'd look like a smoker, though he never was.

"Why don't you just take your time, snoop around," she offered, but he had already started, wending his way along the weedy path, the house now in sight. He stopped short, startled by the carved owl head that was still perched on the top porch step, after all these years.

It hit him hard standing there on that piece of land, almost like he expected the awkward teenage version of himself to pop up at any moment, eyes fixed on the ground scouting for pieces of bark, soft stones, anything malleable that gave his knife something to do. It was the one thing that held his interest during that awful time, his whittling knife.

And it was the whittling that had sealed the deal with him and Ray. He could remember that first time he encountered the sleeping giant, startled by his booming voice.

"Sorry," Robin had stammered, "I was just looking

for wood to carve," which was true, "I wasn't going to rob you or anything." This made the man on the porch break out into a laugh that flung him forward in his chair, threatening to toss him over the edge. Robin didn't think he'd said anything funny.

"You? Rob me? What's your name Sonny?"

As scary as Ray was, somehow Robin began to feel like he didn't have to run off, and pretty soon he learned that this motorcycle guy was also a woodcarver who was more than eager to teach him tricks about carving wood that his dad could never have taught him. Like spitting on the wood first to shine it up and bring out the grain before making the cuts. Like how to cradle the wood against the heel of his hand, how to position the blade slightly sideways and against the grain to shape the feathers.

"Do you live alone here?" Robin had asked him once, feeling brave.

"What's it to you?" the man had responded, but before Robin could figure out an answer that wouldn't make him mad, the man had handed him a skinny cigarette. "Try this, boy," he'd said, and he showed Robin how to breathe it in mixed with air so it wouldn't hurt so much.

Sometimes there was no one around for months at a time, motorcycle gone, no indication whether or not the guy had left for good. Robin would sometimes go over anyway, sit by himself, help himself to some of the larger oak branches, too hard for intricate carving, but Ray had showed him how to use its surfaces as support for the lighter birds, and how to bring out the variations of the grain. There were plenty of days when Robin would sit on the porch, whether Ray was around or not, and wait for the dark to come, or his dad's voice to call him home, whichever came first.

"Can I get you a towel?" The woman's voice interrupted the rush of memories. Robin had been slapping at his thighs, trying to clean off the spider webs that had collected while he walked around the perimeter. He could feel the woman standing right behind him.

"No thanks ma'am, I can wipe them on my jeans." But she had already prepared a dampened cloth, followed by a glass of water. He gulped it down noisily and heard her comment through the gulps.

"Sounds the way my brother used to gulp soda. How do you men manage to make that much noise when you drink?"

"Thanks ma'am." He returned the emptied glass, thinking how there was something of Ray in her face. The heavy eyebrows, the smile that could just as easily have been a scowl, small squinty eyes that seemed to look through you.

"For goodness sake, stop calling me ma'am. Call me Hannah if you're going to call me something."

He responded by moving out of earshot, helping himself to the only ladder he could find, amazed that it hadn't rotted away. It was sturdy enough to allow him a good view of the roof line, cracked gutters, shingles loose around what was left of the fascia boards, patches of bare wood exposed and vulnerable to the wet and cold. He lowered himself to the uneven ground, thudded his foot on the threshold so that puffs of rotted wood broke free. He felt parts of the window ledge dissolve into his fingertips. Shook his head and forced a smile.

"So?" she asked.

"Look here," he started, though it really didn't matter, every inch of the place needed work.

"See this, this is one of your biggest problems." More than a crack in the window, he explained how the window itself had shifted from the frame and the frayed cord sash, which had been providing the rodents with ample nesting materials, snapped off somewhere deep inside the wall frame. The double hung was doubled over in a permanent sideways tilt. Replacing the glass would be easy enough, but it appeared as though both window jambs and part of the wall frame needed replacement.

"And over here," he pointed to the entrance, where fluffy wads of wood chips had settled at the crease of threshold, more evidence that wild creatures were using the infrastructure to build their nests.

"Looks like some critters are eating your house." He picked up the wood shavings, sniffed them, and let them fall away back to the dusty floor.

There was so little room here to maneuver. The woman never left but a few inches of space between them, following him closely from window to door, from porch to gutter to closet and back, using her hands as punctuation marks so he more than once had to duck to avoid getting hit.

"Look over here," she shifted again, causing him to bump into her at the unexpected turn of direction.

"Does it seem this countertop is about to fall through, here, where the wood is wet and black? Isn't it a bad sign when wood turns black?"

"Real bad sign ma'am."

She offered up one of those razor sharp looks, as though daring him to smile, but he didn't.

"Have you considered tearing it down and putting up one of those pre-fab houses? They're not so bad and it would probably be a lot less trouble. Folks across the road from you have one. Big driveway. You might like that kind of thing."

Lying down, legs stretched into the middle of the room, he checked the pipes underneath the kitchen sink, saw where the kitchen trap had broken away from the pipe, just like his dad described.

"Looks like this is where you got busy with a wrench."

She seemed to like his sarcastic tone, took it up a notch.

"Maybe you could use an apprentice."

In fact she had patched something together, it was just the trap she busted and she told him how Len at the hardware store told her which parts she needed, even the white plumbers tape, and she managed to seal it up to where it just leaked a little.

"Hand me my wrench, let me tighten it," he said, and

just like that, the work had already started. Robin finished up the sink trap as Hannah narrowed in on him, her feet so close he couldn't get up without bumping into her.

She reached out her hand to help him upright, as though he needed an old woman's hand to get out from under a sink but he grabbed her hand because she'd left him no option, no room to wiggle past her. Robin sensed that he had been snared. Never even saw the trap.

"So what exactly do you want to do with this place?"

"All I want right now is for the windows to close and stay closed, open and stay opened. The usual. I want the roof sealed. I want to know how much of a meal the mice have made of the rafters. Dry and safe are my priorities. I'd like to return it to whatever state it once might have been, livable at the very minimum, and after that I'll see."

He thought he caught a wink, like she was fishing for a lighter side of him, still unseen.

"I'll need to give it some thought," he offered, but already his mind was racing. Everything his father said about this opportunity was true. How easy this would be, so close to home, and even a bit entertaining. Blackwell's sister, of all people. She didn't seem like she was going to be putting any pressure on him, kept repeating "no hurry" like he needed more convincing, and didn't blink when he told her his hourly rate. Even suggested a few bucks more per hour, which made him wonder if he was charging his other jobs enough.

The woman must have sensed his thinking because she backed away, turning her attention to something outside, maybe the trees, maybe the air. He wandered back around to the storage shed that looked exactly as he remembered it, the door half off. There, leaning behind the door, was the beginning of one of his tortoise heads, mostly rotted, eyes still staring. It was one of his early attempts. Ray never carved tortoises. He stuck to birds. It was Ray who had pointed out the difference between falcon and hawk crowns and why it mattered so much to get it right. Ray had all kinds of books on birds that he had offered Robin but Robin said he'd rather leave them there, gave him a reason to visit again. Funny that one of his old owl heads was still there after all these years. Robin was sure Pete would have taken the last of them by now.

Robin picked the head up, brushed off the dust, imagined finishing the piece, setting it next to Ray's owl head on the top railing. Maybe carve a snakehead or lizard to go beside them.

It was probably time to go. He was making mental notes, windows would need to be first, double hung cords, latches, varnish.

She was waiting for him inside the house. She had poured another glass of water and he gratefully accepted.

"I have no doubt you can handle the work. Come here as often as you can. The only thing I'm sure of is that I'm not planning on tearing it down. I don't know what my brother was doing with it, or why he thought I'd want it, but it's all I have of him. Anything you do will make a difference to me."

He had started in already, writing notes with the pad and pen he had pulled from his back pocket, unhooking a measuring tape that was latched to his belt buckle.

"I can get you a discount on supplies at the hardware store."

He recognized that smile, just like her brother's, you don't quite know what to make of it, but it feels good just the same.

"How about I start a week from Monday, isn't that February 1?" He had to turn away when he noticed tears welling up in her eyes. She wiped them away quickly with the edge of a dirty sleeve.

15.

CALLIE HAD JUST FINISHED cutting back some of the wild rose branches that were creeping into the driveway and just as she began to get up, a thorn snagged her cheek. She slapped at it, like a mosquito, and saw blood on her hand.

"Ouch!" she said, then looked up to see Robin walking down the driveway towards her.

"Are you okay?" He knelt down next to her in the dried brush, pulling a rag out from his back pocket, filthy with sweat, and wiped the blood off her face. Just a tiny red dot of blood, like a firefly, shining up at him.

"Robin, what are you doing here?"

He wanted to help her up, half hoping she'd reach for him so he'd have no choice.

"I'm doing some work for the lady who owns this property. Didn't I tell you that when I saw you last time?"

"No," Callie reminded him, "you only told me you lived with your dad and kids. We didn't really talk much."

It was an invitation, sly and sweet, and he opened it slowly.

"I thought I told you," but no, come to think of it, he hadn't yet begun to work for the woman last time he ran into Callie. "Maybe I didn't." Robin was looking at the ground now, trying to think of what to say next. Its not like he hadn't been rehearsing this moment, secretly to himself, ever since he had run into her a few months back. Its not like he hadn't been trying to drum up reasons to run into her again.

And here it was, the opportunity literally falling on him, as she reached out to him to steady herself, grabbing his arms first so he didn't have to be the one.

"Thanks," she said, as he pulled her gently up and away from the rosebush, pausing longer than he should have, before letting go of her hands. He could smell her perfume, and though he couldn't identify it, it was a smell he wasn't likely to forget any time soon.

"So why are you here?" she asked again, smoothing out her skirt, and he was relieved to have a reasonable answer.

"The new owner hired me to fix the place up. I was coming over today to replace some door hinges. Come on, I'll show you." Robin started up the driveway and Callie wasted no time pulling the baby out from the stroller and following alongside him, sidestepping the litter of logs and saw blades that lay scattered around the property.

"I tried to tell her she ought to fix the roof first so the place doesn't cave in but she wanted me to start on the door hinges and I'm not about to argue with her."

"Don't tell her I was here, please," Callie begged, following him to the back shed where Robin was reaching for bags of nails, handing them to her one at a time, working as a team already, one hand crossed over the other.

"Thanks," he said, as she helped him carry the bags of hardware into the house, setting them down in the bedroom where he had positioned himself to replace the hinges on the closet door.

"And what did you think you were doing back there on the road? Tearing out the rose bushes? Good luck with that!" He was loosening up, the feel of female companionship slowly and sweetly growing familiar again.

"I really wanted to get rid of those weeds while the ground was damp, maybe get a start on some spring seedlings. Some new owner might not be too happy about me digging around on their property."

"Don't you have your own garden?" Robin asked her, emerging from inside the closet in time to see her shift the baby from one hip to the other.

She rolled her eyes hard, like she wanted to be sure he'd notice, and he did notice. He also noticed, among other things, a wet stain forming on the front of her t-shirt.

"Ralph is putting in a sprinkler system, or so he says. For now we've got a lot of dirt and not much else. I'm not going to bother planting when it's all going to be pulled out anyway."

She said it with a little laugh but Robin didn't see any humor in it.

"I take it Ralph's your husband."

Callie wasn't sure if Robin remembered Ralph from high school, he was two years ahead of them. He told her he didn't and she looked relieved.

"You know," he said, "you're pulling her weeds free of charge. My guess is if she met you, she'd offer to pay you."

"Oh no," Callie said. She really seemed upset. She was suddenly standing right beside him and he noticed a small scar above her eyebrow, nothing ugly, just a small scar she might have gotten falling off a bike. Her face was peppered with freckles, a few shades darker than her blond hair. He was remembering her again as Callie Thorpe, sitting in front of him in history class. She looked almost the same except for her breasts, which seemed way too big for her small frame. He tried not looking at them but it was impossible, with those dark stains drawing even more attention to them, like arrows marking the way.

"No," she pleaded again, "please don't tell her."

"Callie, have you taken a good look at this place?" He had taken her hand, not thinking, but she didn't pull away, just held on to the baby with her free arm and followed him easily through the mess of landscape.

"Anything you do can only help. Look," he said, pointing to a thick patch of broken twigs, a winter mess of thorns and thatch and not much else.

"She wants me to fix her place up and all these brambles and God-awful Mountain Misery twigs are in my way. You'd be helping me out if you clipped them back."

He had picked up her pruners, demonstrating what kind of help he needed, and next thing he knew, she had put her sleeping baby down on a blanket in the living room, came back out with a square of sandpaper she must have found in his toolbox, and was smoothing down a rough section of porch railing. Minutes then hours passed, the two of them clipping and sanding and hammering and plucking twigs off dead limbs. And talking all the while.

"I wonder whatever happened to Mr. Hargrove," Robin asked.

"Didn't we have Hargrove for history and science?" Callie asked. "How lucky can you get?"

Robin didn't really give a damn about Mr. Hargrove. He just wanted to hear that little bit of excitement in her voice, the way she ended each sentence with a giggle, like she found herself amusing.

"What a prick he was!" she laughed, then looked up. "Sorry, did I offend you?"

"No," he said. "You're right." It actually turned him on when girls cussed.

"He was a fat prick," she added, spitting the words out, and they both laughed, heartily, and maybe a bit louder than the joke required.

Robin put the screwdriver down, turned toward her. She had taken off her sweatshirt, nothing but a sleeveless top underneath, and he couldn't help notice a thicket of blond hair sticking out from under her armpits, wet with perspiration. Robin thought most women shaved under there, but she seemed fine with it, holding her arms high in the air, pulling at the straggles of hair that had fallen loose from her ponytail. If those hairy armpits didn't bother her, he sure wasn't going to let them bother him.

"I really think you ought to ask her if she needs help outside. I could set up a meeting for you. She'd do anything I suggested." He was pushing now, the idea of them working together fully formed now in his imagination.

He hardly recognized the voice coming out of his mouth, so sure of itself, so strong.

"Are you kidding?" She lowered her arms quickly, and he was afraid she had caught him staring. He turned his attention back to the screwdriver, tightening the last hinge one more time.

"I'm not kidding," he said, keeping his eyes firmly on the hinge. "Why shouldn't you?"

"Ralph would never let me take a job like that. He'd have a fit. I wouldn't even know how to ask him."

"Why not?" It was a good question, and he wanted an answer.

"Ralph doesn't want me to work. He likes taking care of us." She said it with a shrug, her words slower, in measured flattened tones, all the music gone. "Besides, I like hanging out here playing in the weeds. I wouldn't want to think of it as a job."

He was looking at her again, and this time he saw something sad wash over her. This time she was the one who averted her eyes, so he backed off, turning again to the hinges. The low winter sun was cooling quickly and the baby was beginning to stir. He gathered up his tools, the Phillips, sandpaper, some spare screws, filled the loops and holsters that dangled from his belt.

"Look, Callie, don't take offense. I didn't mean to pry. Sorry if it sounded like it. I'm no one to be telling someone what to be doing. My life is a big mess, big mess," he said it twice, once didn't come close to describing it. "I really had no business...."

But Callie had come over to him, close in, and put her hand on his wrist.

"Its OK. I'd just rather not tell Ralph I'm here. It's hard to explain that's all. I shouldn't even be talking about him to you. I really shouldn't."

This was not the way either of them would have written the end of the afternoon, with Ralph, smack in the middle.

It was getting late, they both agreed. The light was changing fast, dark coming earlier in the day, pouring low streaks of orange and purple, making everything look a little more beautiful than it really was.

Callie started pushing the stroller up the driveway, slowly, waving back at him practically the whole way down. Robin stood on the porch like he owned the place. He called out, "Come around any time." And then, "I'm here most afternoons," but she was out of earshot by then, and he hated to admit to himself how badly he wanted her to stay.

Later that night, Ralph came home gruff and fitful.

"What's all that crap on the porch?" was his hello. He didn't wipe his shoes at the door, as he always demanded of her. Just headed straight to the refrigerator to grab a beer.

She knew these evenings. She moved quietly around him like an animal in a hostile jungle, scampering light-footed and low, lest she interfere with his grumbling.

She very carefully opened the front door, pressing softly against the latch to muffle the click. She swept away the day's remains with the porch broom—clods of dirt and a few wilted flowers that had not survived the slow walk home. She'd meant to sweep up earlier but Daphne was having one of her screaming attacks. At least she'd remembered to remove her muddy shoes before she brought the baby into the house.

"Shit," she heard Ralph say. Then she heard a door slam, interrupting the crescendo of evening crickets that had lured her outside.

"Where's the goddamned bottle opener?" he yelled.

She put down the broom and turned from the cricket chorus toward the door. At the threshold she took one deep breath, and then another to propel her inside.

"If it's not in the drawer, look in the dishwasher," she told Ralph. "No, never mind, let me get it." The mood he was in, he shouldn't be rooting around in the dishwasher rack. He'd knock over the nipples or break a glass. Besides, he needed her to do it for him.

"Honey, let me pour it into a glass for you," she said. She easily located the church key, poured the bottle sideways like he'd taught her, just enough foam at the top, and settled him down with minimum effort, hand resting softly on the back of his neck. In no time she whipped out a plate of crackers and cheese, cut a few little squares of cheddar, placed them neatly on a cracker, and nudged it toward his mouth. He closed his lips around her fingers, not noticing the clod of dirt that had fallen loose from her

140

hand, and he ate that too.

"Something happen honey?" she asked and then listened while he guzzled his beer and spat out the horrid details of his day. Some environmental group was pushing drought tolerant alternatives to lawns and the developers were reconsidering the whole sprinkler deal. Thinking about going with sages and cactus gardens to save some money.

"Kids can't run around in cactus gardens!" he yelled at her but he was yelling at the wind, he was yelling at the eco-system, he was yelling at himself for not seeing this obvious curveball aimed right at his perfectly formed plan.

"Shh, its all right," she said, though she hadn't really heard many of the particulars. Her soft voice and the swigs of two beers had begun to do their job. With Callie's fingers stroking the back of his neck, Ralph had calmed slightly, lulled into a quieter, almost pitiful version of his earlier self.

"This is going to kill us," he said, taking her hand, and she was afraid he might cry, "What am I going to do?" She nestled up close, containing the whole of him so he wouldn't spill away altogether.

Later, Ralph curled into a fetus on his side of the bed and fell quickly into a fitful sleep. Callie tiptoed into the baby's room, though the baby was soft and still and didn't need her at all. Through Daphne's small window, she had a better view of the almost full moon that cast a reddish glow in the black sky. She figured the light was likely shining through Robin's window too. She stared at its brilliant light for a long time.

16.

HE KNOCKED LIGHTLY on her front door, then waited. In the window box by the door, a few straggly plants drooped. A baby's rattle crusted with mud poked out from beneath some dead leaves. He used his shirtsleeve to clean it off. When he knocked again, the rattle added a thin snap of sound.

I really should get out of here, Robin told himself, but instead he walked around the corner of the house, careful not to dislodge the stacks of irrigation pipes in the side yard. He peered through the kitchen window, like a prowler. Jesus, what was he doing? He'd scare the hell out of her if she caught him poking around.

"Callie, Callie? It's me, Robin. Callie?" he called out, almost afraid that she might hear him. He walked back around to the front again, carefully stepping over the pipes. He noticed a couple of business cards lying on the ground, Timberline Irrigation Systems, in black embossed letters, then below it, Ralph Daschle, Sales Consultant, in smaller script, but just as shiny. He stared at it for a minute, then folded it up until it couldn't fold any more and stuffed the wad down into the window box dirt.

"Robin?"

She was standing in the doorway, baby in her arms, a cloth draped over her shoulder, stained and giving off a faintly sour smell. She was out of breath.

"Robin, I was just about to put her in the bath. Hope you weren't waiting long. What's up?"

"Is it ok to come in?" She looked both ways, like she was about to cross an imaginary street, shifted the baby onto her hip, and stepped back, making room for him to enter. He hesitated at the door, wishing now that he had thought this crazy idea through.

"Is it a bad time?"

"Oh no, it's fine, come on it. Ralph isn't home or anything."

Why did she have to bring him into the picture? Robin caught a whiff of something cooking, tomatoes, something bitter, was it cabbage? He could see the steam rising in the kitchen, thickening up around the windows. He used it as a way in.

"Is something burning in there?"

She turned to look, kicking the front door open by way of invitation. At least he took it as that, and followed her in.

"Oh NO, I was bathing Daphne. I forgot I had the stew going."

"What's that smell?"

"Turnips. I think Ralph's the only person in the whole world who loves turnips."

Ralph again, she couldn't get through a sentence without him.

"Where is he?" Robin had to ask.

"Sales meeting over in Weaverville. He'll be back late tonight," she added, and he was glad she did.

He followed her into the kitchen, watching the baby bob on her hip. She was wearing a frilly blouse just like the first time he met her, falling loose over her shoulder so her bra strap kept showing, and again he noticed her pull at the blouse so it wouldn't slide down.

He leaned on the counter while she messed with the stew that smelled funny to him, but he wasn't about to say. He noticed the countertop—it was the stuff they were putting into all the new homes lately. Supposed to look like marble, except it was cheap plastic backed with particleboard that would absorb moisture and mold and have to be replaced well before the guarantee date passed. It looked expensive, and that seemed to be all people cared about these days.

"Smells good," he lied, and she put a bit of steaming sauce into a serving spoon, blew on it first then held it up to his mouth.

"Turnips, huh?" He had to admit they tasted sweet, once the smell got past his nose.

Finally finished with whatever tasks brought her over to the stove, she motioned for him to sit down on the couch. She'd been holding on to the baby the whole time but now she plopped her into her rocking seat on the floor beside the bay window.

Robin sat down at the far end of an L-shaped couch that seemed oversized for such a small living room. Just like his father's place next door there were great views here, all windows facing into the backside of endless acres of Bureau of Land Management land. Thick with trees, there was nothing but filtered shade all day long, even during that deadly summer heat.

Suddenly he felt uncomfortable, unsure of what it was he intended to say. It had all been so clear before he came over. But now, watching her in her own house doing those little house things that women do—putting dishes in the sink, opening the pale blue curtains that matched the sofa that matched the trim paint around the faux fireplace—he wasn't sure what he was doing there. All he knew was that she had positioned herself at the far end of the couch, her legs up and stretched out so they were inches from his leg.

He resorted to talk about the weather, about the condition of the roads, the new housing developments over in Lake of the Pines.

"I wish we lived there," she said, "but its way too expensive."

Robin had had a few jobs out that way himself last year, he told her.

Callie got up and disappeared into the kitchen for a second. When she came back she handed the baby one of those teething biscuits he remembered his own kids gumming on. When Callie got back to the couch she sat even closer this time, cross-legged and facing him, her foot touching his leg for real this time.

"So how's it going over at the house?" she asked, looking straight at him, her bare feet in full view, with purple colored nail polish, mostly chipped off, messy looking. He tried not to stare at them but it was pretty hard not to with that silver toe ring on her big toe.

"Uh, well, it's going pretty good. I'm almost finished replacing the sills in the living room, hope to get to the bedroom windows next week." He sat up straighter, trying to stretch out what little distance there was between them.

"I really ought to be working on the roof but that will have to wait until the rains are done. The deck is pretty shaky. I plan to fix the rotten boards next so nobody falls through."

"Has she told you what she wants?"

"Good question. She doesn't seem to know what she wants, just leaves me little notes but half the time they don't make sense. Mildew? Shelf paper? Like that's supposed to tell me something."

"Do you think she's crazy?" Callie was sitting up straight, and Robin now remembered what it was he had come to tell her. The last thing she needed to think was that the woman was crazy.

"No," he assured her. "She's completely harmless. Nice even. I had gotten stuck halfway under the bathroom cabinet, replacing some pipefittings and when I looked up she was holding out a glass of water for me. She's not crazy. Strange maybe, but not crazy."

"What does she do that's so strange?"

"I've seen her do stuff like touch the walls, stare out the windows. She's quiet a lot. Sometimes she sits on the floor while I'm working and talks about her brother."

"Isn't he the motorcycle guy everybody talks about?

The one that got killed?"

"Yeah, that's the one. She told me he left home when he was eighteen, she was in her twenties, over forty years ago, she said. I feel bad for her. It must be spooky being in his old place, not knowing a thing about him. She even asked me if I knew him, but that's a subject I don't want to touch."

"Would you like a beer?" she asked, as though she had read his mind.

"Love one," he said, though she had already gotten up and opened a bottle of dark Irish malt. She set it down, along with a plate of peanut butter cookies, on the coffee table in front of him, as though he had ordered it. He took a long swig.

"Well did you know his brother?"

"When I was a kid, yeah, I used to wander over to his place to get out of my house. He looked a lot worse than he really was."

Robin had helped himself to the cookies, worked on the beer that was too bitter for his taste, but refreshing just the same.

"So," asked Callie, "what did she say when you told her you knew her brother?"

"Are you kidding? I didn't tell her a thing. This is the guy who taught me everything I know about smoking dope."

"Dope?" she perked up, suddenly more interested in his story.

You never knew what people thought about drugs

around here. She might have been one of those Christian types but it didn't seem like it. He was relieved when she raised her eyebrows just slightly. "Go on," she invited him, and he relaxed further into his story.

"I was a bored little kid from across the road, always bothering him with questions. He was good to me, never asked me to leave. He taught me everything I know about carving wood, too."

"That owl head on the porch?"

"That one's his. What's left of mine are tucked away in my place, mostly rotting away."

Neither of them said anything for a long minute. Robin took a few more sips of beer, turned to Callie. She had been staring at him, or so it felt, the empty plate the only thing separating them. He wiped his mouth, suddenly self-conscious that he might have left some crumbs on his lip.

"I'll tell you what I did say to her." And now it was him looking directly into her eyes. "I said that I knew someone who could help her in the yard."

"You did what? Robin, I asked you not to," but he continued with surprising force.

"I've been thinking about it. Ever since I saw you last time. It's a good idea. She keeps asking me to clear away the weeds around the deck and I don't want to waste my time. I've got enough to do on the inside. Do it for nothing if you don't want to take her money. Do it for my sake. It would really help me out."

And there it was, out. She had gotten up to rewind

the baby rocker, her back was to him now and he wished he could read her expression. He waited for the no, but it didn't come.

"What am I supposed to do with Daphne?"

He took a breath, pretending to be figuring out a good answer, but it was a breath of relief. She was warming to the idea. He could feel it.

"Bring her. You told me you love hanging out on that land. Remember, you called it your private playground?"

She sat back down next to him, put her hand on his arm. It might have been nothing more than an innocent gesture of appreciation.

"Callie. Think about it. It's a good idea. I don't get that many of them."

Her arm was still touching his. Before he could stop himself, Robin took hold of her fingers, lifted them to his lips, quickly, about to kiss them but reason somehow stopped him and he put her hands down.

"I'm sorry. I'm so sorry…" he stammered. I didn't mean…"

With uncanny timing Daphne chose that moment to drop her biscuit and set to squalling. Callie jumped up off the sofa, turning away, pulling at her shirt to conceal the wet milk circles triggered by the crying baby.

After she picked the baby up and quieted her, she looked over at Robin.

"I'm sorry, I don't know what I was thinking," he said again, he couldn't stop saying.

He stood up to leave but she stepped toward him,

came up close and reached up to kiss him on the cheek, with the baby in her arms, a soft shield between them. And then, so easily, they started to kiss. Later he replayed it over and over in his head, trying to remember who made the first move. He was the one who had put her fingers up to his mouth. But then she was the one that walked over to him afterwards.

He'd never know, really, how it started. He only knew that it had.

"I'll think about your idea," she whispered, quieting down the confusion in his head. "I promise I will."

17.

HERE IT WAS MID-MARCH and I was still up to my ears in post-holiday season chores. All the junk from last year's Christmas pageants still left to clean up and sort through. I usually finished by the end of January but I'd had a lot on my mind. Its not like anyone was waiting for me to clean up the church basement. The decorations could sit there until the following year for all anybody cared, but I still enjoyed that last vestige of my old job, something I knew I could do better than anyone. The Sisters never seemed to notice that they hadn't purchased new decorations or ornaments for the past few decades. It's all about careful packaging, knowing how to fold bubble wrap to maximize space, (did I pick that up from Pa?) using the right tools (I prefer small watercolor brushes) to dust the insides of the ceramic bells. There are costumes to be mended and folded, new copies of Psalms that needed to be hole-punched and put into binders. Petrified fruitcakes to be tossed.

Most people love Christmas but for some reason, I preferred the aftermath. Ned died the week before Christmas but I wasn't a big fan of the holiday even before that. He wasn't either. Our favorite holiday was Halloween—his birthday coming on the 30th and mine two days later on November 1. We just mashed both our birthdays into one big celebration on Halloween. We'd put on the wigs and costumes he'd collected from when he worked as a stagehand at the local theater company. He had always wanted to go into acting, but working on stage sets was as close as he got. He'd bring home Elizabethan wigs, taffeta skirts, velvet robes, and we'd dress up like we were some kind of royalty, (with the help of a few too many glasses of whiskey), and had us a time. Couple of crazy kids we were, for a few years anyway.

I started to dream about Ned again, something I hadn't done in years. The other night, I dreamt that he and I were driving down a hill. I told him he was going too fast but he kept hitting the gas. I was holding on tight, screaming for him to stop. And then we were in a parking lot, looked like the one at the hardware store up on Highway 49. In the dream, a man was loading up the back of his truck with lumber, piling it higher and higher. I wanted to tell him that the weight was pressing down the wheels on his truck. And then the man turned to me and it was Robin.

Almost every night I found myself waking up bright-eyed, full of energy, the clock flashing 2:15 or some other ridiculous hour. My brain refused to quiet down. One night I'd been tossing around for hours, it was just about 5 am, the sky opening up those first edges of grey. I got out of bed and started digging through the medicine cabinet, looking for something to help me get back to sleep. I picked up one of the plastic bottles, my eyes squinting to see what it was, and what the hell, turned out to be an old prescription with Pa's name on it. Next thing I knew I was tossing everything with an expiration date of more than five years, even found a few of Mother's old medicines mixed in there too.

Seemed like I kept running into more good reasons to move.

The Realtor had been calling me about every other week since my last visit back in February. Just checking in, he'd say, with that singsong salesman voice. I knew it was him even before he started his yakking. I'd pick up the phone and there was that silence, like he'd been scrolling through his address book and forgot what number he dialed.

I helped him out. "Its Hannah Blackwell here," I'd say, and it worked every time, startled him right back into his sales pitch. He always had some kind of news—a similar parcel half mile away just sold with multiple offers. Or there's some developer he knows who was looking for raw land, willing to negotiate, blah blah. "No harm in keeping our options open," he reminded me, same words every time.

"Mr. Lundale," I enunciated clear and slow, "I am not thinking about selling my land. If I decide to sell it, you will be the very first person I call." Now was that so complicated? I had a mind to drive back up there again, but the weather wasn't cooperating. Last week nothing but solid rain, no telling what those roads would be like. At least Robin had been giving me progress reports. The living room windows were mostly sealed, and rotten boards on the deck had been replaced. He hadn't gotten around to the bedroom windows yet, or the kitchen cabinets, said he had run into some dry rot that was taking more time to repair. I appreciated the messages he left on my answering machine, and sometimes didn't even bother to listen to the details. Just glad to hear he was busy working.

Then the other day he left a different kind of message, something about a neighbor woman who could help clear out the weeds. "I think you'll like her very much," he said, but it sounded more like he was the one who liked her, the way his voice suddenly got animated when he mentioned her, not his usual yes ma'am, no ma'am. He even left me her phone number, said she was waiting to hear from me.

I called him back and left a message (he never picks up his phone). Told him I was glad things were moving along.

My plan had been to wait until May before venturing up the mountain again. I wasn't eager to drive those twisty roads in the mud, and it didn't sound like the place was going to be sealed up any time soon. I was busy enough anyway, cleaning out drawers, trying to make sense of all the crap I'd collected over the past forty years.

If you can believe it, I counted five, for God's sake, five end tables that each supported yet more of those dull African Violets, all pale pink, not even those luscious striped purple varieties I'm seeing in the nurseries these days. Wouldn't you know it's the boring pink ones that don't seem to die.

End tables, painted wooden boxes with chipped off scenery (ugly remnants of old family vacations) containing nothing but dust and paper clips, and long-forgotten mystery novels. Was that me that bought the "How-

To" books on growing African Violets? What had I been thinking? And all those floozy handbags lined up along the back shelf of my closet, tucked behind the sweaters I never wore. Designed to hold a lipstick, hankie, maybe a house key. They were gifts mostly, from Mother's friends who thought I should get dressed up once in a while, after Ned died. Never used them back then. Not about to use them now.

The great pile of unwanted things around me swelled. I always hated the coffee table. It was Mother's taste, Danish modern sharp edged and devoid of design. I couldn't lift it so I scraped it along the kitchen floor, bumping it down the three steps that led to the garage, half hoping it would come apart on the way. But it just banged its sharp wooden corner against the kitchen cabinet, snagging a thin slice of Formica on its way out the door, as if to say good riddance to you too.

Outside, it seemed like every single tree was budding. No chance of rain over the weekend, according to the paper. The trunk of my car was loaded with crap, all intended for the Goodwill. I set the box of Melmac dishes aside, a few extra pieces of silverware. Come to think of it, Ray's place could use one of those end tables. Ray's place. Or was it mine. Hell with it. No reason to wait until May, I decided. I would take most of the crap I didn't want to the rummage sale, Goodwill was on the way out of town, and the rest could go up to the mountains. Might as well give that neighbor girl a call while I was at it, let her know I was coming. See if she was all Robin cracked her up to be.

18.

THE SILL COMPLETELY SPLINTERED in his hands. He had pulled too hard, or maybe the wood was more rotten than he imagined. Might as well finish the job, he thought, grabbing now at the entire window frame, releasing a nest of termite eggs that crumpled loose in soft white mounds over his pant legs and shoes.

"Serves me right," he said to himself, brushing off the filth from his already filthy jeans.

"Screw it," he growled, yanking on what was left of the sill. "This whole place needs to come down anyway."

Robin had been in a foul mood all day, couldn't shake it. He had been putting off going back to finishing the bedroom windows. He kept finding things to do in other parts of the house, loose doorknobs that could just have well waited, a broken screen door. He had been avoiding the bedroom and he knew it, but he needed to get things cleaned up in there before more rain came in.

"Son-of-a-bitch," was all he had left to say to himself. He pulled out the tape, measured the sills, both standard thirty-six inch. One of the bedroom windows had been busted out completely, glass so shattered it seemed like a rock had been thrown clear through.

No, he had to finish, had to deal with the mess. He surveyed the damage, sheetrock chunks piled on top of rotted bits of wood. Glass everywhere. He kicked a piece aside, went over to the window, took a long deep breath.

The views from this part of the house were tremendous, brighter than the views from his dad's place, offering more sky than trees. Robin leaned into the opening where glass had fallen out, careful not to get splinters on his hands, enjoying the silence. He picked up a small piece of glass wedged between the sill and window frame, held it up to the light. He fixed his eyes on the distant mountains through the blue and green and purple kaleidoscopic light.

It was about a month ago, he had started in this very room in early February, just after he had gone over to Callie's place. The rain hadn't let up for weeks and Robin wanted to close the place up as soon as possible. He hadn't heard back from her, figured she'd let him know whatever she decided. It had been so strange, their kiss, if it even was a kiss. Stranger still the fact that he had gone over to see her in the first place. It wasn't in his nature to take chances. But the idea of spending time with this woman had taken over his reason. And why shouldn't he have some fun?

There was a lot more in this room to deal with than broken windows. Dry rot alongside the entire baseboard, wood crumbling away to expose foundation. He would have to rip the sheetrock clear to the studs. It was going to be a filthy, exhausting job.

He had picked up his crowbar, started pulling at the

sheetrock, grimacing to the sharp shriek of nails tearing loose from the studs. He hadn't so much as heard her walk into the room.

"It's just me."

He shook the dust off his hands, turned toward her, "Callie?" he questioned, as if it could have been anyone else. He looked for words but she had already moved to within an inch of him, leaned so close he had to back up against the wall, felt a small nail catch against the back of his shirt. So, he thought, this is how it happens.

She was whispering now, "Robin?" so soft, and he tried to push her back, but already her hand was on his cheek, rubbing the stubble slowly with her fingertips, and as she leaned in further he heard a shudder in her breath, or was it his?

They kissed then, one long, sensual, hungry kiss that pushed first him, then her against the broken wall, sharp edges cutting into their skin but he couldn't stop, she couldn't stop, turning, folding into each other, splinters stinging their backs as they pressed harder, the open air rushing through the broken windows cooling them both, pain and pleasure indistinguishable.

"Robin," again she whispered, and he slowly guided her away from the debris, to the one corner of the room where no dust had yet settled. He grabbed a tarp that he had left in the room, unfolded it, and she sat down, one shoe, than another off, looking up at him the whole time. So this is it, he said again, out loud this time, as she started undoing the back of her skirt, taking off her jacket, now her t-shirt, quickly off.

Still standing, Robin watched her, staring down at the space between her breasts, and next thing he knew they were both on their knees, his lips tracing all around the soft lines that joined one breast to the other. Ohmygod how long had it been, he wanted to swallow her whole.

"Aren't you going to take off that damned tool belt?" Callie asked him and they laughed, moved apart briefly. She put a finger to her lips and pointed to Daphne, asleep in the stroller that was parked just outside the bedroom door. He quietly set the tool belt down, gently helped her slip off what was left of her clothing. Quiet, quiet, don't disturb the bird sounds that were traveling now through the open window. He shoved his filthy work boots behind them, and, like dancers, they moved around the rough and splintered floor. Woodchips might as well have been feathers, holding them weightless until the last rush of their breaths emptied at the exact same time.

When finally their breathing returned to an even rhythm, he asked her, "What are we doing?"

She had sat up to brush some sawdust off of her arms. "I don't know."

Not much of an answer, but her whisper was like an invitation, so he leaned in again. And again they explored this dangerous new territory, faster this time, aware of a baby outside the door, and a husband somewhere, no-where near. The daylight was changing fast, it could be any time of day with all the late afternoon shadows playing tricks against the walls.

"That was real nice," he said finally, eyes closed, as he lay back and listened to the sounds of her rooting around, wrestling with her clothes, reaching past him for a sock. Her leg brushed against his, but he kept his eyes closed, as if by doing so, he could keep her there. And then, just as quickly as she had entered the room, Callie stood up, brushed the hair away from her eyes, said, "I've got to go."

"No," Robin answered, but she was facing the door and Daphne's stroller. The baby was still quiet but Callie grabbed her jacket, dressed quickly.

"No, I really have to go," she said as Robin touched her leg.

"No don't," he said, even though he knew it was time. "Will I see you again?"

"When?"

"I'm here every day, until I have to pick up my kids. Early afternoon's are best."

"Ok, they're good for me too."

"So I'll see you again, if you want."

"I want."

Hurried, brief negotiations, it could have been a business deal. He wanted so badly to know what she was thinking even though he didn't know his own thoughts, so blurred by the surprise of it all.

They touched fingers as she slipped out the door.

The next day it happened again, almost the same way,

only in the living room, cleaner this time, where the sills had already been finished. The baby stroller parked safe on the outside porch, within easy earshot. She said she couldn't see him on Friday, Ralph sometimes came home early. But next week was good.

"Ok?"

"Ok."

They saw each other a couple of times the following week, and then the next.

One time Callie had thought to bring a sleeping bag and they made love outside, in the manzanita grove. The ground was still damp from earlier rains so he dragged the plastic tarp out and put it underneath the bag. Even still, with a tarp and thick fabric beneath them, pine needles and that damned groundcover managed to poke through. Their bodies exposed to the warm winter sun, they laughed as they compared all the scratches and scabs they had acquired over their bellies, thighs and arms, over the short course of their lovemaking.

And now Robin was back in the bedroom, looking through the broken window again, listening for her again, in the exact same spot where she had found him that first time.

He picked up the hammer, pulled a few bent nails out of the wall. He was twenty-nine years old, with two kids, and still sleeping on his father's sofa. And now he was fucking a married woman. Well good for him. After Cynthia, he couldn't recall a single woman who wanted to get this close to him, and so what if she was married. That was her problem, not his. He couldn't stay away from women forever.

A finishing nail had come loose and rather than try to pull it out, he decided it would be easier just to pound it back in. He took aim, hit the wall hard, causing the other window, the one that had only a slight crack, to shatter.

"Way to go," he admonished himself, staring into yet another gaping hole.

19.

I STOPPED at the hardware store again on the way up. I remembered the signage out front that first time when the Lundale fellow pointed it out to me, after he stopped for gas. They had a big sign out front — *Free bag of birdseed with purchase of Birdfeeder* — and I'm a sucker for birdfeeders, but the Realtor was in no mind to take me shopping.

This time, a flurry of brightly colored signs out front announced *Paint Sale; Saturday Only—all hoses 10% off*, a festival of gifts tempting every car that sped down Highway 49. A bright red banner advertised 50% off all baskets, with Easter already a few weeks past.

I felt right at home inside. The plumbing guy saved my neck back when I broke the kitchen trap. I was in such a hurry last time I came in, racing right over to the plumbing department, then out again to try to hook everything up, which I managed to do, and have been bragging about ever since. Darlene didn't believe me when I told her I fixed a broken kitchen trap, but what do I care what she thinks. I got it to work well enough so the water stopped spraying all over the floor, until Robin got to it and fixed it for real.

But now I was free to poke around. I didn't even own a hammer. The mystery of coming into this piece of land I could blather on about back home, where the only thing

I managed to get excited about was new drip nozzles for my watering system. Walking into Highway Hardware this time around, I suddenly became aware of the world of possibilities opening up to me. Every aisle tempting me with endless choices. Starting with shelf paper.

The store was bigger than I remembered. That first time I didn't stick around long enough to notice the wide long aisles with brightly colored signs—Electrical; Paint; Gardening—so it was pretty easy to find whatever you came in for, if you were lucky enough to know. Under the window, an entire wall was devoted to bird feeders. I had no idea there were so many kinds. I checked my watch, still early enough, though I did need to meet that girl at 2:00. Wishing now I hadn't made the appointment. I could have easily spent all day in there.

First off aisle 1-A. I was smart to grab a shopping cart, just in case I got carried away, which I did. I discovered small screwdriver kits, (seemed like a handy thing to have around), too many sizes and shapes of batteries to make sense of, large metal sheets that had no purpose I could think of, and a wall of nails so vast and varied in shape that I found myself opening each little drawer to see what was inside. Wood screws. Metal screws. Roofing nails. Finishing nails. No wonder men spent so much time in these places. It wasn't enough to say nails and screws. No, there was a whole world of sharp metal doo dads to consider. I filled a couple of small paper bags with some finishing nails, and an assortment of wood screws for no reason whatsoever, moved the shopping cart on to the next aisle.

A man wearing a bright green nametag reading Hi— I'm Leonard was helping another customer picking out L brackets. I moved to within earshot of him. Maybe I could learn a thing or two about L brackets. An impressive array of weather proofing options filled the shelves before me, at least five kinds, and I wanted to know why.

Hi—I'm Leonard must have noticed me looking confused, because he came right up next to me to offer his services.

"Can I help you find something ma'am?"

He was slow of speech, but he quickly proved extremely knowledgeable on the subject of weatherproofing. He introduced me to rubberized and metal plated, one-quarter and five-eighths. "Will this be for inside or out?" he asked.

"I'm not sure," I answered, revealing my foolishness, even to myself. I started to feel guilty leading him on.

He looked at me in that funny way men sometimes have, polite but tense, and I can only imagine that whatever he wished he could say to me was burning the insides of his mouth.

"You've been a great help," I backed up, releasing him gently from his duties, and he gratefully moved on to the next customer.

Over on Aisle 4 I wandered into more familiar territory: Ajax, grout cleaners (I put a bottle in my shopping basket, in case the kitchen tiles ever got finished), and a couple of dish towels, on sale, no pretty floral designs or scalloped edges this time, just regulation terry cloth.

And, what do you know, a selection of Dr. Bronner's, the very same soap my mother used to bathe with. They had all kinds of flavors now, Almond, Vanilla-Apricot, Lotus. Couldn't imagine what that last one smelled like. I unscrewed the cap and inhaled the familiar Peppermint, let a bit of the goo slide on to my fingers.

On and on I rolled, down 6C, up 7B, and here was the cat litter—oh Amos, what would you think of this?—a whole shelf of catnip toys. I grabbed one shaped like a mouse, he can always use an extra, and rolled the cart on.

Turned the next corner and almost swerved into the wall. Who was that mess of a woman coming at me, with straggly grey hairs poking every which way? She had no business wearing that sloppy faded sweatshirt out in public. It was me, that's who. I had turned the cart into the aisle of bathroom mirrors and like it or not, faced into at least five slightly bent versions of myself pushing a shopping cart. Those jowls, way too big for the face. The bent shoulders, like they were carrying an invisible backpack. Holy crap, when did I get so old?

I quickly pushed past the mirror section, found myself at the end of 8B. I noticed a sign on a closed door—Winston Till, Store Manager. Isn't that what they say about small towns? Everybody knows everybody. Almost made me feel like I belonged here.

After the end of 10C there were no more aisles. The cart was getting too heavy to push anyway, what with the garden hose, 2 packages of light bulbs (were there even any overhead fixtures in the place?) and a couple of bags of bone and blood meal, something Wilbur would have been proud I remembered. "You can always use bone and blood meal," he had said to me more times than I could count, not that the wild mess of landscape I was heading to needed any fertilizing help.

By the time I finally came to a halt at the checkout counter, I had learned the distinctions between inside and outside thresholds and picked out a no-nonsense green stripe plastic shelf liner for the kitchen drawers.

One by one I set my acquisitions on the counter. Hi–I'm Lindsay rang me up. "Don't you love this soap?" she asked me, but she smiled at me a little too sweetly and I didn't have it in me to return the kindness. I gave her my usual "mm hmm," and she returned fully to the task of scanning and bagging and sighing at the sheer unfriendliness of some people.

I wasn't being unfriendly. I just wanted to be left alone. Was I required to explain this to every young smiling thing at every cash register? I did not want to continue my life-long state of perfunctory politeness. I don't need to explain, I told myself, as I pushed aside the few things I had brought from home to make room in the sagging truck for my latest purchases.

Driving on toward the land, I could feel how familiar Highway 49 had become. No wonder. This was my fifth trip to the land. I passed the Chinese restaurant, the church that looked abandoned, counted a few cows on the pasture that wound on for a few turns until the field of junked cars appeared around the next bend. Passed the sign for Golden Oaks Retirement Home tucked away behind some trees. Maybe that's where I should be going.

I was already anticipating that sharp left turn at the juncture to Blind Shady where asphalt turned to gravel. The hard grind of bumps and jolts down the unpaved stretch of road leading to the land seemed longer this time, but somehow easier because I knew it wouldn't get any worse, and that the worst of it wasn't so bad really. I knew exactly where I was headed.

Despite the dust, I rolled my windows down to let in the spicy air. Drifts of white flower tips settled on the dashboard. Queen Anne's lace. I'd learned a few more names from a book I purchased back home, Wildflowers of the Sierra Nevada. Now I recognized trillium, bindweed and those sticky monkey flowers growing every which way along the roadsides. I had no idea what plant produced that bitter burnt smell that filled the air. Some kind of strange groundcover that grew all over the place. It smelled like gym socks mixed with cotton candy.

I had arranged to meet the neighbor woman at 2:00, but the time got away from me at the hardware store. No way I could get there any faster on this stretch of road. The car made horrible squeaking sounds if I tried anything over 15mph and why should I? She'd either be there or she wouldn't. I wasn't about to worry. I started singing I been Working on the Railroad, can't say why, heard the melody break and snap in the back of my throat as bumpy pockets of gravel and dirt sent the car chassis into raucous spasms.

My tire hit a rock in the road, luckily not a disaster, but I pulled over to assess the damage. It was a good opportunity to sit down for a few minutes. A nice shady spot on the side of the road with a broad smooth rock invited me to rest a while and catch my breath. Far enough away from the main highway, there wasn't a soul in sight, just me and some birds that I couldn't see but could hear flittering loudly in the nearby trees.

I forget sometimes how old I am. All this twisting and turning of the steering wheel, all this lifting and dragging, wasn't helping my back any. Sitting on top of the rock, it felt good to stretch out my legs, reach for my toes, unhinge my neck muscles. Looking up, I could make out the tops of the pines that grew thicker with the changes in altitude. I still didn't know ponderosa from pinyon (it was in the book I bought, just hadn't read it all yet) but there would be time for that. I did recognize the twisted red arms of the madrones and the waxy leaves of the toyon, and though they weren't yet in bloom, patches of thistle and bluebells and monkshood, weeks away from bursting. The air stung my nostrils.

I didn't want to get up but I got up anyway. Only a few more minutes of driving before the entrance to Ray's place. No. My place.

20.

CALLIE CHOSE the flowered hippie skirt and a lacey Indian blouse she picked up for nothing at the flea market, just in case Robin would be there. It was the kind of outfit that used to set her mother off into a fit. "Your tits are showing," she'd yell at Callie, as if Callie didn't know.

She kept thinking about calling her mother, first when she found out she was pregnant, and then after the baby came. Ralph tried to convince her to make amends, especially now, when she could use a mother's help. But Callie knew what it would be like: one insult after another, one great big opportunity to be told how irresponsible she was. She could just imagine her mother's voice—*You can't hold a job and now you're having a baby?* No, she wouldn't give her mother the chance to gloat over all her mistakes. And Daphne wasn't exactly a mistake. Certainly not today, all yummy from her bath, smiling at nothing in particular, just plain smiling.

"Call your mother," Ralph kept bugging her after the baby was born, but Callie wouldn't risk it. Who knows, maybe her mother wouldn't have chastised her for getting pregnant. Maybe for some crazy reason her mother would actually enjoy her little granddaughter. The truth was that Callie had no intention of providing her with that pleasure. No. You get none of this, Callie said to the phantom mother, who managed to make her presence felt even when she lived fifty miles away.

Callie took one last glance in the mirror, deciding not to tie her hair up but leave it loose. Most men liked it that way. She assumed Robin would be there to introduce her to this Mrs. Blackwell. He had given Callie's number to the woman but Callie never really expected anything to come of it, just thought it was an excuse Robin came up with to hang out with her. But sure enough, the woman had called, taking Callie by surprise. She sounded friendly enough, said she had heard so many good things about her. What ever did Robin tell her? It made her nervous. Like what was she supposed to do, dress for a job interview, brush up on her botany? She twirled around one more time, pulled the skirt down a bit in back, approved. Robin would be there. He had to be.

She couldn't stop thinking about him. Couldn't stop thinking about those first few times when it had been practically all talk, the nervous kind. But they'd created a routine pretty early on. Afternoon nap for Daphne, she set the stroller outside the bedroom, covered her up nice and warm, then tiptoed into where Robin would be waiting, sometimes just a tool belt on, it had become a joke between them. Daylight hours growing every week keeping Ralph at work until dark, they had plenty of time, and yet never enough time. They hardly spoke anymore. Except for that first time when he went to her house, he never said much period. And she was the married one. No way she wanted to talk about whatever it was they were doing together.

She hadn't seen him working or anything at the old house for almost three weeks. Not since right after Easter. She had left him a basket, tucked it behind his toolbox in the shed. She'd filled it with chocolates and condoms. Not even a card. She had weighed the idea back and forth and finally decided yes. They'd been having a great time lately, seemed like the fun was outweighing the confusion, and Callie thought it was a pretty cute idea. Ralph would have cracked up if she'd ever left him a basket of condoms. That kind of stuff turned him on big time.

But Robin hadn't surfaced since Easter, and she wondered if maybe her little joke had put him off.

Three weeks. Maybe it was just a coincidence that they kept missing each other. For those first few weeks they'd met up every day, except weekends of course. And then Daphne had a fever, poor little thing. Callie had stayed in with her for a couple of days, she was afraid to leave a message on his phone, but they had missed other days here and there, he had other jobs to go to, it wasn't like they had a schedule or anything. There was that week of solid storms in March, but then there were the afternoons when the weather cleared and the smells from the new leaves and sawdust and cool fresh earth felt like some kind of drug. They made love outside once, right out in the open in the grove of manzanitas, the ground still damp but he had that heavy plastic tarp and she brought blankets and for a few luxurious hours the land belonged to them. And then Easter.

She made one last turnaround in front of the mirror and decided against the see-through peasant blouse, went for a clean boring light blue t-shirt, her gold dolphin pendant. Wholesome, that's what she was, nothing like the stupid slut her mother called her.

She turned the corner up the driveway and pushed the stroller to the top of the path. The place felt as desolate as ever. Didn't the woman say 2:00? It was twenty minutes after and not a soul around. Daphne was fiddling with a set of plastic keys so Callie set the stroller brake and left her within earshot, at the base of the porch steps. Alone, she detoured through the manzanita grove and stood there for a moment before tromping back to the driveway, headed into the house and straight to the bedroom. She just wanted to be sure they hadn't left any traces, a hair clip or her purple thong. She sniffed the air, as though she might detect the scent of their last time together.

That last time could have been their last time, for real. They had just finished up the afternoon 'roll in the sawdust,' as Robin called it, with all the building debris sticking to their clothes. Callie had to brush bits of wood chips out from inside her crotch, sawdust from the crease between her breasts, even with the blankets she had set down. Making love to Robin was a messy business.

And then, when Robin was just about to come, making that horrid sound like he was choking, (Ralph sounded more like a screeching pig), Callie was sure she heard the crunch of gravel outside, like someone was out there.

Could be that jerk Pete next door, who always seemed to be sneaking around. She jumped off Robin and reached for her pants at the same time, somehow managing to knock her knee into his groin.

"Shit" he screamed, doubling over.

"Oh, God, I'm sorry!" she said, but didn't stop to soothe him, because Daphne, wakened by their noises, had started building to a full-on wail.

Holding Daphne close against her, Callie walked outside to check behind the shack. All quiet out there. Back inside, Daphne still in her arms, she found Robin leaning doubled up against the doorway.

"Sorry" she called to him. "Are you ok?" By now the baby was just whimpering.

"Fine" he muttered.

"Sorry," again she said, but he waved her off, didn't so much as look up. Fair enough, Callie thought, collecting her jacket, a plastic toy, folding up the blankets. It was about time to leave anyway. When she stopped to think about what the two of them were doing together, it occurred to her that maybe her mother was right. She was a little slut.

Callie decided to check out behind the house just in case she and Robin had left any traces back there, not likely, but she needed to kill time. She checked her phone in case he had left a message, but all she had was a text from Ralph saying he'd be home late again. Forget dinner. She was hanging up a rake that had been left on the ground, closing the shed door, when she got the first whiff of a stinking gassy fume. She didn't connect the stink with car exhaust right away, but then heard a rattle of engine and brake noises and realized it must be the woman pulling up the driveway.

Callie ran around to the front of the house, suddenly aware that Daphne was screaming. My God, did she remember to set the stroller brakes? But no, the stroller was right where she left it, and the baby was very much alive, screeching the screech of someone startled by a very loud car.

"Oh, I'm sorry. I didn't mean to wake her," the old woman's voice bellowed in horror.

"Oh, no, sorry, I shouldn't have left the stroller out in the driveway."

"My gosh is she all right? I'm so sorry" again.

"You're sorry, I'm the one who should be sorry" and on like that, a few more sorry's, Callie hoping the woman would please say something else already, since Callie had nothing to say to her. What was she doing there anyway? No Robin. Just this old woman wearing a ridiculous pair of baggy pants, army type, and a huge backpack filled with God knows what. Right then Callie wanted to whisk the baby out of there and run home. This whole thing was a bad idea. And where was Robin?

Callie lifted Daphne out of her stroller and held her tightly as the sobs subsided.

"Oh," the woman looked flustered, "My dear, is there

something I can do to help?" but Daphne had already settled into Callie's breast, as Callie slowly walked her up and down the driveway to calm her down.

"You're good with her," the woman called out, but Callie's attention was on the driveway, looking toward the road, searching for signs of Robin. He should have been here by now.

"We can meet another time," the woman offered, but Daphne had quieted down finally, and Callie wanted to get this ridiculous meeting over with.

"Its OK," she replied. "I hope Robin told you I didn't mean any harm here. I just wandered over here one day and…"

"Shh shh" the woman said, and Callie realized the woman was speaking to the baby, not listening to a word she said.

She went on anyway. "I'm sorry about trespassing on your land but I didn't know anyone lived here. I mean I heard it might belong to someone but I never saw anybody here and it seemed the place could use some tidying up because the weeds are pretty bad and…"

Callie's nervous excuses were wasted on the woman who had leaned in and started clicking her tongue at the baby who was now attempting her own sloppy versions.

"Do you want to hold her?" Callie offered, because Daphne seemed transfixed by this new face that was making silly clacking noises with her tongue. The baby was reaching for the woman with thick rubbery fingers.

"I don't have much experience with babies. If it starts

to fuss, I wouldn't know what to do."

"She seems to like you," Callie assured her. Hannah reached out and took the baby who was now giggling so hard the spittle was sliding down the side of her chubby chin. The woman used the side of her sleeve to wipe it up. "There there," she said, and Callie started thinking maybe she could do a trade. Leave the baby with her while she and Robin take off for the afternoon, maybe one of those boat trips he kept talking about.

Where was Robin, anyway? This woman was nothing like he had described. Just at that moment Hannah looked up at her, for the first time, and Callie saw the deep grey eyes Robin had warned her about, "she looks scary but she's not," he had told her, and she could see exactly what he meant. Callie wasn't the slightest bit scared.

"And where exactly is it that you live?"

"Right across the road."

"That place with the big antenna?"

Why did everyone have to mention that thing? It made Callie cringe to think what people must say about them.

"When are you moving in?" Callie returned, mostly just to change the subject.

"Do I look like someone who would live in a place like this?" the woman asked, but her smile was now broad and unmistakable so Callie knew it was a kind of joke, and she allowed herself to let out a smile, too. And then she noticed that the old lady had a mole over her eyebrow exactly like her Aunt Daphne's mole. She was pretty wrinkled, but Callie had a hard time guessing old people's ages.

"Well, are you?" Callie pushed, more playful now, feeling both expanded and sheltered in the soft afternoon air.

The woman stopped still and stared hard into Callie's eyes. "I don't know if I'm going to live here. It belongs to me, that's all I know." And now she handed the baby back, brushed the sleeves of her shirt down, and Callie caught a whiff of the woman's soap, Peppermint, spicy and inviting, nothing like the sickening stuff most old ladies seemed to like.

"I'm just fixing it up for now, then I may sell it. It's too soon for me to know anything other than I like the smells around here. I like having a change of scenery. I even like not knowing. The place belonged to my brother and when he died, it was left to me. That's about all I'm sure of, stupid as that may sound."

Callie took Daphne back, following the woman up the steps to the front door and into the house. "That doesn't sound stupid at all. This place is like a secret hideaway. It is for me anyway."

"Come on in, the woman motioned. "It's a bit of a wreck but Robin keeps working on it. Well you know that, I suppose."

Callie hoped her face didn't look as guilty as she suddenly felt. The woman was pointing out the living room, the laundry area, telling her what Robin was up to, but

Callie wasn't listening, too busy scanning the rooms for evidence.

"Robin has only nice things to say about you," Hannah said, and Callie tried to keep her face neutral. She steered them back outside, and Hannah offered her the one wicker chair that sat on the porch. Callie had already plopped herself down on the steps, Daphne on her lap, mother and baby looking quite at home.

"Be careful of splinters, the floor is filthy. I wish I had a blanket I could give her. It's a her, isn't it?"

Callie knew exactly where the blankets were, but wouldn't dare say. "Her name is Daphne. She's just starting to sit up by herself. It's fine down here if I hold her."

"Daphne isn't a name you hear much these days."

"She's named for my favorite great-aunt."

"Your great-aunt must love that baby."

Callie looked down. "Well, no, she had to move into a nursing home about the time I found out I was pregnant. She never knew the baby was coming, and then she died just before Daphne was born."

"That's too bad."

"I like to think her free spirit passed into my baby."

"Well, from what I can tell, you seem to have a pretty bright spirit yourself. Look at all you've done around here."

Callie was embarrassed and pleased by the unexpected praise. "I didn't really do anything," she said. "Just push some weeds around, give myself something to fill up the time instead of pacing around my house all day. I really appreciate having this place to go to. I really hope you don't mind."

The woman clearly didn't mind. It was one of those polite things that Callie was so good at saying, knowing the answer all along.

"Of course I don't mind. I hope you like tea and bread sticks, it's all I've got. Can the baby eat these?"

"She could suck on one. She doesn't have teeth."

"Lord what I don't know about babies."

"Its ok," Callie assured her, "she really liked when you were playing with her back there."

It wasn't a typical picnic, the woman handing Callie a couple of breadsticks on a paper towel, on a very dirty porch. But Callie realized she had stopped looking for Robin. Now she kind of hoped he wouldn't show up. The breadsticks were a bit stale, but they had currants in them, sweet, more like a cookie.

"So are you from around here?" the woman asked.

"I grew up a few miles from here, closer to town. I met my husband in high school and we were planning on moving to Sacramento but then he got a great job selling sprinkler systems for new housing developments. It's kind of a booming industry out here, or so he tells me."

Callie took another bite of breadstick, and the woman got up, went back inside briefly and came back with a spoon and some almond butter.

"Here, dip it in this."

By now Callie had figured out what had been weighing

down the woman's backpack. "Wow, Mrs. Blackwell, this is great!" and before she could stop herself, "do you have any jelly?"

"Coming right up," and unbelievably, the woman produced a jar of loganberry, Callie's favorite. She dipped her finger into the jam, let the baby lick it off.

"Please call me Hannah," the woman sat down next to her, on the step, taking hold of Daphne's little feet.

"How long have you lived across the road?"

"My husband bought the place as an investment. He promises that we're going to move into one of those big new developments by the time Daphne is ready for school. He says these country properties are where the fast money gets made."

The crumbs from Hannah's breadstick were landing all over the baby's feet, and Daphne kept trying to pick them up but her fingers were too fat for the job. It seemed to Callie that Hannah was paying more attention to feeding the baby bread crumbs than listening to her talk about Ralph's plans. She thought she heard Hannah say 'um hum' so she went on, trying to convince herself at least, that Ralph's plans made sense.

"Ralph says it's just until he gets his sprinkler business going. Then we'll be able to afford anything we want.

"Don't you have any gardening to do at your house?"

"Ralph says I can only plant begonias or things that don't clog up the water lines since we won't be living there forever anyway and...."

Callie stopped mid-sentence, as the woman pulled in

a noisy breath, then a long exhale.

"Are you all right?"

"Do you hate begonias as much as I do?" was all she said.

She had never admitted it to anyone but now she could full on confess. Callie killed begonias on purpose. Put salt in the soil.

And what did Hannah think about azaleas?

"Hate them," the old woman announced.

"Me too," Callie laughed out the words as she stood up to brush the crumbs off her pants, which signaled Hannah to get up too, and lead the way down the path toward the back of the house.

"Was that you who cleared all the weeds away from the shed?"

"Yes, that was me. You couldn't open the door the weeds were so high.

"What else have you done around here?"

They talked plants some more, the woman knew the names of a couple of the wildflowers that were growing, but talk somehow shifted to African Violets. Now it was Hannah's turn to confess, she recently tossed out six perfectly healthy plants.

"You just threw them away?"

"Didn't even save them for the church bazaar!" Hannah admitted and Callie cracked up. "You really threw them away?"

Just then Daphne started to squirm and Hannah surprised all three of them by reaching out and grabbing the wriggly little thing from her mother's arms.

"I can take her," and she did, easily this time, as the baby wrapped her thick little arms around the woman's neck.

"So what do you think about my hiring you to do some work around here?"

"It's just a hobby, working in the garden. I just don't think I could accept payment from you."

Hannah was jiggling the baby, and, as she did so, the last of the crumbs dropped from her slacks. Callie experienced a sudden urge to hug this strange woman.

"And just why is that?"

"I'd feel funny taking money from you for something I do for fun. And my husband would kill me if he knew." She hadn't meant to say that but it just came out.

"You don't really mean he'd kill you, do you?"

"No, no," Callie assured her. "He's a good guy really. He just likes to think he's taking care of me. He's old fashioned that way."

"Well you can tell your husband that you're doing an old lady a favor. I invited you here, you can tell him that. I don't see my way into this bramble patch any time soon and far as I can tell, whatever you do will be an improvement. Of course you ought to get something for your labor."

"Oh no I ought to be paying you something."

"Silly girl." Hannah said, looking at the baby, but Callie knew the woman was referring to her. Hannah didn't seem in any hurry to give the baby back.

"I'd better be going." Callie wheeled the stroller over. Hannah gently set the baby down, and managed to strap her in. Without a word they walked together, Hannah supporting the front of the stroller, Callie lifting it down the steps to the walkway, a silent, slow motion journey to cushion the sleeping child. Hannah leaned over to pick rocks away from the path before they set the stroller back down.

"I guess I can keep clearing weeds around the deck and driveway." Callie whispered.

"I guess I can leave some cash in an envelope on the kitchen counter," Hannah whispered back.

"I guess Ralph doesn't have to know."

"I guess not."

It was a funny way to end the visit, deciding without deciding that a deal had been made.

"You can leave me lists if you want me to buy any materials."

"I'll just keep on clearing, like I've been doing, and maybe plant more."

"I'll see you next time then."

"Next time." Callie walked up the driveway, waving, waving.

"And you can leave your gardening tools here if you'd like," Hannah called out.

When she reached the road, Callie turned back and watched as the old woman disappeared down her driveway. Daphne was still asleep. The short walk home would be slow, as slow as possible, one stroller wheel bump at a time. She took a deep breath, hoping to hold on to that mysterious scent of peppermint and dark tea.

21.

DUSK WAS PETE'S TIME of day. Just him, the lizards and the occasional woodpecker settling in for the night. Once in a while, off in the distance, an owl hooted a greeting. Turkey vultures swirled overhead for one last shot at a meal. If Pete was lucky, he'd catch a glimpse of a red-tailed hawk swooping down to grab its prey.

On this particular evening in mid-May, with daylight savings time pushing his visits later and later, Pete tilted back in the old wicker chair that miraculously, after all these years, had survived the elements. Already 7:30, and he could still catch a glimpse of what was left of the daylight as it slowly crept behind the grove of buckeyes, settling between the manzanita branches, hot streaks of sun bleeding the bark from pink to purple as blackness and chill descended. He preferred the sweep of views from Ray's porch to looking at the panorama of crap that had been slowly collecting on his own broken down porch ever since Beverly moved out. She had kept the place up nice, he had to admit that much, changing the pads on the porch chairs every few years, planting those pretty flowers in pots that Pete enjoyed watering, one of the few chores she assigned him that he took pleasure in. He had lost track of how many years since she'd finally left him. It was around the time Winston's wife passed. Pete was pretty sure the only reason Beverly stuck around that last year was to help take care of her sick friend, bring her all those stinky home brewed medicines the two women loved to concoct. She was barely talking to him by then, only shouting orders at him to clean up his crap on the porch.

Pete didn't miss her one bit, but in the last few years he had to admit his porch had become uninhabitable. There wasn't so much as a free spot to set up a lousy fold-up chair. The squirrels had helped themselves to the last of the cushion stuffing on the chaise lounge, which now was loaded down with mildewed magazines and boxes filled with who knows what. Even if there had been a decent place to sit, the only view from his porch was the stupid satellite dish of those young idiots that moved in across the road.

No, he was glad he had thought to move his wicker chair over to Ray's place. He'd carried it over after that first time Ray disappeared back in the late 1980's. By then, the two men had already forged an agreement. Pete kept an eye on the place whenever Ray left town (which was more often than not), maintained the fences, and poked his head in if anyone suspicious showed up. He never knew where Ray went for months at a time, never asked. He figured if Ray wanted him to know, he'd have told him. Just said 'got some business,' and sometimes left Pete a phone number, in case Pete might need to get hold of him.

Then out of the blue Pete would hear that familiar roar of Ray's motorcycle and, soon enough, smell the old familiar smoke wafting through the trees again.

Pete had lost track of how many years since Ray had last come around. He had been surprised to read about Ray's death, especially since the crash happened not five miles from here. Pete wondered if Ray was about to move back to his land when he crashed, or maybe just coming to pay a quick visit. Hard to ever know what that man was up to and now Pete would never know. All he knew was that Ray's place had always felt like it was Pete's place too. More so in the years that he had it all to himself. And this particular evening, sitting in his own wicker chair on Ray's front porch, he felt all the more justified making himself at home. Who knew how long this would last, with all the recent goings on around the property?

Pete alternated swigs from his bottle and slow inhalations of mountain air. The changes were coming fast, starting with the day Lundale first drove that woman on to the property. Pete had heard the truck that day as soon as it rounded the bend right past his house and immediately knew something was up. He suspected it was Lundale, with that fancy hydraulic system, pretty much announcing his arrival. Pete hoisted himself to his feet and peered out through the coyote brush hedge that bordered their properties. Sure enough, there was Lundale, cowboy hat and all, carrying his clipboard in case anyone doubted he had important business to take care of. And there was that old lady with him, the one Lundale told him about, it had to be Ray's long-lost sister.

He watched as they got out of the truck and started walking up Ray's driveway. He had to think fast. He tiptoed around to the back end of his property that offered up a wider view of Ray's old shack, then positioned himself low behind the coyote brush that marked where his property ended and Ray's began. He crouched down at the spot where borer beetles had eaten through a clump of branches, swept the mess aside so he could sit comfortably on a log and have a straight-on view of the two of them, though it was the woman he really wanted to see.

Straining to hear, he leaned into the hedge as close as he dared, careful not to get caught by the prickly wild roses. All he managed to take in were sounds of the woman muttering to herself. He couldn't make out a word. She walked around the house, leaning over to touch the plants, looking inside windows, looking up at the trees, poking her head into the toolshed like she was looking for something. It had been nearly impossible to know exactly what she looked like with that flopping straw hat on her head.

And then she disappeared from his view. But he held his position, didn't dare move, and when she reappeared, it looked like she was staring straight at him through the coyote brush. He ducked down lower and luckily she turned away. Lundale had called out to her about something, Pete couldn't hear, but it had been a close call. No telling what would have happened had she seen him there.

"What the hell," Pete had thought to himself that day, and was thinking still, seven months later. Made him miss his old pal Ray, all mellow on his white wicker chair. Those were the days all right, the two of them trading swigs off the same bottle. Ray would natter on and on about his wild women or near misses with the cops, and Pete would slap his thigh in approval. All Ray's talk somehow made Pete feel younger than his years, and he felt inclined to spin a few stories of his own, exaggerating and inventing some doozies even he himself wouldn't have believed.

Sometimes they didn't say much at all. Just an occasional "Yep," or "Those were some good times," or a quiet nodding of the head, not remembering exactly what they were agreeing on.

Pete missed those days, more and more it seemed.

Recently people had started messing with him, poking him on the shoulder, yelling out from their car windows, "Hey Pete, hear you're getting yourself a new neighbor." He ignored them, or tried to, sometimes offering up a curse or hand gesture that didn't do much to quell his disgust. Everyone in town knew how Pete still used that piece of land to collect the crap he sold at the flea market. He was proud of his reputation for making money off of things most folks just threw away. They were envious of his talent, and now, with this buzz about someone looking to buy the place, they were eager to rub it in.

Lundale was no use, claiming the woman never returned his phone calls, though Pete suspected George wouldn't have told him if she did.

Well he didn't need George to tell him the woman was interested. Not two weeks after he had driven her up that first time, she was back again, this time by herself, poking around, and then again, unbelievable, Pete caught sight of her slogging through the mud in what had been their wettest winter in years, clanking and banging away inside. How the hell she could stay dry in that dilapidated old shack he couldn't imagine.

Then Winston's boy started coming around with tools, making so much noise Pete couldn't do anything but look through the hedges to see what was going on. And now that young woman who lived across the road flitting around, what the hell was she doing? It was becoming a regular circus over there and Pete couldn't keep track of all the comings and goings since the days started getting longer. He never knew when the old woman would show up and he couldn't be too careful. In the beginning it was just weekends, but there was one time she got there on a Monday. He'd watched her unload her car, backpacks full to bursting slung over her shoulders, yanking boxes out of the back seat.

On that particular occasion he'd been rooting around in the gully when he heard her car pulling onto the land. He'd had to race back to his side of the property line quick—those stinking Mountain Misery flowers sticking to his socks—so she wouldn't catch him on her property. It threw his whole week off.

So far she hadn't spent the night, he was glad of that. So far, on the days she did come around, she arrived in the morning and left early afternoon, giving him plenty of time to enjoy the dusk hours all to himself. But with the longer days coming, activity was picking up. Winston's son working, tossing piles of old wood and glass in the gully, busted floorboards, bent hinges, leaving bits of sandpaper all over the place, making a mess. The old woman was clearly fixing the place up but to what end Pete could not say. Even now, the porch didn't feel quite like his any more, his wicker chair threatened by all the recent comings and goings.

Maybe I ought to just go over and introduce myself.

It was the whisky talking. Getting involved with that woman could only be trouble. She'd likely ask questions Pete could just hear himself answering. "Yeah, I knew your brother. Back in the old days we'd hang out on his porch, get shitfaced. We were business partners, of sorts." Yeah, over his dead body would he tell her about that.

Ray and him weren't exactly business partners. What they had was an I'll-scratch-your-back-you-scratch-mine kind of deal. Ray had been in and out of jail a few times over the years, never for too long, and Pete always kept up his end of the bargain, keeping an eye out, making sure the place was quiet. In return, Pete got free rein to mine Ray's gully. Pete wasn't even interested in the stinking weed Ray grew on his land. He was a Canadian Club man himself. He could care less about Ray's crop, not about selling it, not about smoking it, certainly not about stealing it.

Pete sometimes wondered if Ray ever blamed him for the times he got busted. But whenever he came back, he acted like nothing happened. He'd even plant another crop, like he hadn't learned a thing.

By now Pete had pretty much scavenged the place dry. Still he enjoyed snooping around the edges from time to time and sure enough, just the other evening a jawbone turned up, and a rusted coin, couldn't make out the date but shined up it would bring in a couple of dollars. It usually happened after the rainy season, flotsam from the river pushing crap through the tributaries, eventually winding up in Blind Shady Creek. A lady's hatpin appeared last winter, pretty worthless, but always some fool around to buy it. He still thought about that '48 Nevada license plate Ray himself had found years back, a real rarity, not a bit of rust on it, and barely bent. What Pete wouldn't have given for it! But Ray said he was saving it for his big sister, which was the first Pete heard about him having any kind of family.

Pete wished he could have told Ray it wasn't him that turned him in. He knew people assumed he did it. He heard the whispers and under-the-breath jabs. As if anyone around there even cared about what happened to Ray. But damn it, he had kept his word until the end, with nothing to show for it. Too late now. The guy was dead.

An owl called out in the distance and Pete took it as a sign. There was less than a swig left in the bottle, not so much as a gulp. He inhaled what was left, stood up and stretched. The cool air was doing its job of sobering him up a bit, and he thought maybe it wouldn't be such a bad idea to introduce himself to his new neighbor. Get on her good side. Keep your enemies close, he remembered someone saying over at the Nugget, never quite sure what it meant, until now. He picked up his empty bottle and straightened the chair back to exactly where it had been, afraid she might notice someone had moved it. At least for the time being, the gully and the porch were still his. He made his way to the back of Ray's land, crossed over into his place, dragging a stick behind him to rub out his footprints, something he figured Ray would have wanted him to do.

Spring

22.

THE TIME HAD GOTTEN AWAY from me. It was just after Easter I think I recall, when I first met with that girl on the land.

She certainly made it hard to forget her. Phone messages practically every other day with updates on her progress. Yesterday she had left me yet another one. "Hi, its me, Callie, I hope you don't mind I bought some seeds for the planter boxes." That first time she called, just after I got back home, it took me a minute to figure out what she was talking about. I didn't know anyone named Callie, but then that singsong voice of hers came right back to me. Goodness, had I really hired her? I couldn't even remember what she and I had decided. I just remembered that cute little baby and what a nice afternoon we spent together.

Once I came back to my real life, the one with the refrigerator that needed to be cleaned out, the one where Wilbur forgot again to bring the splicer to fix my busted garden hose, I'd all but forgotten about whatever small connections I had made for myself on Ray's bit of land.

And somehow my life had gotten busy again. When I returned from that last visit to the land, I got an unexpected but welcomed call from Sister Eugenia. "Only for a few weeks," she promised, until the school year ends. They had just lost the latest in a string of less-than-stellar secretaries to maternity leave. I never minded filling in as a substitute from time to time. I was glad to have the diversion of cleaning up their year-end messes, feeling needed for a change. I was relieved to sleep in a clean bed again, and wear clothes that didn't have stickers in them.

So those occasional calls from Callie, I had to stop and think sometimes where I knew her from. That's how fickle my old brain has become.

And then there was Robin. I certainly hadn't forgotten about him, but he hadn't been leaving any messages lately and I wasn't in a hurry to find anything new out about the place. What would I do if he told me the roof had caved in? I wasn't in the least bit interested, now that I was back in my quiet, clean, predictable house, to find out if the roof had caved in.

Robin, sweet sad Robin. I found myself growing concerned about him, not even sure why. There's some sadness there he keeps to himself. He mumbles when he talks, just like Ned did. That time I met with him, I accidentally said "Honey, speak up," that's how much he reminded me of Ned. I have a mind to wrap my big flabby arms around him and give him a squeeze but of course I never would.

But here I was, sorting through last year's report cards, sweeping up year end school reports into neat little piles, no time to think about giving anyone a squeeze. The people I had met on Blind Shady Bend could just as well have been characters from one of those TV shows I watch when I can't find a decent book to read.

It happened one morning, while I was getting ready for work. I had broken my nail trying to fix a zipper on that fuzzy jacket that tries to look like real fur but doesn't fool anyone. I picked it up at a garage sale for practically nothing and it's become my absolute favorite. No accounting for my taste in clothes. Anyhow, the damned zipper had caught on some of the fuzz and wouldn't budge. Pulling at it practically ripped my nail clear off.

I went looking for my nail file that wasn't in any of the five places it should have been in, hoping I could salvage what was left of my nail. I finally tried the top desk drawer, just in case I put the nail file in the wrong place. Wouldn't have been the first time. The drawer was jammed, and I had to pull hard to get it open. And then I was sorry I succeeded.

Ever since I met with the lawyer back in October, mail concerning Ray's property had been piling up: Nevada County Tax Collector, Law Offices of Hanover Combs and Greer, Placerville Mining, Nevada County Assessor's Office, not to mention hordes of advertisements for tree trimmers, well diggers, and who knows what else.

Couldn't bear to read them and couldn't bear to throw them out, so instead I stuffed them all into the top drawer of my desk, like they belonged to someone else who might someday come for them. I must have figured that if I didn't know what was in those envelopes, I didn't need to make any decisions. And maybe, just maybe, if they piled up long enough, the decisions might go away by themselves.

This time though, I couldn't pretend not to see the Nevada County Tax Collector envelope staring up at me. I gave in and pulled the whole wad of unopened mail out of the drawer. What the hell, maybe there was a check inside one of them.

It was as though someone hit me over the head with one of those giant hammers from Highway Hardware. What an idiot I'd been. This land wasn't a gift my renegade brother had dearly bestowed on me. No. It was one last shining dose of his mean spirited jokes, even better than the time he loosened the handlebars on my bicycle. I could almost hear him laughing, picturing me slogging through his weed patch, scratching my head at the impossibility of it all.

Plain and simple, Ray owed back taxes. What a shock. And pursuant to the terms of some Proposition B from last November's election in Nevada County, a new assessment had been added on for electrical lines that were going to be installed for the upcoming tax year 2008. Back taxes (and penalties) along with next year's first installment, came to just under $4,000.00.

Let's see, what else. A letter from Placerville Mining and Well Company. How did they get my name and address? It would appear that the warranty on the well on Ray's property was long past expired, and they'd be happy to offer a one time only 10% discount to the new owner for the necessary replacement. For only $1,500, they'd throw in an inspection of the generator.

And there was more.

That little weasel of a lawyer had charged me $350 to pass me a couple of Kleenexes. And would you believe, he tacked on finance charges for late payments. Balance due was now a whopping $462.50.

I was looking at $4,000, plus $462.50, plus $1,500, not to mention whatever I still owed Robin, though so far it hadn't been much.

Those bills sure woke me up.

For God's sake SELL THE PLACE, I yelled into the empty room. Take the money and maybe sell my folks' place too, get one of those new condos with flags flying out front and a patio just big enough for my one lousy fuchsia.

Lucky Lundale's business card was right where I had left it, in my nightstand, near the telephone. I had picked it up more than once over these past eight months, not even knowing what I wanted to say. I've decided I'm not going to put the property on the market. I've decided to sell the property. I'd practice saying both sentences out loud and they both made perfect sense. One time I got all the way to dialing and once he picked up after a few rings, but I quickly hung up before he could get to his happy little greeting.

Maybe it was time. Past time. Before Robin and Callie got too deep into their work. Before I got too deep into this folly.

What a foolish old woman I had become. Thinking I might actually reconnect with Ray somehow, with this 'gift' he bequeathed to me. I should have known better than to look back. All I've ever seen when I look back at my past is nothing but nothing. What a foolish, bored, silly old woman I'd become.

My fingernail started to throb. I must have been picking hard at it because there was a bit of blood on my hand that I sucked away, glad none of it had dripped on to that jacket. Broken zipper or not, I didn't want it stained with blood. I was going to be late to work but I didn't care. The time had gotten away from me while I was opening all that mail but I was glad I had finally figured it out. I would call the Realtor first thing tomorrow. Put a stop to this once and for all.

I set Lucky Lundale's business card back where it was supposed to be and breathed in one long relaxed breath. Ray, that son of a gun, my father was right about him after all. Dead in the ground and still he was capable of pulling the rug out from under me. No, Ray. Not this time. Somebody else can fix the well pump and pay the property taxes and figure out how to get that stinky groundcover smell out of their socks.

When I got to the church, Sister Eugenia was waiting for me.

"I thought you were coming at 9:00," she said, almost a scold, but we played around like that so I knew she wasn't angry.

"I'm sorry, I got stuck in traffic," I replied, part of our

joke, because we both knew I had a three block walk to get there.

I sat down at my old desk, ruffling through piles of paperwork that had gotten out of hand while the nuns were busy tending to more urgent matters.

I picked up a stack of report cards, gracious me they were dated from last year, and still not filed. In my day I had no need for a filing basket, whisked those papers into their proper spot as soon as they hit my desk. Sitting there brought up so many memories—the smells of bananas and peanut butter, the noises of jackets flapping against the sides of lockers, high pitched voices echoing in the hallways long after the kids had left the building. This was good for me, this pushing papers around. A gentle kind of a medicine.

"You seem quiet," she was leaning over my desk, and I was pretending not to notice, looking extremely busy 3-hole punching last year's choir song sheets back into their proper folders.

"Is everything all right?" she asked again. Sister Eugenia had what they call a sixth sense, and I knew she'd never let me get back to my work until I told her.

Back when I first learned I had inherited my brother's land, she had listened intently to all the details and pronounced, "Maybe it's a sign." She always spoke in that soft voice of hers, the one that makes you have to strain to hear what she was saying.

It sounded a little bit dingy, like that New Age crap I sometimes hear on TV if I don't flip the channels fast enough. But I couldn't get her words out of my head. There haven't been too many people in my life that cared about me for my sake and not theirs. Sister Eugenia had grown up in a rural town somewhere outside of Portland, I've forgotten the name. She wanted me to show her pictures of the place, disappointed that I hadn't taken any. She was much more enthralled with the idea of living off a dirt road than I was. I'd brush her off, saying I had no idea what I was going to do with the place. I tossed and turned some nights thinking about what she said to me— *You must follow every path that is presented to you*— playing her words back over and over in my head until they finally put me to sleep.

I hate to admit it was because of her that I had picked up the phone and called Mr. Lundale in the first place.

But this time was different. A reasonable amount of time had passed and I'd given the place a chance. I didn't have the energy or money to deal with that rambling spread of country property. No regrets for whatever Robin's efforts cost me. It could only help the selling price, and either way, I could at least look myself in the eye and say that I'd gone in with an open mind.

"I've decided not to keep the land." I blurted out. Hoping this would make her go away and let me get back to my work.

But she didn't go away. That's another thing church people do. Just when you want to sneak past them, they bore their deep-set eyes into you and stop you in your tracks.

"This must be so hard."

I grunted something, can't recall what, but she just stood there, still and determined. She wasn't yet finished with me.

"Maybe you should go there one more time, if for no other reason than to say goodbye."

I dug deeper into the piles of papers, changed the subject on her.

"Do you really need to keep copies of last year's report cards?" I asked, but all she answered was "you must say goodbye."

So there you have it. I take the advice of a nun and decide that the call to the Realtor can wait until one more visit.

"OK, OK." I have to tell her or she won't leave my desk. "I'll go up there one more time. Say my goodbyes. That's it."

And it most likely would have been it, had I not run into the man in the gully.

23.

CRIB SHEETS FOLDED, shirts stacked, Callie set her nose down on the soft clean pile, took in a long deep breath, enjoying a brief sense of contentment for this one small event. Every single sock matched up this time. Even the tiny baby socks that don't ever stay on those rubbery feet of hers, this time, each tiny sock found its match. And Ralph's black socks—seemed like he had hundreds of them—added up to an even number. So this is right where she was supposed to be. Inhaling dryer sheet perfume, she gave herself a moment to feel the warmth of fresh soft clothes permeate the folds of her wrists.

Once the baby things were all put away, Callie picked up the stack of Ralph's t-shirts. No amount of laundry soap could remove the familiar lime scent that permanently adhered itself to the fibers of his clothing. He'd been wearing Old Spice since their high school days. She used to spray her sheets with cheap perfume so her mother wouldn't suspect he'd been in Callie's bed.

And Ralph had been looking different lately. Handsome even. Last night she noticed something new on the back of his neck, faint blond hairs, baby hairs, like peach fuzz, looking out of place against the thick sinew of his muscles. She rubbed her fingers up and back on the thin threads, wondering if they'd been there all these years and she was just now noticing them.

"Feels good baby." He liked what she was doing, rolled into her more gently than usual, and she wondered what other little details about Ralph she hadn't yet discovered. Callie loved the smell of Ralph, the smell that mixed well with the lavender oil she bought at the flea market. Tart and fresh, the Callie-Ralph smell, brewing and blending for twelve years now, she'd bottle it if she thought it would put her mind to rest.

She closed her eyes and tried to remember what Robin smelled like, but all that came to her was the dry scratch of sawdust that caught in her throat as she gasped for breath every time, hot and dry and wrung from exhaustion.

Still more weeks had passed. Robin hadn't called, hadn't come by. Was never there when she went over to pull weeds. It was obvious that he wasn't waiting for her like she kept waiting for him, at every turn, looking out her windows as she passed from one room to another, just in case. She couldn't say what she was waiting for exactly. It wasn't like she was about to leave Ralph for him. No, it was the idea of him she waited for, waiting beyond how long she thought it possible to wait. And still he hadn't come around, hadn't so much as called.

Well what did she expect? She was the one who had started the whole thing, surprising him that first time, pushing him into the windowsill so hard he cut his hands.

Callie was used to Ralph taking charge of things but Robin wasn't that way. He was quiet and seemed far away in his thoughts, talking to the ground so much she had to reach over and pull his chin up so her eyes could meet his. Maybe she mistook his softness for something more interesting. More she thought about it, this affair had become work, and the work had become tedious. Here, she had to tell him, putting his hand on exactly the spot that Ralph knew by heart.

Her very first affair and who would have thought it would be such hard work. Keep an eye out for the baby, check her phone for messages from Ralph in case he decided to come home midday (he never did). Always always it was she that made the first move. Of course there was the baby to think about. If Daphne hadn't been such a good napper, the whole affair may never even happened. A cranky colicky baby would have prevented the whole mess from starting in the first place.

And it was so awkward, sawdust all over his behind and her having to extricate her Velcro bra straps from his tool belt. It was a great adventure at first, they laughed about it, but sometimes when they finished she wanted to get out of the room so fast she didn't even bother to pick up her barrettes. She even left her panties there on purpose once and who cared. Let him use them for a dust cloth, maybe get a little thrill when he cleaned the windows.

Damned if she was going to chase him down anymore.

But now here she was, sniffing at her husband's t-shirts and thinking about Robin, looking out the window again like she was still in seventh grade. Wondering why men disappear so easily while women hold on for dear life to practically nothing at all.

A new crop of seeds had arrived in the mail a couple of weeks ago, nasturtium that would open quickly, and sweet alyssum, the most foolproof things she could find. They should have been put into those flower boxes right away. She had promised Hannah she'd spruce the place up but the woman never returned her calls so maybe it didn't matter.

Callie left her messages just about every week. "I pulled the rest of the monkey flowers away from the driveway." "I should be getting nasturtium seeds in the mail soon, I'll tell you after I've planted them."

She could hear herself rambling on too long, sounding needy. How lonely must she be if she was already missing some old woman she didn't even know. "I hope you like penstemon, they were on sale and I got a couple of purples and a couple of deep reds. They don't need much tending to, I hope you like them." She had immediately regretted saying "I hope you like them." She was pretty sure she had already said that earlier in the message. What was she so anxious about?

It had surprised Callie how much she enjoyed meeting Hannah, how much she found herself looking forward to more of her company. It was too corny to think of her as the mother she never had. She had a mother, not fifty miles from here, but her mother didn't exactly show interest in anything Callie had to say. Her mother never finished Callie's sentences in ways that made her feel better instead of worse about whatever was on her mind.

Callie hadn't made much of a dent in the garden. She

had big plans right after Robin had found those perfect rectangular planting boxes under the deck, which was amazing considering how long they must have been buried under there. Callie got excited, immediately deciding to set them around the deck so the old lady could have some color waiting for her on her next visit.

Robin had started working on them right away, gently brushing the dirt from the bases while she swept cobwebs away from around the deck. Together they had set and twisted and maneuvered the flower boxes until they were just exactly in the right spot. Callie remembered thinking back then how easy it was to be with him, without questions or opinions or insults. It was his quietness, when she thought about it, that attracted her most. The way she could work beside him and still feel like herself. It had been one of their best days together. If only she hadn't gone and bungled things up, those nasturtium seeds would have been planted weeks ago.

24.

"WHERE'S GRANDPA?" Timothy jumped out of the car first, hoping to beat him at their usual hide and seek game. Timothy ran behind the magnolia tree where Grandpa often called out "surprise" even before Timothy saw him there. When the tree came up empty, he turned toward the wiry clump of tomato stakes behind the shed where Grandpa sometimes crouched, like a broken scarecrow.

Grace usually spotted him first, pant legs jutting out from his hiding place. Grandpa couldn't hide from a flea. She would race to get the first juicy, sweater-fuzzy squeeze from Grandpa's arms, and sometimes he slipped her a hard candy that she popped into her mouth real fast so Timothy wouldn't see.

But not this time. Grandpa was not behind the tree, not inside the tool shed, not squatting by the tomato cages or under the back porch rail.

"Dad," called Robin, stepping inside the house and then "Dad?" again, louder, a slight strain of worry creeping into his throat.

"In here," came a voice that seemed like it was underground. Robin traced the muffled sound to the back laundry room, what used to be his mother's sewing room, now loaded down with papers and junk from the hardware store, stuff he used to keep in the kids room before they all moved in on him. His father was slumped over a makeshift desk, really just an old hollow door atop two metal file cabinets. Boxes of papers lay scattered on the floor beside him. His fingers rested on the keys of his adding machine but didn't move.

"Dad, what are you doing?" Robin called out, startling his father upright so the resting fingers momentarily sprung to life, hitting the keys haphazardly

"Look what you made me do" Winston yelled back, now clicking furiously at the machine to fix whatever numbers he accidentally entered when Robin surprised him.

"Dad, we've been calling you. What's going on?"

"I'm busy, can't you see that?" he growled back in a voice that was harsh and unfamiliar.

"Dad, are you all right?" Robin did not want to hear if he wasn't, but something seemed off about the old man. He'd been falling asleep earlier, sometimes even before Robin got home, and Robin would find him snoring on the couch and rush panicked into the kids' room to be sure they were all right.

"I fell behind with the books and need to get everything to the accountant by Monday. I tried to tell you." Maybe he just thought he had told him, or more likely Robin had his mind on all the crazy shit he'd been doing across the road and wasn't listening.

"Dad, I told you before I left this morning, I have to do an estimate over in Sierraville this evening. It might be a huge job, the people wanted to meet me there after six. The kids need to take a bath, and after that they can keep themselves busy."

"Have you finished that woman's house across the road already?"

Finished? Was he kidding? The windows still needed caulking and he hadn't even begun to deal with the kitchen cabinets. But instead of tearing out the old cabinets (he had already ordered new ones) he'd been staying away, dreading bumping into Callie, wishing he could take the whole last couple of months and rewind them. That idiotic basket full of condoms, Jesus, anyone could have found it. Who knew if her husband wasn't on to something? And Pete right next door, Robin could smell traces of him lingering in the air in the mornings when he did make it over there. Cigarette butts and an occasional bottle of Jack Daniels under the porch steps, a few clear drops of the liquid still in the bottom of the bottle. No way Pete wasn't on to him and Callie.

Robin had lots of good reasons to avoid Callie. So many he didn't have to admit the best reason of all. He was a coward. Always was a coward. His father knew it. He just was too kind a man to say.

"No Dad, I'm not nearly finished. Won't be finished there any time soon."

"Why not?" grumbled Winston.

Robin preferred not to tell his father much, which seemed to make the questions come all the more.

"I just need to take a break, change scenery for a while. The old woman's not in any hurry. If this Sierraville job pans out, I could be thinking about getting my own place."

That was a lie but if he said it often enough, maybe he'd start to believe it. Maybe. There were jobs over by the lake, boatbuilding jobs, he'd heard about them from some of the guys he worked with back when he was still living with Cynthia. Jobs with benefits, full time real jobs, not this piecemeal crap he'd been forced to take so he could juggle the kids.

His father had turned back to the adding machine, furiously working his fingers over the keys. He had refused to learn the computer. It was hard for Robin to imagine how his dad could handle managing a hardware store in this day and age. Sometimes Robin wondered if they kept him on out of pity.

"What the hell," Robin muttered, backing away from his father, feeling the beginning of a headache forming at the edge of his eyelids. He stretched out on the sofa, legs flopped over the edge, squeezed his eyes shut tight as they'd go, something that usually helped ease the headaches that seemed to be coming more often lately. The kids would be getting hungry soon. He should just call it a night. He probably wouldn't have gotten the Sierraville job anyway.

"I hope it all turns out for you," Winston finally got around to answering, unaware that his son had already left the room. He wasn't so much talking to his son as to himself anyway. So hard to know what to say to the boy.

Those first weeks when he'd started on that job across the road he'd been waking up early, sometimes before the kids were up, then going back again in the late afternoon. He'd drop the kids off after school and take a sander over, a skill saw, said he just had to finish up whatever he was working on. Sometimes he stayed until dark. Had a little spring in his step when he'd get home, like he was finally coming back to life, first time since that horrible woman left him.

But something had changed again. The boy rarely made eye contact. He could even smell it on him—a smell Winston didn't recognize. He couldn't tell if Robin was doing well or doing worse. More distant was the only thing he was sure of. The boy didn't answer his questions except to grunt, like he was a teenager again, off in some distance that Winston could never reach. He shook his head, trying to dispel his worries about Robin, but when he turned his attention back to the string of numbers he had entered on the adding machine tape, they made absolutely no sense. He wasn't even sure what the figures represented, sales for the month, supply orders? A thick pile of receipts had dropped on the floor and when he picked them up, he could see they were all mixed in with some grocery bills (he didn't know why he held on to them but he did. Vera always had.) How was he supposed to make sense of any of this?

He could hear the children's high voices skittering around in the kitchen and the sounds of chairs scraping along the linoleum. He knew that sound. The kids were trying to reach for something they weren't supposed to have.

"Robin?" Winston called. No answer. Can't the boy at least give his kids some snacks? Winston got up and pushed his chair away from the mess of papers, pulled on his sweater and trudged down the hall to see what the ruckus was all about.

"We're hungry. Why can't we have some snacks?"

Winston looked over at his son, slumped on the sofa, his head in his hands, mumbling something about a headache.

"OK OK, here" he said, tossing some kind of power bar at them, mostly sugar as far as he could make out, told them to go watch something on TV. Winston couldn't believe how fast he had changed horses on that score. Used to be he had a strict rule. One half hour a day. Now they could stare at the stupid screen all day long for all he cared.

"What kind of headache?" He approached his son now, carefully, uncertain of how close in he should get.

"Just a headache, Dad. I'm jammed up trying to get the place tight across the road and I never finished the deck over in Langston. And now this thing in Sierraville, looks like I won't be able to get over there tonight to bid on it. I know you're busy too but I'm just jammed right now. And I have this headache."

So the headache was Winston's fault. "Let me go see what I've got."

"And maybe give the kids something to eat while

you're at it." Hands back on his brow.

"Sure son," Winston unbent his shoulders, no sense telling the boy his kids already got their snacks. He was feeling the circulation coming back into his hands and feet now, feeling a bit more awake than he had when he was sorting through all that impossible paperwork.

"Stay there son, I'll see what I can do."

Tylenol, Excedrin PM, Advil, he didn't know one from the other. Maybe bring them all, let Robin decide. He pushed the bottles into his sweater pockets, headed back to the living room. Then he remembered that natural remedy stuff downstairs in the basement, the stuff Vera and Pete's wife concocted together. What was her name? He couldn't remember. What an odd couple, Vera and her. They'd spend hours together stinking up the kitchen, cooking up thick soupy syrups from plants they collected all around the area.

Winston turned to the basement stairs, pulled the overhead switch, and slowly walked down, eyes adjusting to the bright light, there had to be something down there for headaches. After Vera died, he considered throwing the whole lot of her medicine jars out, but kept them instead out of respect to her memory.

She had come up with the names, carefully labeled all the jars with her perfect hand: Get To Sleep Sip, Funny Tummy Tonic. He still used that Goop Gargle mixture she concocted just for him, enough to last many lifetimes, just like Vera had promised. Coughing kept him up many nights, that thick endless coughing that came not from illness, but from some unconfirmed condition that seemed to grow denser with age. The stuff smelled like a cigar butt and stung his throat, resulting in yet more coughing, but after a while, he had to admit it really helped. He used to give her such a hard time about it, but by golly, one swig and the coughing stopped.

Winston located the jar marked Hot Eyes – that had to be the headache remedy. He unscrewed the top, took a deep hard smell. Maybe it had turned to poison over the fifteen-year fermenting process. Maybe having merely sniffed it, he was already doomed.

He closed the jar and wondered if he shouldn't just throw it out, along with the other several dozen dust-covered jars that were probably either poisonous or useless by now. But somehow he couldn't dare throw them out. It was really all he had left of her. Let Robin choose between the Tylenol and the Hot Eyes. Hell, the smell alone might knock his headache out.

By the time Winston got back upstairs, Robin was laid out flat on the sofa. Winston had the feeling the boy wouldn't wake up until morning.

"Robin? Robin?" he shook the boy lightly on the shoulder, "Here's some things for your headache." But Robin was in a deep sleep, his breath slow and silent. Winston emptied his pockets of the medicines, set them all down on the table next to him, tiptoed out of the living room. Had he remembered to turn the light off in the basement? And where were the children? He couldn't hear them but he could hear the television coming from their bedroom and was grateful for that one, sure sign that things were in order.

A hasty dinner served and forgotten (Robin slept right through it all) Winston returned to his desk in the laundry room office. The kids were off getting ready for their bath. Robin was right, they were big enough to do it all by themselves. Even read themselves stories, now that Grace was in second grade. She used to be afraid of the dark but not any more, no longer asking to be tucked in or cuddled like her brother. Yet not so old that Grandpa's arms were no longer called upon once in a while, when dreams woke her up and her father was not yet home to comfort her. She was somewhere in between small child and budding young girl, and fast growing. Eight now, and just the other day she made her own sandwich, one for her brother, without needing a bit of help, and the two set off on a walk and didn't tell him where they were going.

The big bed was still wide enough for them to squirrel around in but Winston wondered if it might be time to separate them. He had a cot in the basement, it could squeeze in next to the double bed, but when he showed it to them, they said no, they preferred to pile in together. The girl jumped in first, her brother would pile on after her, taking turns jumping, knocking heads, laughing, tickling each other into sleep.

Winston suddenly caught himself about to doze off again. It seemed to be happening more and more lately, and he thought, I've got no business taking care of young children. He listened for their voices. Were they already in the bathtub? Shouldn't I be checking up on them? "Grace? Timmy?"

Robin was still sound asleep on the sofa and he wouldn't dare wake him. Didn't need to. Everything seemed to be under control.

"Grandpa, can you help us? The stopper doesn't work."

The stopper had indeed disintegrated into a mass of rubber flecks, crusted on to the side of the porcelain.

"I think there's another one downstairs. Stay put, I'll get it." And down to the basement again, wasn't he just down there? Winston was feeling too tired for all this.

Half way down the basement stairs, Winston realized he didn't know what he was going down there for, or why he was in such a hurry. He must have been in a hurry because he had skipped a few steps at the top, then had to steady himself with the banister to keep from falling. It was that very thought, to slow down and not do anything stupid, that hijacked the memory of whatever purpose led him to the basement stairs in the first place. Looking for something, but what? He started opening drawers, hoping the thing he was looking for would reveal itself.

Why were all of Vera's medicine jars out? Now he would need to put them back on their shelves, but he knew that wasn't why he'd come down here. Why did he come down here?

His eyes scanned the crowded wooden shelves. Hammers, screwdrivers, little pieces of screening that he had cut in 2" and 4" squares in case something needed to be patched. He had been so meticulous at one time, nails and drill bits all sorted and labeled.

It was impossible now for him to find anything, with those old medicine jars open and contents spilled, even if he could remember what he was looking for he'd have trouble finding it in this mess. Measuring tape? Wrench?

A nest of wires hung loose from a heavy bottom drawer that never did close, and now the mess of its contents corralled his attention. While he waited for his mind to give him clues, he sat himself down on the cold concrete floor, helpless against the mess of tangles and dust. And once he was down there, he had no choice but to start picking through the dislodged debris.

Why on earth was he saving that old address book? Everyone inside it most likely was dead by now. What's this? A small dust-covered box sealed with rubber bands revealed silver-engraved napkins and matchbooks. All fancy with a couple of doves and *Robin and Cynthia ~ forever* inscribed underneath. Forever my ass, he said to himself, under his breath, as though someone might be listening from behind the dusty corners.

He had never trusted that woman. That crazy wedding of theirs! All her doing. She had hired a minister who looked like he was about to perform magic tricks, all decked out with a long ponytail and purple satin robe—Winston half-expected him to pull a rabbit out of his sleeve. And then in the middle of the ceremony, this so-called minister had begun to whisper some nonsense about goddesses of the east and west and Winston had to manufacture a coughing fit trying to cover up his laughter.

Made him laugh right now, just to think about it. This minister had to be someone Cynthia dredged out of one of her spirituality classes. "Reverend Aimes communicates with dead people," she had told her father-in-law to be, trying to impress him he assumed. She said the minister confirmed that she and Robin knew each other from a past life. Winston replied with dead silence, wondering if this reverend so and so could hear what he was thinking.

That horrible wedding. Winston couldn't forget the sickly sweet smell of the lilies, and the florist's bill. All that money for bunches of stinking flowers that drooped by the end of the ceremony. He could envision, clear as the engraved matchbook in his hand, Cynthia fooling with her shoulder strap right when she was supposed to be saying the "I Do" part. He was relieved that Vera wasn't alive to see the debacle, though she would have at least tried to put a stop to it.

Stop to it. Stop. Stopper. He had come down looking for the tub stopper. There was one down here somewhere, now where was it? Up on the top shelf he saw the plastic bin marked BATHROOM. Some things were still where they belonged. He opened the box and sure enough, three different sized stoppers to choose from, he'd take them all.

But the kids. The bathtub. Water running. Winston froze, listened, how long had he been down there? He thought he felt a drop on his head. Yes, it was water.

He looked up and saw the dark glistening beads forming above him, could hear the sounds now, small drops hitting the floor, the stair railing, water dripping faster and the kids! He felt a sharp pain in his leg. In his shoulder now. Moving fast like a knife but he pushed it away. Where were the kids?

Winston darted toward the stairs. The bathtub! His heart was pounding loud and the room swayed so he grabbed for the railing, sharp pain, drops of water falling harder, pounding in his eardrums so he couldn't hear,

"Grandpa!" it was Grace's voice. "We can't turn the water off its too hot!" and he did hear her now, took the steps two at a time, slippery steps, Grace, Timmy! He grabbed the railing, foot caught on that third step, twisted in, stuck.

"Grandpa!"

That damned third step, ears ringing, he never fixed it, kept meaning to, never fixed it, down on his knee, can't move, Timothy, Grace, and right before the room went black, he thought he heard a voice so loud it knocked him out.

"Graaaaandpaaaaaa!"

25.

THE LAST OF RALPH'S SOCKS were put away, just one more stack of her jeans, when she thought she heard a voice. Then she heard it again, heard her name, loud, *Callie.* She looked out the window and saw Robin running up her driveway. Robin?

Callie dropped the pile of clothes and got to the door before he had a chance to knock, but it wasn't just Robin standing there. He had his children with him. The little boy was crying, and his sister's head hung down so Callie couldn't see the girl's face.

"Callie, I'm so sorry. I had no other choice. I know this is awkward Callie but you have to help me. I need your help."

She let them in, reached for the little boy's hand and he took it eagerly. The girl, still not looking up, clung to Robin.

"Its my dad," Robin said, then repeated, "my dad. He fell down, blacked out. The kids" and Callie missed a few words, he was talking so fast. She heard him say "bathtub" and then "unconscious when I got to him."

"Is he ok now?" she asked.

"He's awake now, just babbling."

Robin was the one babbling. His face was shiny with tears or sweat, she couldn't tell, but the poor guy obviously needed help.

"Please Callie." His voice faded to a faint monotone, like he was the one who was about to pass out. "I need to take him to the hospital. Can I leave the kids with you for a couple of hours?"

The little girl finally lifted her head, and Callie could see the blue-green eyes, her father's eyes.

"Grandpa was supposed to get us a stopper so we could stop the water but he never came up and Timothy put a towel over the drain so we could take our bath but then we couldn't take the towel off because the hot got too hot."

"Were you burned?" Callie asked. It was evident that the girl had a very exciting story to tell, and wanted to tell it.

"No, but we almost got burned. I turned off the cold water but I couldn't touch the hot water and Timothy put a towel on the drain and we almost got burned."

"It sounds terrible," Callie encouraged her, all the while keeping her arm around the little boy, who didn't seem to want to leave her side.

"Don't worry about them, Robin. They'll be fine here. They can play with Daphne. Give me a call when you know something."

He turned to leave and she stood there for a few long breaths, a child on either side of her, staring at the closed door. Robin was back. Not exactly how she imagined, but it didn't matter really. He was back. And this was even better than she might have imagined. He had asked her to do something only a friend would do. She no longer had to wait for the next time. The next time had happened without her having to do a thing.

"Who's Daphne?" the girl asked.

"She's my baby. She'll really like playing with you. What's your name?"

"Grace. And that's my brother Timothy."

Timothy had stopped crying but didn't let go of Callie's hand.

"I have a cousin named Timothy," Callie told him, on their way into the baby's room. She squeezed his hand when she said it, and he looked up at her, offering what little smile he had.

Daphne was lying in her crib, enraptured by the dangling mobile animals that hung above her head. She was squealing in high pitched yelps as her little hands batted furiously at the hanging elephants and giraffes that she would have greedily stuffed into her mouth, had they been within reach. Callie hated to disturb her, but as soon as she picked her up and set her down on the floor, the baby found something even more interesting to capture her attention. Grace had pulled the stacking plastic blocks out from beneath the crib and Daphne fell into helpless peels of laughter as the blocks tumbled to the ground, over and over again. Daphne's chin was wet from laughing and Grace insisted on wiping the baby's face dry, her eight year old interpretation of mothering.

Timothy quickly discovered the library of cardboard

baby books and eagerly showed off his rudimentary reading skills, offering Callie his best attempt at the *Big Brown Bear* and *What Makes Ostrich Laugh?* Very good, Callie admired.

"He's not really reading. He just knows them by heart."

"I too am reading" he insisted and nudged himself a bit closer to where Callie and the baby were sitting in the middle of the floor, her arm now around him and the baby, stroking the top of his head while he sounded out *One Fish Two Fish Red Fish Blue.*

Then Grace found the box of music toys and soon she and Timothy were banging on the toy xylophone, banging the wooden sticks, the plastic drum, using them all to capture the baby's attention. Callie sat with the children on the floor, clapping Daphne's hands in time to the banging, enjoying this room full of children so much she could even imagine having another one. Her head was filled with the sounds of clanking toys and squealing little voices so she didn't hear Ralph's truck pull into the driveway.

"What the hell is going on in here?"

"Ralph, honey." Callie tried to stand up but the baby fell forward, bumping her head on the base of the changing table and now the only sound in the room was Daphne wailing. The children looked up, silenced immediately by the presence of this stranger.

"So glad you're home, honey." The words sounded

silly, unauthentic, even to her. She tried to mask the lie with high sweet notes "its OK honey," nervous empty words that only made her sound all the more ridiculous.

"What are these kids doing here?" His voice was a thin, taut line edged in anger or fatigue, she couldn't quite tell which.

"Our neighbor up the road. You know, that old guy who runs the hardware store." Everyone knew the old guy who ran the hardware store. Better talk about him and not the children's father.

"Whose kids are these?" Ralph asked again, growing impatient now. Callie launched into the whole story.

"His son came over a few hours ago. He was in a big fix. He found his dad passed out on the basement stairs. It was terrible Ralph. The kids were crying. He had to drive his dad to the hospital and he was desperate. He seemed like a nice person. The kids were crying Ralph, I couldn't say no."

Ralph didn't move, didn't change position. She continued on.

"Look honey, they've been playing so nicely together. Daphne loves them. The kids are fine here. We've been having a good time. Timothy, this is my husband, Ralph. Ralph, this is…"

"Are you Daphne's daddy?" Grace asked but Ralph had already walked away from the bedroom door, headed for the kitchen, the refrigerator, cracking open a beer, sucking it down.

"When are they getting picked up?" was all he could

muster, the beer more important to him for the moment. He sank down on the sofa, she could hear his shoes tossed against the wall, then he aimed the remote control at some sports station, volume up to high.

Callie went back to the bedroom, asked the girl to start picking up toys. She lifted Daphne into her arms, the magical energy now completely dissolved and the real story beginning again. Why hadn't Robin called? What had it been now, two, three, hours? It was getting late. Was she supposed to put his kids to sleep here? Had they eaten dinner? She had some cookies and pineapple juice that they used for pina coladas, but nothing really for kids. Zweiback teething crackers.

She went back to the kitchen, Ralph would need to eat something, though he was catatonic in front of the TV and didn't show any signs of wanting anything. Still, she put a pot of water on, some quick pasta dish always worked for him, suddenly aware that Robin's kids were in her way. Ralph was being terribly quiet.

"Honey," she brought the baby over to the sofa, "He'll be back soon. Don't be mad."

"Why would he ask you? He doesn't even know you."

"He met me once when I was taking the baby for a walk. He was taking his kids home from school. Just being neighborly," she started, all the while rubbing his shoulders, she was good at that, while he held the remote up, raised the volume so the baby's cooing sounds were drowned out by a Chevy truck commercial.

"I've never seen Daphne so happy," changing the subject back to the kids, "they kept her giggling for hours. You should see honey, she tried to hit the peg with the hammer. Grace, the little girl, was showing her how. See?" manipulating the babies hands up and down, "see how she can hammer? She's so cute now, honey, she's starting to do lots more things. Grace got her to topple the stack of blocks, you should see...," she was non-stop talking and she knew he wasn't listening as she kept on rubbing his shoulders, rubbing, rubbing, feeling him soften under her fingers.

Just then came the sound of a truck turning into their driveway. Callie rushed to the front room window and saw Robin's headlights, thank goodness, as he pulled to a stop. She walked out on to their porch before he got a chance to get out of his truck, calling out to the kids "your dad's here!" She made sure the front door was closed in case Ralph decided to get up and see what was going on. She doubted he would, but still. And did the kids have their shoes on? Callie's heart was racing, suddenly caught in a scene she hadn't had time to rehearse.

"Wait there, I'll get them," she called out to Robin. Ralph was still stuck on the sofa. She gathered up Grace and Timothy. "Coming!" she yelled again, and thank goodness Robin stayed in his truck.

"Is he ok?"
"Daddy, where's Grandpa?"
"Were they good?"

"They were great. The kids entertained Daphne all evening. We had so much fun, honestly it was no trouble at all."

"I read the baby stories."

"You did not."

"I did too."

"Is your dad ok?"

She leaned into the back seat and strapped the kids in, buckles buckled, she could have been their mom she was so efficient at it. Callie glanced quickly back to the house in case Ralph decided to get up and see what was going on but there was no sign of him, they were safe.

"Thank you Callie, I don't know what I would have done."

"Is he ok?"

"The doctor says he had a stroke. He doesn't remember a thing. He can't talk, doesn't seem to understand my questions. Doctor said they're going to keep him for a while. It's hard to say."

"Do you need me to take the kids again? Really, it was no trouble at all."

"I'll let you know. I can't think right now."

"Callie?" Ralph's voice, loud. They both knew it was time for Robin to leave.

"Coming honey. I'll be right there." Why had she called him honey in front of Robin?

"I can take them again," she repeated, "if you need me to. Really, its no trouble."

Robin's head was cradled on the steering wheel. She

put her hand on his back and heard a stifled sob, felt his whole body heave, remembered now the faint smell of his cologne, more a soap, like sandalwood, a clean smell, something from the earth. She may have kissed the back of his neck or maybe just thought to.

"Call me," she whispered so low she wasn't sure if he heard. "Its ok. I'm here."

Callie tiptoed back into the house. Ralph must have put the baby in her crib while she was outside with Robin. He hardly ever did things like that. She sat down on the rocking chair beside the sleeping baby, rocked and rocked herself calm, trying to make sense of all the conflicting emotions that were colliding like pinballs inside her. She hugged herself, rocking ever so slowly, wishing someone would rock her to sleep.

Much later, after their dinner dishes were cleared and washed and dried, the salad scraps spooned into plastic tubs and the beer cans crushed and tossed into the recycling bin, Callie finally broke through her husband's silence.

"Ralph. What on earth is going on? This can't be about the kids."

He just shook his head. No, it wasn't the kids. His hands were clenched but she came in closer anyway, something a wife just knows, this wasn't about her at all. And then he reached for her and she sat down beside him and he put his arms around her, more like a child than a man, and she held him for a sweet long while.

"Ralph, what is it?"

"They changed their minds about the contract."

"What contract?"

"The contract Callie. You know, the contract I've been busting my ass on for the last year. The sprinkler contract. Have you even been listening to me?"

It was her turn to be quiet now. She sat on the side of the bed and listened while he spilled the horrible details of how this goddamned environmental group from the city, bunch of rich kids, finally succeeded in convincing the developers that lawns required too much water and cost the county too much money. Instead, they decided to go with native plants and cactus.

"Can you picture Daphne crawling around on a square of cactus plants? Jesus, these people don't know what they're talking about, but they're scaring everyone into thinking there's a water shortage."

Callie leaned in closer to him, trying to take in his words, relieved that it wasn't Robin's kids that had put him in this state.

"'Lawns are a thing of the past,' that's what they told me. They don't think there's a market for underground sprinkler systems anymore, don't think people are going for big lawns anymore. Just like that. A bunch of crack-pots with big ideas and lots of money, thinking they know what people want." He stood up, shook himself away from her comfort, pacing around the room like some wild man about to strike.

"People want green lawns, that's what people want." He was yelling now. "A place for their kids to play ball and let their dogs take a crap." Callie couldn't help but laugh at that last remark.

"This isn't one Goddamned bit funny Cal. You hear me? We moved to this shit hole of a place for one reason. There was a load of money to be made with all these new mountain developments. I can't afford to live here much longer if I don't close any deals. Do you think that's funny too?"

"No Ralph, I don't. But maybe you're..."

"Maybe I'm what?" he yelled, not waiting for an answer, turning to the bathroom, slamming the door shut. She could hear the shower running. She had a few minutes to herself but what would she do with them? Daphne was sound asleep, nothing to do there. Callie's heart was no longer racing but she felt a knot in her throat. If it were up to her she'd walk out the front door and keep walking, the direction didn't even matter, just keep walking out of this life and maybe find another one that didn't feel so small. But instead she walked into the kitchen, picked up a sponge, doused it with dish soap and let the water run through it until the last frothy bubble dissolved.

By the time Ralph got out of the shower the tension of the evening's events had calmed down and there they were, side by side under the covers, just another night, toes touching.

"There's an area south of here may have some opportunities. I ran into Lundale, and he says housing prices are much lower there. He gave me the name of a Realtor, over near Folsom. I don't know what we could get for this place but I may have to move fast."

Folsom. Where Callie's mother lived. Where her mother moved after Callie finished high school for what she called a dream job with the prison system. She'd had the nerve to suggest to Callie that she should apply. "There's tons of jobs, administrative stuff, things even you could do," were her mother's exact words.

Last time she saw her mother was at Aunt Daphne's funeral. At the time, her mother hadn't known Callie was four months pregnant. Callie had come so close to telling her about the baby, but then her mom chose that moment to say "You look like you've put on a few. Watch out girl, at the rate you're going, you're going to look like me before you know it."

Callie got out of bed and walked over to the window, checking to see if any lights were coming through from the direction of Robin's place. He would have put the kids to sleep by now. He'd be alone up there, maybe looking out his own window, trying to figure out what he was going to do next. How many more people were looking out their windows right this very minute, wondering how they got themselves stuck so deep in what once seemed like a good life?

She strained her eyes for some glint of light coming her way, but there was way too much thicket separating her parcel from his. Too many high piles of rotting wood and gnarled wire fences overrun with tree limbs and hedges and whatever all crapped up the spaces where people didn't have the luxury of clean square lawns.

Callie pushed the curtain closed. Pulled the bed covers back. Ralph was deep in sleep or pretending to be. He'd been saying all along that once her mother saw Daphne for the first time, she would soften up, even be nice to her. People can change, he said. Maybe he was right. He was right about so many things. Maybe it wouldn't be such a terrible idea.

A faint woodsy smell lingered on Callie's fingers. She imagined it had somehow transferred from Robin's jacket when she'd touched him. She pushed her hands down under the blankets to cover up all traces, and forced herself to sleep.

26.

SCHOOL WAS OUT, my work at the church finally finished, and so I chose the Tuesday after Memorial Day, figured the roads would be quiet by then, to make my last sweep of the place, and put an end to this folly once and for all. This time I came prepared to spend the night, something I had yet to do, and why not? The place was still mine, at least for now anyway. I took the Realtor's card along with me, maybe I'd go see him on the way home to start the paperwork, or whatever it was he needed to get this place off my back.

I'd been having crazy dreams, like the other night the one where me and Ray are hiding in an alleyway, I've got his hand held tight in mine (like that would have ever happened). They were just dreams. They didn't mean a damn thing.

I couldn't quite bring myself to throw out the cardboard box of his bird carvings, but I did move it to the back of the garage, behind where I kept extra packing supplies and other things I'd never use and should have thrown out years ago. Maybe the birds would rot back there. At least they weren't taking up space in the house any more.

The ride up to the land was uneventful. Same old landmarks, the Chinese restaurant popping up out of nowhere, a few cows grazing in and around a field of busted out cars. Somehow those sites lost the quaintness I'd experienced on my previous trips up the mountain. My car had no problem with the sharp left on to Blind Shady. I only had to back up twice to clear the turn. Just another ho hum country road, nothing to feel adventurous about. I made a point of looking straight ahead this time. No sense getting sentimental about the blooming lupine and monkshood along the side of the road. Veer left again, a few more rights, say my goodbyes, and thank you very much Ray, for that strange little detour.

I'd hoped more of the trash would have been cleared away, but I was grateful I didn't have to strain my wrists any more pushing up the bedroom windows. The back porch appeared to have a new threshold. Go slow, I kept telling Robin, so I guess I had no business complaining. Especially not now.

I wandered around from room to room, curious to see if he'd made any progress. Other than the bedroom windows, it didn't seem like he had. Before I set down my sleeping bag I swept the bedroom floor clear of dust, and what do you know, I uncovered a couple of hair clips on the floor, a few stray blond hairs still attached. And then, when I opened the closet to set my overnight bag down, I noticed what I thought was an old rag that turned out to be a pair of flimsy undies young girls wear, nothing but a thin strip of cloth to cover the behind. Made me itch just to think about it.

So what do you know. I suppose I should have figured it out, the way Robin went on and on about how great that neighbor girl was. A married woman, with a baby no less.

Well I certainly wasn't sorry now that I hadn't called her back. She did seem like such a sweet thing, lonely for sure. But even before my change of heart about keeping the place, all those chatty messages of hers were starting to annoy me. She'd been moving a little too fast for my taste.

I did notice that the shrubs and gravel had been cleared away from the porch, so she was doing something constructive around here, at least when she kept her panties on. Under the side bedroom window stood a flower box I hadn't seen before, the wood cleaned and shined, emptied and ready to be planted. I wondered if that was her work or Robin's.

The deck looked a whole lot better, but I have to say that owl carving struck me as strange. Polished and placed perfectly centered on the top shelf of the deck railing so it appeared to greet you when you walked up the steps. Made me wonder about Robin. He's a nice enough young man, but first this Callie nonsense, and then his silly priorities. The owl was about the only thing that looked finished on the whole property. He'd certainly done a good job on it—the eyes seemed to be winking at me. But why on earth would he spend so much time shining up that stupid owl when the kitchen cabinets needed to be torn out.

I remember asking him about how that owl got there, that first time we met. At the time it was lying loose on the deck, filthy with dust and I figured it had to be one of Ray's birds. Robin lowered his head when I asked, mumbled "don't know" so softly I had to strain to hear him.

"Did you know him? The last owner?" I tried.

"Not really. I was just a kid."

"Do you remember anything about him?" Pushing, but to no avail.

"No ma'am" came out in a whisper.

It was like pulling teeth, trying to find out if he knew anything about the property, about Ray, about anything.

The small closet of four shelves and three large wall hooks turned out to be more than adequate for my few overnight belongings. I wondered if it was Robin or the girl who thought to hang the hooks. Or maybe they were always there. So many details I had yet to notice. There was ample space on the shelf above the sink to hold my toothbrush and toothpaste, and the mirrored cabinet above the sink, I'm not sure I remembered there was one, sure enough the three narrow shelves were intact. Just wide enough for my jar of Noxzema cream that stinks like some kind of medicine, but keeps my face feeling smooth, considering. And Vaseline for my feet at night. I even found a closet for linens, how had I missed that? Tucked behind the bathroom door, I wouldn't have expected a place this small to offer up a linen closet. But no matter now. Maybe the next owner would appreciate it.

After the two-hour drive, unpacking and putting away what provisions I had brought for an overnight stay, I had earned a nap, even though it wasn't even noon yet. Nothing too long, just to get some strength back. I lay down on my sleeping bag, in what was once Ray's bedroom, and found myself picturing him, lying there. Did he come straight to this land after he ran away? What would he have been, nineteen? Where on earth did he get the money to buy this place? Did he live alone? Did he have a woman in his life? Staring up at the ceiling, trying to quiet my mind against the onslaught of questions, more questions came. Was he happy here?

Hell, for all I knew he didn't live there at all, just rented it out, or who knows what else. More I thought about it, I didn't know a thing about my brother's adult life. Only the boy, Ray, kicking and screaming his way through adolescence, quieted only when he held a whittling knife and a piece of wood in his hands. And where was I while he was making all that noise? I closed my eyes trying to remember, but nothing came.

Still, looking out the bedroom window, Ray's bedroom window, I couldn't help but think he may have had some good years here. He always loved the outdoors. Nobody here to fight with. No one to tell him what a disappointment he was.

It occurred to me that one person who might know something about Ray was that man who lived on the other side of the hedge. I'd seen him sneaking around, boots squeaking, spying on me through the bushes. He'd have to know something.

I must have drifted off to sleep because next thing I knew I was startled awake by strange sounds I couldn't quite place. A chainsaw so distant it sounded like a swarm of bees. A deep bark from some far away mutt, or maybe it was a wolf. Crisp crunching of tire treads over loose gravel. It wasn't until I set my feet down square on the wood floor and got nicked by a splinter, that I remembered where I was. And then my stomach reminded me I hadn't eaten since leaving home that morning.

It didn't look like Robin had so much as touched the kitchen counters, which seemed designed to hold a pot of coffee and not much else. There was but one working narrow drawer for utensils and two cabinets deep enough for a couple of plates and bowls, if that. The tiles at the base of the cabinets were either streaked with mold or coming loose. It wasn't the most appealing place to prepare the cheese and radish sandwich I had planned to make myself for lunch.

Inside the pantry closet it appeared as though someone hung four new handy little plastic hooks for dishtowels. A nice touch, seemed to me they might've been another one of the girl's ideas. I decided to brew some tea and reached under the counter for where I thought I had stashed a couple of teabags last time I was here, but the drawer was stuck shut. I yanked hard with both hands and sure enough it opened, or rather crash landed, two sides split clean down the center, releasing a fluff of dust, a paring knife gray with time, and one petrified rat pellet sprinkled in the mix. Oh yes, and two torn tea bags, releasing a few wrinkled leaves on top of the rest of the debris scattered across the floor. The cold porcelain knob, all that remained of the busted drawer, slid from my hand and landed loud on the wooden floor, before rolling out of sight beneath the stove.

And now the kitchen was filthier than before. The old drawer had also released an empty matchbook, a penny turned blue, a small square of soap thick with grime. Could this have been Ray's soap? No sense getting sentimental about that now. I grabbed all the crap up from the floor and stuffed it into a couple of plastic trash bags I remembered to bring. Give me a good excuse to visit that famous ravine I'd heard so much about.

"No garbage pick-up in these parts," I remember the Realtor telling me, "but you do have what once had been a gold mining tributary, your own private gold mine right back there," adding to his sales pitch, as he pointed to the ravine which wasn't visible through the trees. Said it with a smirk, like it would impress me.

The only value I could see when I got to the ravine was half a steering wheel stuck upright catching a ray of sun, and beside it a hubcap stained black by time. Turns out the back of this property was a veritable trash museum, displaying a scattering of car parts, bits of leather boot, stones and concrete chunks embedded in mud, fork tines sticking up out of clumps of dirt, like arthritic hands, bent every which way. Everywhere I turned, more broken tree limbs and boulders decorated with bits of jagged metal long past rusted. The afternoon sun was starting to dip down, and deep shadows were overtaking the sunlight, interfering with my aim. "Well here goes," I shouted out into the air, tossing the first of two garbage bags into the pile.

I heard the crash of wood hitting glass, and then a loud yell. A man appeared out of nowhere, covered in dust, his hand pressed against his forehead. "What the hell," he shouted, before lifting his head up from a pile of bramble. His hand hadn't left his forehead so I gathered the bag must have hit him square in the head. I dropped the other bag on the ground in front of me, somehow managing not to fall into the ravine alongside him.

"Who the hell are you?" I shouted, anger leaping out ahead of fear.

There he stood, stuck silly inside a snatch of weeds, at the bottom of the gully, not four feet in front of me. Mostly protected by the shade of the underbrush, he was hard to see. I could make out his hair, jutting out in asymmetrical tufts beneath a red bandana, looking a lot like a patch of weeds. Red splotches, the sure work of alcohol, decorated his nose and cheeks. By the depth of the ravine, I judged that he was in no immediate position to harm me, and seeing him stuck down there with a clump of twigs hanging off his shoulder made me feel more amused than threatened.

"Name's Pete." He righted himself. "And I'd have to ask you the same thing."

"I believe this is my property. It's pretty well marked with those yellow posts in case you hadn't noticed," and I pointed a few feet behind him to the county markers that ran parallel to the culvert.

"So I don't really see why I need to introduce myself to you. You are trespassing on my property and you're the one with some explaining to do."

Once I got started, I must say I surprised myself. I hadn't intended to get so huffy but he'd given me a scare startling me like that, all covered in filth, popping up in the ravine, my ravine. While he wrested himself loose from the thorns and brush, I could see he was quite a bit larger when not protected by the surrounding under-growth. I edged backwards a few paces, scanning for a rock or large stick, should it come to that.

"Name's Pete," he said again "and it looks like you must be my new neighbor. I heard you might be taking over this place but didn't know when that might occur. I've got the place over there." He pointed to the hedge of honeysuckle that blocked the view beyond.

By now I stepped back far enough to let him clear the height, and next thing I knew, he was standing right next to me, smacking his pant legs to shake off the dust.

"I've lived here near twenty years. I make my living digging around these parts."

I turned away to avoid inhaling his dust but he con-tinued on.

"Yes ma'am, I know every hill, gully, trap and sand pit around here. I know where the gold used to be and still find some from time to time. That's my business here. I take what other people toss. People's garbage is my gold."

"Gold," I said, unable to find a single other word to utter.

"You got quite a gully here ma'am, probably don't know it. This here streambed was a main artery back in the heyday, twice as wide as it is now, twice as deep. That old shack you've got there used to be a miner's cabin at one time. At least that's what they tell me. Miners used to set up camp right here on this spot, pulled nuggets out of the gully like they was acorns."

"Really." Still unable to talk, though his chatter was beginning to pique my interest.

"Just look," and he reached over to extricate a glass bottle stuck behind a log, not a nick on it, "looks like 1915," trace of lettering still clear like it had been etched that same day—alcohol content 15%—must have been some kind of medicine. "This bottle will bring $30 maybe $50 if I could get it to shine up well enough. Tourists so dumb, thinking they're so smart. I'll make $50 on it. Make it easy."

While he continued on his rant, I began to notice the shape of him, wide and thick, arms tight from a lifetime of heaving and hauling. Men like him, the kind that weren't afraid to work in the dirt, never aged gradually. Their muscles seemed to hold them together like vise grips, preserving them through their middle years and disguising the latter years sometimes by a decade or two. This one could be forty, could be eighty, the deep ruts of sun and dirt marbleized by muscle so it was difficult to place him in time. Lucky son-of-a-gun.

"That's all very interesting," I interjected. He had finally gone on too long for my taste. "So, you think you can just trespass, root around in someone else's garbage pile whenever you feel like it, because you make some kind of living at it?"

"I'm sorry ma'am, I guess I need to call you ma'am since you haven't told me your name. I didn't mean to scare you, that's all I'm trying to say."

"You didn't scare me."

"This land's been empty for years now, more than I can remember. You might want to know it's been me keeping those hedges down so that house of yours wouldn't catch fire. It's also been me taming back those wild roses you're now enjoying. I have some stake in this fine piece of land I think I can say."

Those roses—the ones that stung my feet and snagged my hands first time I started exploring around. He should have pulled them out altogether.

"This property is a special place, ma'am, and I'm awful glad to know it finally has someone here now that deserves it."

Poor guy was trying hard to make some headway.

"Are you trying to wiggle out of this?"

"Wiggle out of what?" he said, as he brushed more dirt off his clothes, wiping the sweat off his forehead with a rag he had pulled out of his back pocket. In full view now, I could see he wasn't particularly tall, just a few inches more than me, but sturdy enough. He carried with him a faintly unpleasant odor of clothes that had not fully finished the laundry cycle.

Suddenly I felt an urge to ask him questions, pump him a bit about whatever he might know of Ray's life here. What if he knew something that would make me change my mind? Maybe there was still gold here? Would that make me change my mind?

But no. I shook my head, as though the physical act might shake away this sudden surge of curiosity. I had come here to say goodbye, to the land, to Ray, and to any notion that I ought to be grateful for this so-called gift of his.

"Here's something you ought to know," I informed him. "I don't like surprises. If you got some reason for rooting around here, I expect you to come knock on my door and ask permission. And let me know exactly what you're taking in case I decide I want it back." I do get carried away sometimes.

"OK ma'am, if that's the way you want it."

"And you can call me Hannah," my mouth rushing out ahead of my better judgment.

"Hannah," he repeated, then walked back toward the grove of shrubs that bordered our properties, looking back one more time, as if to be sure I wasn't a figment of his imagination, before slipping into the brush. If he'd been wearing a hat, he surely would have tipped it.

27.

ROBIN MANAGED TO REMEMBER to pick up a plant at the hardware store after dropping the kids off at Callie's, on his way over to the nursing home. His dad's favorite, a tall purple hyacinth, on sale for Hyacinth Month, maybe it would cheer the old man up. But when he got to his father's room, the nightstand was filled with curdled wads of napkins, not a square inch to spare for a plant. Never mind. His dad wouldn't have noticed anyway. He set the plant on the floor beside the doorway. Maybe one of the attendants would take it.

Robin gently uncrooked his father's awkwardly dangling arm, and set it back on top of the blanket. Like one of those ragdolls that Grace used to play with, the arm flopped right back down, landing like a twisted L bracket against the side of the bed.

"Dad?"

One of the attendants, this must be a new one, he didn't remember seeing her before, entered the room, rushing past him with crisp efficiency, to adjust the window blinds. "Just about time for your dinner," she sang out, before rushing back out the door. The late afternoon sun had been streaking down on his dad's bed and Robin noticed an immediate difference after the blinds had been adjusted. The room felt cooler now, calmer, without the play of shadows, more lifeless than before.

Robin leaned down and gathered his father's lanky body in his arms, as gently as he knew how, propped him up against his pillows.

"Look, Dad," he said. "I brought some magazines for you. And a box of Fig Newtons."

Winston sputtered some incomprehensible sounds, opened his eyes bright. "Vera?" he asked, his voice raised for a brief moment to a normal, familiar pitch. And then he closed his eyes again.

"How are you feeling?" Robin knew no answer would come, but maybe the sound of his voice would give his dad some comfort. If only it would. Robin never had brought his dad much comfort, certainly not in recent years, moving in on him with the kids, not at all what the old man needed at a time in his life where he was finally slowing down. For all Robin knew, it was the stress of all of them living there that contributed to his stroke.

"Here Dad," lifting his father's chin up a bit, holding a glass of water to his lips, but the water dribbled down his cheek, then slid down the side of his face, landing in a small perfect drop inside his ear.

At least Robin had managed to find a suitable nursing home. The doctors assured him that his fall was a result of a massive stroke, and that even if Robin had been able to get him to the hospital quicker, it would have made no difference. But the prognosis was poor. They doubted he would ever be able to live independently.

"Dad?" he asked again and this time his father stirred, opened his eyes, uttered "where's my" followed by a word

Robin couldn't decipher. Yet another attendant, this one he remembered, Melanie, who was sure she knew Robin from soccer practice back in high school. She walked in carrying a tray of food that she placed on a wheeled table and set beside Winston's bed.

"Time for dinner," she sing-songed, as she swung the tray table around so the plate was within Winston's reach, flashing Robin a huge smile, like she was hoping for an invitation to join them for dinner. Robin didn't meet her gaze, just told her thanks, they were fine, he could feed his father.

"All right then," she answered, then added, "He loves his applesauce," before closing the door behind her. Robin imagined she probably said that to everybody.

He picked up the small container of applesauce, pulling back the aluminum cover. He unfolded the tightly wrapped napkin and peeled the plastic off the fork and spoon. "I can do this, Dad," as if he were fishing for approval. As though spooning lukewarm food into flaccid lips was some kind of challenge that Robin was at last up for.

Had he ever done anything to help his father before now? Robin tried to think but nothing came to mind. Sure he did his share of handy work around the house, but he was living there for God's sake. He had replaced the back porch steps when they rotted out, and as long as he could remember, his dad called on him to replace the fence posts whenever the time came. So that was something.

But now Robin was in charge, he was the father to

this weak man lying in front of him, pathetic as a baby. His father seemed to be comfortable enough. The nursing home Robin found was clean, didn't smell like piss and ammonia. He had been given a number of places to choose from, and he chose this one. So that was something too.

"Here you go," Robin whispered, spooning applesauce into his father's waiting mouth, one tiny teaspoon at a time. His dad sucked it down, the nurse was right, he did like it. Robin began to relax into this strange new role.

"Good job, Dad." He could have been talking to Timothy. He patted his dad's mouth, a slurp of applesauce, now a sip of water, "good job," he said again, one sloppy slurp at a time.

Last week Robin saw something that made him stir. A notice on the bulletin board at Yancey's—*Boat Builders wanted. Experience in fine woodworking preferred. Will train.* He had heard of the company, saw their advertisements in the local paper, but this was the first time he saw them advertising for jobs. Robin had ripped the notice from the bulletin board, folded it neatly and pushed it down deep into his jacket pocket. Sierra Boat Designs was about an hour's drive south on Route 50, over in Carnelian Bay, one of many small vacation towns dotting the greater Lake Tahoe resort area. Lots of rich folks out that way with second homes on the lake. Lots of money floating around. The boat business was all about rich people looking for ways to unload all their excess money.

Not that he'd had much experience with sailboats, just the canoes he'd taken out from time to time over at Fordyce Lake. But Robin knew his way around wood. He could carve just about anything. Back in junior high and high school he used to sell his owls and herons to other kids, saving the money and telling nobody.

Ray had bought one of his starlings outright. The two of them had been sitting on Ray's deck, whittling away, Robin had set out to make a falcon but his knife slipped and one of the heavy wings broke off. Robin remembered throwing the bird into the bushes but Ray went over and picked the bird up and handed it right back to him.

"Make a starling, they've got shorter wings," he'd said, and then Ray had showed him how to change the body shape so the broken thing could be saved. When it was finished, Ray actually handed him a ten, said, "You're too good at carving to let one little mistake discourage you."

Robin never forgot that. He could still hear the man's deep voice, almost angry, bellowing down at him, "You've got a gift. Now use it."

The words came back to him in hollow echoes every so often, like now, tucking a napkin under his father's bed shirt, pulling the lukewarm lunch tray up close so the food wouldn't spill on its way to the slack mouth. He wondered what it would be like to have a father that said things like that to him. You've got a gift, use it.

"You think I have a gift, Dad?" he said to the slumped over figure beside him, faded and shapeless like the cushions that supported him.

Some gift. Robin shrugged, then pushed the spoon into the lumpy mound of cold mashed potatoes. "Eat this. It'll do you good."

The potatoes went down faster than the applesauce. Robin spooned slowly, steadily, creamed corn following the potatoes.

"Eat up Dad, go on, you're doing good." Winston forced a smile, attempting to speak with a slither of creamed corn streaming from his lips.

"Vera?" he slurred. "Is that you Vera?"

"Its me, Dad. Robin." He knew it was useless. He rested his hand on his father's chest, felt the light steady breaths. After he dabbed the wet spots of corn from his father's lips, he checked his watch against the clock on the wall. Still twenty minutes before he had to pick up the kids at Callie's. They agreed he'd get them before six, so she didn't have to bother with Ralph knowing the details of their arrangement. It was just easier all around. Though easy was hardly the right word for it.

He hated being in this position with Callie, hated feeling beholden to her. But he had nowhere else to turn. She had offered to help and he was pretty desperate, with school out, and that measly half-day summer school program barely giving him enough time to finish the few carpentry jobs he had, check on his dad, not to mention pick up food, be a father. She had insisted, wouldn't take no for an answer, and now every afternoon he dropped them over to her house so he could have a couple of extra hours before dinner. There was no question that he needed her now. Trapped by her kindness, he could barely look at her.

There was a time he had wanted her so badly he had to stop himself from walking over there, husband or no husband, and tell her he was all hers if she ever decided to leave. Perfect was what she was, in those first few months, when he'd wake up feeling wanted, maybe for the first time ever, and go to sleep feeling hungry for the next day to start. Perfect, yeah, except for one tiny little glitch. No thank you. Busting up another man's family was one fuck-up he wasn't interested in adding to his list.

The first attendant, the one who had fixed the blinds, came in to pick up the food tray. Robin didn't bother to look up, just sank into the fake leather chair next to his father's bed and tilted back his head, trying to loosen his cramped neck. He almost envied the old man, not a care in the world, while Robin himself was more trapped than ever. How was it he always felt trapped?

The old headache was back, the one that never completely left. Robin rubbed his temples, squeezed hard in the crook between his thumb and forefinger, a maneuver he vaguely remembered Cynthia telling him stimulated something or other. Anyhow it did seem to take the sharp edge off his headache. He'd even been thinking about calling the bitch. If he could even figure out where she was living now. Denver still? Montana? She wrote him a letter every six months or so, having the nerve to ask about the kids. Cynthia. It wasn't out of the question. Maybe she was set up to take the kids again. Maybe by now she had a change of heart. Maybe he should call her.

Who he really should call was the old woman. He'd probably already blown it with her. She never even called to check up on him. Maybe she really didn't give a damn one way or another about that property. Maybe she'd already found someone else to finish the job. He wouldn't blame her if she did.

"Vera?" his dad called out. Robin sat up and adjusted the pillow a bit, pulled the covers up over his father's shoulders.

"I'm here Dad."

Last thing he'd done over at her place was finish the thresholds. He had planned to start in on the kitchen next, had even ordered cabinets. He never did get the receipts to her. That would be reason enough to give her a call. And also, he'd left his power sander in her living room, intending to go back for it, but then this business with his father, and everything afterwards a blur.

Just call her, he heard the words in his head, what would have been his father's words, but now were his own.

"All right, Dad, I'll call her," he said to the sleeping man, who made a little noise, like a child dreaming, and then quieted again. Robin picked up his father's hand, cool to the touch, and rubbed his thumb all along the translucent blue lines that ran across the top. "Dad," he whispered, feeling the coolness of tears beginning to pool in the corner of his eyes.

"Hey Dad, any chance you want to come live with me and the kids over at Carnelian Bay?"

Robin set his father's hand down gently again on top of the blanket. He wanted to break down and cry so bad his throat burned, but he didn't dare.

"I'll see you later," he said instead, and then touched his lips to his father's forehead, on the outside chance the old man might know he was there.

28.

A WEEK, THEN TWO WEEKS passed since my last visit, but instead of pushing ahead with selling the place, I found myself daydreaming about the gully, thinking about bringing some digging tools next time, maybe climbing down into it myself. Who knows what I might come up with? Just last week I read about a couple who stumbled on a box of old coins buried in their backyard. They were planting an apple tree, next thing they knew they had over $100,000 worth of coins. It happens. Who says I can't try my hand at digging up some treasures from that gully? So why the big hurry to sell?

It was dangerous for me to daydream, but hard as I tried to keep my resolve, all kinds of foolish thoughts kept bubbling to the surface, thoughts I couldn't seem to silence. Like that Pete character—he had to have known my long lost brother. No harm digging around in that direction a bit longer.

I thought I was making progress, having stashed the Realtor's card in my handbag, in the slot where I kept my credit cards so I'd see it every time I went to pay for something. But then whenever I pulled the damned card out, intending fully to get the ball rolling, I'd hear a voice in my head, thick and gravelly, (could have been Ray's ghost for all I know) sneering, "Don't do it."

One thing hadn't changed. That fat stack of bills. They

were still there.

And then Robin called. Out of the blue, it felt like. I had pretty much given up on hearing from him again, and certainly didn't need to chase him down, seeing as how I had no reason for him to finish what he'd started. Last time he called was right after that trip I took when I met the girl. He had left me a message saying something had come up, something about another job he had started, they needed it finished before the end of summer and would I mind if he took a break for a while. "Something's come up" he said one too many times, and I couldn't help thinking about those blond hairs on the hair clip. Something's come up all right.

Instead of being disappointed, I found myself relieved. What did I care how long it took him to finish. Finish what? I wasn't even sure at this point why I had bothered to hire him in the first place.

So hearing his voice again came as a bit of a surprise. We didn't actually speak. He left me another message, saying there had been some problem in his family, he apologized over and over but he wasn't making any sense. He had already told me he had other jobs to finish. What was this business about his family? It was hard to understand his words, he kept repeating himself but mumbling the whole time. He sounded nervous, distracted. That much I could hear plain as day.

His message went on to say that he had a number of receipts for some materials he had purchased and wanted to square things up with me. I had completely lost track of what I had paid him and what I owed him. "Sure," I answered him back, voicemail replying to voicemail. (Do people ever actually talk to each other anymore?) I said I could meet him at the property the following Sunday morning. It was just the excuse I needed to go back up the mountain. I'd remember to bring my garden trowel this time, some thick gloves, maybe a bunch of those thick garden bags to hold all the gold coins I was sure to unearth.

Pulling into the driveway late Friday, I still had a good two more hours of daylight left to enjoy the sounds and smells of a summer evening. June's the nicest month of the year. All the colors of summer without the blasted heat. I'd decided to make a weekend of it, square things up with Robin, and once and for all make an end to this foolishness. I had exhausted myself with indecision. Finally, one simple decision even I could stick to: I'd spend a couple of days, one last final couple of days, on this particularly odd inheritance that I had neither the means nor abilities to manage. Just one more weekend. Out of respect for my brother's memory.

And then I would start up the engines to sell.

By the time I finished unpacking the car, putting away the clothes and food I had brought, and sweeping up the latest two weeks' worth of dust on the floor, the sky was already beginning to turn grey. I brewed myself a nice dark pot of tea, glad I'd remembered the honey, changed into my flannel nightshirt, and wandered outside, feeling lucky to have the full moon to guide me around the logs and debris. There was light enough to navigate through the mess of ground cover and I realized that in all the visits I'd made so far, I hadn't ever actually paced the perimeters. Here it was mid-June, nine months since I first got the lawyer's letter, and still so much about this place I hadn't bothered to notice. Like the huge flat rock at the uphill corner, farthest from the road. Even with the dark approaching, its smooth surface still felt warm to the touch.

I hoisted myself up and sat cross-legged, looking out at what was left of the views. From that vantage point I could easily make out the twisted limbs of madrones, and that wild thicket of penstemon, even in the encroaching dark I could make out their red and purple shoots. I sprawled myself up onto the warm rock, picturing the old neighbors on Meadowbrook Lane, the Hunnicuts and Whidbeys with their perfunctory petunia pots and poodle-cut camellias. What I'd give to have them see me now.

I rubbed my fingers into the dust and soaked it all in. I picked up a smooth stick nearby and found myself drawing squiggles in the dirt. Aimless, I know that. The dust that kicked up smelled sharp and sweet. It was the smell of that groundcover grows everywhere, even under the porch slats. Kit-kit-dizze. The girl across the road told me that's the name the Native Americans gave it, but she said everyone around here calls it Mountain Misery.

The name did make sense. You can't get the damned smell out. On my previous visits to the land I must have carried the smell on my clothing and, somehow, managed to transfer it from my clothes to Amos's fur. He'd spent days trying to lick it off. When the sun hits it just right, the smell reminds me of my Lapsang Souchong if its been steeping for too long. The smell defines the air, competes and wins over every other growing thing, not to mention the insoles of your shoes. It had already started to work its way into my skin.

In the moonlight, I noticed for the first time a thin trace of the beginnings of varicosity, legs otherwise smooth, thick blue lines slightly above my knee, colors shifting from blue to white and back to blue. I unbuttoned my shirt to scratch an itch, noticed several tiny red spots, like those spicy red candies, popping up across my belly and down toward that nether region that grows increasingly hairless and childlike with each passing year. The doctor assured me the red spots were nothing but age. No cure for that, he added. Smart aleck.

I was getting old, no doubt about that. But I did feel like a kid right then, and one who had just run away from home to boot.

Lying back on the rock, feeling the darkness cover me, I closed my eyes and imagined that Ned was there with me. It was a luxury I rarely allowed myself. But my hand went to my heart and as silly as this sounds, I pretended like he was lying next to me, right on this rock, just the two of us lying there looking up at the moon.

The next morning I slept in. The sun was already blasting its rays through the bedroom window. Who knows how much longer I might have slept if I hadn't been on that flimsy mattress. My head was wedged tight against the wall and the scratch of rough wood against my cheek startling me awake. It took a few minutes to uncreak my bones before opening the bedroom windows, grateful that Robin had at least gotten around to fixing them. I leaned my head out and sucked in the luxurious smells of morning. The field outside offered a constant simmer of sharply competing perfumes but inside still stank of old cigarette smoke and pine tar on the doorknobs that I couldn't rub out.

Something about waking up alone to the sounds of buzzing insects, distant birds, and this symphony of sweet dark smells, felt like a swig of strong coffee. I walked out onto the porch, stretched my arms overhead, wishing there was a folding table out here, a couple of folding chairs would be nice, so I wouldn't have to sit on that rickety wicker chair to drink my tea, wishing I had brought up a real whistling teakettle, not that old bent up aluminum pot I discovered in the back of the pantry. I took a piece of paper out of my purse, wrote down tea kettle, and added can opener, then thought about Sister Eugenia, how she'd be looking at me right about now, with that smile on her face that's way older than she is.

I crumpled up the list and threw it across the deck, watched it roll into a patch of weeds. Good place for it. I noticed an old broom leaning against the side of the house, looking like it was attached to the place, and proceeded to sweep the front porch yet again, swept it until every last snatch of leaf unstuck from the surface.

I wondered if there was a possibility I was in the beginning stages of dementia. Because after a fierce porch cleaning, I plopped myself back down on the living room floor, couldn't stop smiling, picturing the place with a fresh coat of paint, my claw foot chair would fit just right over there, centered, no maybe more over to the left, facing up the driveway so I could see if anyone was coming. As though anyone would be coming up this driveway at this time of morning.

And just at the moment, as if on cue, I heard something breaking through the dense quiet. Yes, there it was again, the distinct sound of shoes on dirt.

And there he stood. Mr. Trash. I wasn't half surprised.

"You again?" This time, Pete was wearing a baseball cap and damned if he didn't put his hand on the brim and tip it toward me.

"Heard your car pull up last night. Thought I'd pay a visit." He looked like an overgrown schoolboy drumming up the nerve for a first dance.

Well, what was I supposed to do, leave him standing out there like a wet puppy?

"Come in," I waved, "sit down," wondering what he'd do with that invitation, since there wasn't a seat to be had.

"Looks like you've got some work here," he said, hat in hand, eyes darting every which way. I almost expected him to bump into a wall.

"Yes, it looks like I do. But I imagine you've spent plenty of time rummaging around here and already knew that."

Pete walked over to the window, impervious to my rudeness.

"Over there, in a few more hours, sun's going to light up the back side of the madrones."

"I've already seen the view," I told him, my voice too sharp even for my ears.

"What about at sunset? Have you seen it at sunset? The whole place turns red just after sunset."

It sounded like he was planning on staying until then, just so he could show it to me.

"Sunset's a way's off, and I've got a day's full of things to do around here," I grunted, though at that moment I couldn't say what those things might be. I was almost wishing I did have a chair to offer him. What else was I doing today?

But it didn't really matter what I said to the man. It seemed like the more I tried to be rude, the friendlier he became.

"Too bad," he came right back. "I've got a few extra chairs at my place, nothing fancy, I'd be glad to bring them by later this afternoon. That is, if you're planning on staying 'til then."

"Excuse me, but what did you say your name was?" I asked him, just a ploy to make him mad. I remembered his name all right, but more I remembered his fingers, creased and hard and one knuckle badly out of joint like it had been smashed by a hammer.

"Pete. And you're Hannah, if I'm not mistaken."

"You're not."

"Well how about I bring some of my extra chairs over so you can use them whenever you're here."

He wasn't a stupid man, already turning for the door, heading for the shrub line that separated our parcels.

"Wait," I stumbled, almost tripping on the bottom porch step. He didn't stop walking.

"Pete," now I was almost in a run, "that would be very nice. I will take you up on that offer. That is, if it's no trouble."

Just a nod of the head was all he gave me. All I deserved. By the time I thought to say thank you, he was out of sight.

The chairs were a nice touch. Two rickety bentwoods and he even went back for a second trip, hauling over a small table to fit between them. It was mid-afternoon by then, sun high overhead, the dense cluster of trees surrounding the property punctuated by flashes of light that swerved and dipped over every single leaf. From the porch steps, I could make out where the road turned at the top of the long driveway. We sat out on the deck and watched the sun play in and out of the madrones, just like he said they would. Streaks of light appeared then disappeared like headlights on a foggy road. Or it might have been birds we were watching, fluttering around like tiny

Adina Sara

mobiles in the wind.

Pete's hands were folded behind his head, leaning back on a chair that didn't look like it could hold him. He pointed out the various barks that turned neon from the glow of sunlight, hot streaks bleeding red to purple. Occasional knife-like cuts of yellow. He knew a lot about the trees, every single name, better than that book I purchased.

Every once in a while he asked me again if I was sure I didn't want to stick around to watch the sunset.

"I've really got work to do," I said every hour or so.

Once he went back to his place, to fetch some peaches and dark bread. "These are from my tree," he gloated, and I had to admit I'd never tasted sweeter. Later on, he left again and returned with some whiskey.

Of course I told him no, I didn't dare in the middle of the day, but instead brewed my darkest tea, which he spit out. It didn't take us too long to discover that a little whisky mixed in with the Lapsang improved the quality of both.

Somewhere along the day, Pete started in about his booth at the Saturday flea market. Said a good lot of his inventory had come from my gully over the years. Said that lately business had been slowing. Seemed like the locals were tapped out of their interest in old junk and he might do better taking his junk to a less rural area, where he could call it 'antiques' and no one would know enough to argue.

I was no stranger to flea markets myself. Kind of a

269

weekend hobby, though in recent years I had trained my-self not to buy a thing, enjoying looking at what kind of crap people buy and sell. I added my own flea market wis-dom, whenever he gave me space to sneak a word or two in, which wasn't often. The man did know his junk, I had to give him that.

While he rambled on, another screwball idea entered my head. Maybe he'd want to buy the place? Or rent it from me. He could keep his little gold mine and hell, I could have my cake and eat it.

Grateful for his endless jabbering, I closed my eyes on this new idea, took another sip of that spiked tea of his, aware that he kept refilling my mug since it should have been empty with all the sipping I'd been doing. At this point he was talking to himself, because I had stopped listening. I was concentrating instead on the grand variety of sounds that wind makes, the endless chatter of flying things.

After a while I picked myself up out of the chair and walked the short distance over to the edge of the porch. Was I wobbling or did it just feel like I was wobbling? Ei-ther way I was glad to have the owl head to lean on for support.

"Did you know my brother?"

The sentence came out of nowhere, and I couldn't possibly take it back.

The man who hadn't stopped talking was suddenly

silent.

"Did you hear me?" I repeated, in the off chance he didn't.

"Who was your brother?" he asked.

"Ray. Ray Blackwell. He used to own this property and I suspect you lived here at the time."

"Oh yeah, I remember him."

"And?"

"And I hardly knew him."

"And?"

"The man pretty much kept to himself. Its been years." he said, immediately changing the subject right back to his flea market findings.

Fine then.

As sometimes happens in the mountains, even in the summer, the winds changed quickly. Unless my eyes were playing tricks, my watch read well past five o'clock. How many hours had we been rambling on there? Whatever long it was, it was too long. I for one was getting cold.

We didn't fuss around with goodbyes. I must have looked as tired as I felt, and he apologized for going on so long.

"Remember, flea market every Saturday, 9-4, where Highway 49 hits Anderson Road. I'll give you a great deal." He had stepped off the porch, turning to go.

"Seeing how half your merchandise was buried on my property, I should say so."

By the time I made it to the front door, certain now that I might be just a little bit drunk, he was already out of sight.

Back inside the cabin, I tended to my poor hands that were cut in places where I had grabbed before looking, those damned wild rose thorns, splinters painfully tucked beneath filthy fingernails. My hands were beginning to look like roadmaps, lined and linked in endless directions. I turned on the tap, watched the mud break loose from my fingers, and allowed the cold flow of water to cool the top of my head, run down along the sides of my neck, then slide into the crease of chin all the way down to where I could almost taste it.

My head was spinning and it wasn't altogether the whiskey. When was the last time I'd had a day like this? Doing nothing but talking to a stranger, staring at shadows and leaves, not caring about what I said or who was listening.

When was the last time I felt this utterly and completely content?

I didn't bother to dry myself off, just went outside and let the cool air wash over me, hoping the chill might bring some clarity to my confusion. I looked up at the sky but with the brightness of the full moon, there was not a star to be seen. Not a sign, not a hint of direction. The sweat under my armpits had come and gone, leaving behind an acrid scent I didn't recognize. Who was this woman standing in the dark, on a splintered deck, reeking of a strange bitter groundcover? I noticed that wooden owl, perched on the top step like he owned the place. I could have sworn he turned his head and looked straight at me.

I surveyed the landscape one last time before heading back to the bedroom, and collapsing on the mattress. What a foolish old woman I'd grown into. Tomorrow I would meet with Robin, pay him whatever I owed him. Then stop by the Realtor on my way down the mountain.

29.

ROBIN SMELLED SOMETHING burning coming from inside the shack when he stepped on to the porch. From the outside, it appeared as though the old woman had cleared things up quite a bit. Some deck chairs, a folding table, and a pair of slippers on the porch railing made it seem like someone actually lived there. It made him feel less guilty for telling her he had another job to work on, when he really just needed things to cool down with Callie. It wasn't completely a lie. The couple out in Peardale changed their minds and decided they wanted that hot tub after all. Then one of their neighbors poked his head over the fence and asked him to build a play structure for their kids. He had plenty of other things to do. And it's not as though the Blackwell woman had been after him for progress reports.

And now this thing with his father. If nothing else, he finally had the excuse he needed to be done with her.

"Stay in the truck" he motioned to the kids, not intending to be inside with her too long. He brought his clipboard, hoping to look official, along with receipts for a couple of dowels he had bought for the bedroom and broom closets, and the order form for the kitchen cabinets, which he had paid for but never picked up. Considering how he had flaked on her, he could see why she might not want to reimburse him for any of it, but in her voicemail she'd insisted on paying him every dime she owed him.

He approached the front door and was greeted by her backside. She was squatting on the floor in front of the stove, cursing so loudly he was pretty sure she didn't notice him. He immediately identified the source of the burning smell—remnants of a platter of black-edged cookies, now cookie crumbs, littered the floor. She was on her knees, more or less cleaning the mess up.

The front door was wide open and he knocked softly on the doorframe, not wanting to startle her.

"Can I give you a hand there?" he called out. She had gotten up and turned around, her hair all wild and flecked with ash, a painful expression on her face. She motioned him inside, less interested in his arrival than on the filthy floor.

"Blasted kitchen isn't built for cooking. Here I was going to make some cookies for you but this oven doesn't exactly know what its doing and then I put the darned platter on the counter, except I forgot there isn't enough room on the counter for so much as a teacup." Robin knelt down to help pick up the scramble of broken cookies and pottery shards that littered the floor.

"I thought I shut the oven off and I think maybe I did but I don't know, there it is, a broken plate of ruined cookies."

Robin relaxed, relieved that it was the stove, and not him, that caused her fury.

"That's a pretty old stove. I'm surprised you got it

to work at all. Those things need to be refurbished every century or so and from the looks of it, it missed its last tune-up." He hoped a little bit of humor would help speed things up a bit, get this business over with.

The mess cleared, she put what crumbs were marginally edible onto another plate, motioned for him to sit down. "So how much more do I owe you?" she asked, not wasting any time, and he took a seat, as she directed, looking for the right words to express what he had been dreading to say.

"I'm sorry I had to stop working here, I should have called you sooner," Robin began, but she waved him off.

"No need to apologize. You got plenty done already, my windows and doors all work, that's what I wanted most."

"Here, I managed to salvage a few." She pushed the plate of broken cookie bits in front of him. "Tell me what you think?"

They sat down at the table, the platter of mildly burned cookie pieces wedged next to his clipboard, and he opened the envelope of receipts, laying them out in front of her, one by one. But before he could even begin showing her what was what, they were interrupted.

"Daddy?" came a small voice, quickly followed by another, softer "Dad?" They stepped into the kitchen and flanked their father, eyes on the cookie plate, waiting for an invitation.

"Well it looks like we have some hungry visitors here."

"I told you guys to stay in the truck," he scolded, rustling them back to the door but Hannah would not allow it.

"They can't sit in the truck. We need somebody to finish up these crumbs." She handed the children what was left of her baking fiasco.

Grace was not shy and took the largest pieces, leaving Timothy to try and lift up the meager remains with wet fingertips.

"Daddy, can we go across the street and see if the lady with the baby is home, please?"

"This is my daughter, Grace. And this is Timothy. This is Mrs..." but Hannah cut him off before he could finish.

"We've already met. Don't you remember, that time your grandpa gave me pancakes?"

Of course they remembered, and Grace added, "That time you broke your sink?" which made all of them laugh.

Then right away Grace started in again, "Please Daddy?"

"Please can we go across the street," Timothy this time, but Robin wouldn't hear of it.

"Now what's across the street that's more interesting than my cookies?"

Robin began to explain about the woman across the way, the woman with the baby, yes, Callie, of course Hannah knew her, of course Robin remembered, he had introduced them, of course.

"She's been helping me take care of my kids ever since

my father went to the hospital."

"Your father's in the hospital?"

And so he finally began to explain the reason for his lack of progress on her house. She interrupted him mid-sentence.

"For goodness sakes, no wonder you stopped working, what with kids to take care of, and now your father. How long ago did this happen?"

As Robin went into detail about the fall, the stroke, moving his dad to a nursing home, Hannah reached out and encircled the children, an arm around each one of them. Timothy sidled up closer and closer to Hannah while Grace managed to sneak the last of the cookie crumbs into her mouth.

"I found him first," Grace said, adding in the part about Grandpa lying on the stair landing.

"Was he unconscious?" Hannah asked, stroking the back of Grace's hair.

"He needs to sleep a lot," Timothy offered, and Hannah lowered her eyes with the understanding that the old man's condition was serious.

"We almost drowned," the boy went on. That was his favorite part of the story, gaining dramatic fervor in each retelling.

Seeing how the cookie plate had been licked clean, Hannah got up and took it over to the sink. The children followed like ducklings.

"Do you have anymore?" Grace asked.

"Grace," Robin admonished but Hannah didn't mind

at all. "Its OK. They're paying me a compliment. First time anyone ever wanted seconds on my cookies." She refilled the plate with a few more bits and pieces, then walked over to the door, motioning to the children to come over.

"Do you like treasure hunts?"

The children looked at their father, eyes wide, and he decided to let the woman go ahead with whatever she had in mind.

"See out there," she told them, bending down to meet them eye to eye, "there's a gully out back, just loaded with treasures, if you know where to dig." She handed them both spoons that were bent and crusty with dirt.

"Be careful, now. Don't climb down into the gully. There's broken glass down there. And nothing good anyway. The good stuff is on top. You never know what you'll find."

Again they looked over at their father for permission.

"Go on, but stay close so we can hear you," Robin finally ordered.

"We promise we'll be careful," Grace shouted as they dashed outside, leaving Hannah and Robin at the small table.

An uncomfortable silence filled the room. Robin turned to the window and stared out, not sure what more there was for them to talk about.

"So how is your father doing now?" Hannah asked after a couple of awkward moments.

"Well," said Robin, and once he started, he just kept

going, like he was talking to himself, as much as to the woman next to him. She kept leaning in closer so he had no choice but to continue, filling her in on the medical details, more than he ever intended to say.

"Looks like I'll be moving out of the area. I may need to sell my father's place to pay for his nursing home care. I need to find a regular job, a better place for the kids."

"Stay right there Robin." Hannah got up and started fussing around again in the kitchen. He was glad for the interruption. It gave him an opportunity to collect himself, seeing how far he had strayed from his purpose here. The receipts. He needed to get back to the receipts.

"I'd like to go over these receipts with you. Some of those things can be returned if you don't want them."

But she had her back toward him, pulling a couple of mugs out of the overhead cabinet. He really wanted this meeting to be over, but now she was firing up the tea-kettle, dropping a tea bag in each mug. She hadn't even asked him if wanted some.

Finally, after an uncomfortably long pause, she turned to him.

"What happened to the children's mother?"

Now that was a question out of left field. How would he begin to answer? He tried to think of a polite way of saying it was none of her business, but when he made the mistake of looking up and seeing her eyes narrow, it seemed as though they were about to drill right through him.

"That first time I met you, you told me your wife left

you with two little kids. I never forgot that."

Robin couldn't remember telling her about Cynthia. It wasn't like him to talk to strangers about his problems.

She placed the cup of steaming tea in front of him, "hope you like it strong" she said, and he felt like there was no choice now but to tell her the whole sickening story.

"A guy named Jason teaches a class, some kind of spirituality bull she said she needed to get her back on track after Timmy was born. So this Jason tells her she's a gifted healer, teaches her some new meditation technique supposed to get rid of pain forever. Called the Hobart Method. 'Gifted healer,' she told me, like that was enough of a reason to leave your kids. She followed him back to Indiana, then Denver last I heard."

Hannah was silent for a bit. Robin didn't dare look up to catch her eye.

"I just don't understand how a mother could walk away from two babies—her own babies." Her throat seemed to snag on the words, and she excused herself, got up and walked back over to the sink.

"Geez ma'am. I can't believe I've been telling you all this."

"Why do you insist on calling me ma'am? My name is Hannah." She seemed to be shouting at him, and he immediately regretted opening up to her.

"I'm sorry to have gone on. All the stuff that's happened to me isn't your concern. I didn't mean to burden you with this."

"I didn't see any burden in it. You've got a lot going on young man. You don't owe me any apologies."

"Well, I want you to know I did enjoy working on your place, getting to fix it up, even a little. I've always liked this place. I have some of my own memories here."

It came out like some things do, unintended, and now he couldn't take it back.

"So you do know this place. I've asked you a number of times but you never said a word."

"I used to come here when I was a kid. All those shrubs make great hiding places." He was backing up now but she stayed in close, looked hard at him, and though he wanted to, he couldn't look away.

"Then you must know something about my brother."

Robin was shuffling the small pieces of paper around, trying to buy a little time, but she walked over to the table and covered the piles of receipts with both hands.

"Tell me," she demanded. "You knew him, didn't you?"

Robin measured every word before speaking.

"Not really. I was a kid when he lived here. My mom was sick and I'd sneak out of the house because it was hard with her in bed all the time. I'd come over here and hang out with him. He was nice to me."

"So you knew him."

"Not really," was all he answered. He had said too much already. He gathered up the receipts like a pack of cards, hoping the gesture would get them back to where he wanted to be. She leaned in too close for his comfort, her voice a gravelly mixture of fierceness and sorrow.

"Anything you could tell me about him would be appreciated. He ran away when he was about your age, maybe younger, but no sign of him since then. Until he turned up dead, and left me this property. Anything you know about him would mean a great deal to me."

Robin considered her words but didn't dare speak. He had so much to say about Ray, none of it what she'd want to hear. Still, the woman deserved some consideration. He granted that he remembered Ray a little.

"A little?" She was hanging on each word. "A little, how?"

He could hear her taking in sharp breaths, like she was getting ready to swallow his every word.

"He was a nice enough man, but again, like I told you, I was just a kid."

"What do you remember about him?"

"He was nice to me, let me hang around his place. He didn't think I was a pesky kid, which I probably was. That's really all I remember. He gave me a safe place to play when I didn't want to be home. I remember he scared me at first but he really turned out to be nice." It was more than he intended to say, but not too much. Maybe it would stop her questions.

Hannah picked up the packet of receipts, went to the bedroom to get her purse, leaving him alone at the table. He became aware of an uncomfortable stillness in the room, like a cloud forming but not yet formed, leaving a heavy thickness in the air. He wished he could up and bolt out of there but already she was back, checkbook in hand, and he sat back down again.

"So when exactly are you planning to move?"

She didn't sit with him at the table but mercifully stood next to the sink, making it easier for him to answer.

"I found a boat building apprenticeship over near Tahoe. They want me to start in September. Between now and then I'll have to get settled into a new place before their new school starts.

"What are they going to do until then?"

"They've got summer school but it gets out early. I'll be able to do small jobs here and there, and Callie said she could take the kids once in a while, whenever I needed it. I wish I could have helped you more but there won't be nearly enough time for me to do all the things you need finished around here."

She was still at the sink, looking out the window, and he wished he could read the expression on her face.

A long silence fell, and heavy, as she stood not three feet away from him, holding on to the sink counter like she needed it to hold her up.

She somehow seemed larger from this angle, her arms outspread could almost reach to both ends of the kitchen counter. A strong woman, Robin could see that, even with her baggy grey trousers and oversized t-shirt. Why did Ray run away? he wondered. What was he like as a kid? But he wouldn't dare ask.

But now she turned around to face him and when she spoke, he wasn't at all prepared for what she had to say.

"You say you need to find work between now and September?"

He didn't answer, just looked at her.

"And you need as much childcare as you can get?"

He shifted in his chair. Why was she asking all these questions?

Suddenly she walked right over to the table, pulled out her chair and sat down, facing him full on.

"I'll take care of them. I'll move some more of my things up here and spend the rest of the summer. You can keep plugging away around here, finish up whatever time allows. The kitchen's still a mess. Start there. I don't care if you finish or not. Whatever progress you make between now and September will be fine with me."

He looked at her, stared right into her eyes this time. It was his turn to speak but he couldn't find a single word to say.

"So it's settled then."

30.

I RAN INTO DARLENE in the Pay 'n Save parking lot. I'd been avoiding passing her hair salon. When I needed to take in some cleaning, or go to the pharmacy that shared the same lot, I made it a point to park my car on the other side of the strip mall, as far away from her shop as possible. Since the last time I saw her, my hair's turned into a thicket, not unlike the weeds that run along the driveway on Blind Shady. I knew if she saw me she'd throw a fit, and that's exactly what she did.

"Whatever happened to you?" That pretty much said it all.

I kind of liked my new look. My hair had gotten long enough in back that I could keep it together with one of those fat hairclips I'd taken a liking to. I bought a bunch of flashy bright colored ones, pretty much the only bright colors I allowed myself. The grey hairs had been filling in steadily since I stopped letting Darlene dye it, and the new colorless strands grew out wiry, twisting every which way so it really was no use to try to smooth them down.

"Nothing happened to me," I responded curtly. "Just stopped getting my hair cut is all."

"Well where the hell have you been?" she continued, as though my business was her business.

In a way it was her business. Every other week since before my father died I had kept my standing appointment with her. And then I up and disappeared without a word.

"Just here and there," I said, "been busy with this land I got from my brother. I told you about it...," rambling out excuses that even I thought were weak.

She stood in front of me, arms across her chest, shaking her head. She couldn't help herself, reached over and tried to smooth some hairs that had pulled loose from my hairclip. Always Darlene. She looked more sad than angry.

"I just hope you're OK," she said, before moving on to her car.

She cared about me. All those years, of course she cared about me. I was just too thickheaded to notice. I did owe her an explanation. But how could I have explained to her what I couldn't explain to myself? Because, try as I might, I still couldn't make sense of how I had jumped into Robin's life uninvited, just blurted out my plan like it was the most natural solution in the world, like it was something I had been thinking about all along. And maybe I had been, just didn't know it.

I couldn't get Robin's expression out of my mind. I'd like to say he looked like a deer in headlights but that's more fear than amazement. I could see the muscles in his shoulders drop, like some weight had been removed that he wasn't aware of. He looked like he would burst into tears if those kids hadn't come in just when they did.

When the poor boy finally got around to talking, (I think I knocked the wind out of him), he stammered more than talked.

"But, but, I don't need you to. I already have child-care." Nonsense, I said, because my mind had been made up and there was no going back.

"You just told me you needed help with the kids," I shot back, "and the few hours Callie helps out isn't exact-ly enough time for you to accomplish much, now is it?" I was in high gear by then, because the more the words spilled out of me, the more I grew excited about the whole idea.

But he wasn't going for it. He stood up from the table so he was now peering down on me. "I can't ask you to watch my kids."

"You didn't ask. I offered. It's a win-win as far as I can see."

"I said I can't ask you do to that," Robin repeated, his voice shaking and I wanted to get up and hug him to piec-es. Poor boy. About Ned's age when Ned died. Not that he reminded me of him in the least bit, well maybe a little, but my heart went out to him nonetheless. Still a boy, bearing the weight of an old man.

I began to add up the receipts that covered the table, double-checked the numbers while I sensed him staring at me. I wrote out a check, Robin Till, even threw in an ex-tra couple of dollars for good measure. Maybe he'd figure it out, maybe he wouldn't.

He picked up his mug of tea, I could see his hands shaking, so I pushed on.

"Seems to me the kids would be quite happy with this arrangement. There are plenty of things for us to do in town and I'll bet they can show me more than I can show them. What sorts of things do they like to eat?"

Again, nothing.

I handed him the check and he took it, put it in his pocket.

He took a deep breath, I could see his shoulder blades tighten, then relax. It was a good idea and he knew it. Maybe I had crossed a line. Once I got going on something, I did have that tendency.

"Well that's perfect then," I concluded.

It was as though a gale wind had blown through the window, without warning, pushing us both over, yet leaving us surprisingly upright.

It wasn't a gale wind, more like a whiff of breeze that blew through the window, carrying the squeals of Timothy's find, a caterpillar, and now Grace walked in with a glass bottle she found but the opening was too small for the caterpillar's head.

Robin told the children to put the bottle and caterpillar outside and the children complied without protest. I couldn't help but interject.

"Let's put the bottle down on the step and see if he crawls into it by himself. Then we'll know for sure if he wants to be in there."

"Do you think he will?"

"We'll check on him next time you come over."

"When's that? Daddy, when can we come back?"

Robin looked at me and I just smiled back at him, my biggest fattest grin smeared across my face, and I could see the beginning of a smile trying to poke its way through his stubborn pride.

"Looks like Miss Blackwell will be taking care of you while Daddy has to finish up some work around her house. How does that sound?"

"Really?" both of them said at once, turning their heads towards me as their father ushered them back into the truck. I couldn't tell if they were happy or upset about the idea, but then Timothy asked me if they could hunt for more caterpillars next time.

"Of course we can," I called out to him, waving long past the time the truck backed down the driveway and turned out of sight.

Summer

31.

THE VERY FIRST DAY that they stayed with the lady, she drove them over to Grandpa's hardware store. She gave Grace a pad of lined paper and a green sharpie pen, and asked her to write down the shopping list, even if she wasn't sure how to spell the words.

Grace was tired of that old hardware store. Grandpa used to take them there all the time before he got sick. They'd sit in his office and draw pictures with his stubby old pencils and leaky pens until he was finished working. It was boring.

The place kind of smelled like Grandpa and going back there without him just made Grace sad. But then the lady turned the hardware store visit into kind of a game, see who could find the things on the list first. She had Grace read the shopping list out loud and then she and Timothy would race to find whatever thing it was she wanted to buy. Timothy got to pick it off the shelf and put it in the cart.

She made everything into a game, asking questions that only Grace could answer. "Which of these bolts is three-quarter inches?" Grace was learning fractions in school and Timothy didn't even know what a fraction was.

The lady, who asked them to call her Hannah, even though their dad said to call her Miss Blackwell, kept a point system in a little red notepad. Every right answer got a point. Grace already had way more points than Timothy. She got points for finding how many things in a store started with the letter B and she even got extra points for running back to the restaurant and grabbing Timothy's jacket, which he had left on his chair. The games she made up never seemed to end. So far there hadn't been any prizes for winning.

After the first couple of weeks, Grace started looking forward to going places with Hannah, though it still felt weird to say her name like that, so mostly Grace didn't call her anything. Once Hannah took them to a movie in Grass Valley and then last week they got to take a hike along the river. They found long twisted branches along the riverbank and the lady showed them how to use them as walking sticks to help keep their balance on the rocky paths. Back at Hannah's place, they found some really cool rocks underneath her trees and Timmy got extra points for coming up with the idea of using them to build a giant snake.

This week was Timothy's turn to ride in the front seat. What was so important about them taking turns anyway? Grace was pretty sure that Hannah liked Timothy better, the way she picked him up (he was plenty big enough to climb in by himself) and buckled him into his car seat, even sometimes kissing him on the top of his head. With Dad it was the other way around. Grace got special treats after Timothy went to sleep. She was the only one who got to turn the radio dials.

Sitting in the back seat, her seat belt tight across her lap, Grace decided she liked it back there. She got to be more like a grown-up, rolling the windows up and down however way she wanted, getting to stretch her legs out, having the wind all to herself.

Last week they went to Train Town and Grace won a stuffed panda bear and a Pez dispenser (that she had to share with Timothy) and Hannah got into one of the bumper cars with them and screamed as loud as they did. Hannah gave them whole dollar bills to buy anything they wanted, not the pennies and nickels and dimes Grandpa said added up to a dollar.

And today they were going to Grace's favorite place of all, the flea market.

Dad usually asked Hannah where she was planning on taking them, but this morning he just dashed them through breakfast and dropped them on her porch, honking his horn instead of getting out, like he usually did.

"We'll be back some time around dinner," Hannah yelled out to him from the porch, as he backed the truck down her driveway. It didn't seem like he even heard.

Maybe it had something to do with Grandpa. Maybe today Dad was finally going to bring him home. Or maybe Grandpa already died. Dad never answered her questions about Grandpa. Always something stupid like "he's not feeling very well" or "he's not better yet."

Grace knew what it was like to not feel well. That

time her throat was so sore she couldn't swallow and didn't go to school for a whole week. But Dad didn't send her away to some place where nobody could visit her. She got to stay in her own bed and got to drink sodas in the middle of the day. So she knew her dad was lying about Grandpa. He was really sick and maybe was going to die. She wished Dad would just tell her the truth, stop making up that Grandpa needed to rest in a special place. Like she didn't know what was really happening to him.

"Enough about Grandpa," he'd scold her whenever she asked about him. "Get your shoes on." Like Grandpa didn't matter any more.

Timothy never asked questions about Grandpa. He didn't even seem to notice he was gone.

"Going to have our friends come along with us today," Hannah told them as she pulled up into the driveway across the road. It was Daphne's house, Grace's favorite place in the whole world. She kind of wished that they lived there instead of with their dad in Grandpa's old house.

Hannah drove the car across the road into Daphne's driveway. Callie was standing outside, holding the baby in her arms, both of them waving and waving. All of a sudden it felt like going from having no mom at all to a mom and a grandma, all at the same time.

Callie asked if Grace would mind if she put the baby's car seat next to her. Mind? She wiggled over as far to the door as she could, and soon they were off, the baby next to her, Callie on the far side, each holding one of the baby's tiny hands. Grace rolled the window up just a little, afraid the wind would be too much in the baby's eyes. She made sure the pacifier stayed in the baby's mouth. She pretended it was her baby sister, but only to herself.

At the flea market, Hannah told her she could pick out one thing if it was under five dollars. But the only thing Grace wanted to do was push the stroller, taking great care that no one bumped into it. Callie showed her how to adjust the top to give the baby shade and how to push the seat back if the baby wanted to sleep. But the baby didn't want to sleep. The baby was having way too much fun laughing at the funny clicking noises Grace made with her tongue.

In her mind Grace made up a story that they were a real family, a mom, a grandma, a baby sister, and Timmy was just some kid who was visiting. She closed her eyes and tried to wish away her real family, but then felt bad and opened them quick.

When Grace turned the stroller down one aisle, she fell into step with Hannah, who held Timothy's hand tight. Grace wished Callie would grab her hand and hold it. She wished her dad wouldn't get that new job he kept talking about. They'd have to move, he said, and Grace didn't even care when he said maybe she could get her own room.

They walked up and down, aisle after aisle, passing displays of used car parts, beads and necklaces, baskets overflowing with socks, belts, old comic books. They came to a table where a man sold toy cars and trucks, and Timothy sprawled on the ground, feet splayed out amid rusty old hot wheels.

Callie knelt down beside him to help him choose. She pointed to the coins in his hand. "You can choose three," she said. Grace knew from experience it was going to take forever for him to choose only three.

Right next to the guy with the car stuff was a booth filled with jewelry, ribbons, beads and old stuff that Grace couldn't figure why anyone would want. She locked the brake on the stroller, (Callie had taught her how) and started poking through squares of yarn and the ugliest junk you could imagine, the kind of stuff Grandpa kept crammed in the kitchen drawers but never used. She picked up a round piece of cloth that had holes in it, and stuck her fingers through, trying to figure out what on earth anyone would want with it. She wished Callie would leave Timothy to his stupid cars, maybe come over and talk to her. But instead it was Hannah who came over, resting her hand on Grace's shoulder.

"That's a doily. People used to put them under things to keep the furniture clean."

"What kind of things?"

"Wet things, hot things that make marks in wood furniture. This keeps the wood protected."

Grace thought that was the stupidest thing she had ever heard. The doilies were ugly and they looked dirty too. Something dirty to keep something else clean. Who would want to buy them, she couldn't imagine.

"Look at these," Hannah went on, "you don't see these anymore." She was fingering a thick piece of cloth, just as ugly as the doily, "an old fashioned hot pad, haven't seen these in a while." Grace didn't want to sound stupid so she didn't bother to ask what a hot pad was for.

"Are you going to buy it?" she asked Hannah, but it was too late, Hannah had already moved on, drawn by something at the next booth over, tucked behind the table.

"And what kind of priceless garbage are you featuring today?" Grace turned to see who Hannah was talking to. It was that creepy man Pete who lived down the road, with that same red bandana he always wore around his frizzy old hair. His booth looked just like the front of his house, all wadded up with broken bottles, chunks of metal, stacks of magazines wrapped in rope. Grandpa and Dad liked to make jokes about him, how one of these days they wouldn't be able to find him buried under all his junk.

Hannah seemed to be friends with him. Sometimes when Grace and Timothy were playing outside, he'd come over to Hannah's house, and then she'd send him home with a plate of something to eat, both of them laughing while he carried it down the porch steps. Grace wished she could know what that jerky man said that was so funny.

Hannah picked up some really ugly thing that was on his table and moved it over to another place in his booth, in the back where you couldn't see it. The man didn't say a word, just watched her with his arms folded in front of him. Grace couldn't tell if he was mad or not, but then he said, "You break it you buy it!" and Hannah cracked up. What was so funny about that?

After a while, Pete came over to Grace, handed her a rusted old button. "How would you like this, young lady? Its real brass."

She didn't know what to say. What was she supposed to do with a stupid button? Then he handed Timothy some old rocks, and a dented toy car.

"Say thank you," Hannah said, and they both did. Grace wanted so badly to move on to the next booth.

"Why you're welcome," he said. He was leaning against the back of one of his display tables, looking a lot like one of the pieces of junk he was trying to sell.

"Can I get you anything ladies? Some lace curtains here might look nice in your bedroom." He was holding up a raggedy piece of cloth, more holes than thread.

"This is ripped," Grace pointed out and Hannah got a big laugh out of that.

"She's got better taste than you do," Hannah said and Grace hoped that wouldn't make the man angry.

"You just don't know quality when you see it." Pete answered, showing them a hand-written tag that verified the curtains were from the 1890's.

"Looks like it died and got resurrected," Hannah shot back, and this time Pete had to laugh. Grace loved that she was able to understand some of the jokes between them, even guessed at the word quality.

Grace picked up a tattered square of fabric and held it over her head.

"Looks like I got spiders in my hair!" she said, and now they were all laughing.

"Put that back Grace." Hannah shouted at her. "He's likely to charge you if you rip it."

"But it's already ripped." She loved being part of all this teasing.

"If you don't recognize quality," he winked at her, "you best find another place to shop." Maybe he wasn't such a jerk after all, even though her dad said he was.

Just then Pete turned away, drawn to a customer eyeing the glass bottle collection at the far end of his display table.

"Anyone getting hungry?" Callie asked, which was just what Grace was thinking, but Hannah was bending down at one of Pete's tables and didn't seem to hear the question. When she stood up she pulled something out of a box that had been hidden beneath one of the side tables. She held it up with both her hands, held it high up to the light, turning it back and forth, like there might be something hidden inside it.

"Where did you get this?" She was loud, almost shouting, but Pete was talking to other customers so she marched over and interrupted them.

"I said where did you get this?" She was yelling for sure, this was definitely not joking around.

"Now pipe down, Hannah, let's see what you've got

there. Do you think I remember where I get every piece of merchandise? I trade with lots of dealers, it could have come from anywhere."

Grace looked at the thing Hannah was holding up and knew exactly where it came from. Her dad made it. He made lots of things like that, they were all stacked in the back corner of Grandpa's tool shed, half-finished, some of them broken. She couldn't believe Hannah was interested in that old owl head.

"I know who made that" Grace chimed in.

"You do?"

"My dad. He makes those things all the time. We've got lots of them. I'll bet he'll make one for you if you ask him."

Hannah bent down so her eyes met Grace's full on. It was the longest time any one ever looked straight at her, that she could remember. The woman's stare was so hard it made Grace blink, and she felt like it feels right before crying starts, tight in her throat and hard to breathe.

But Hannah wasn't staring in a mad way. To Grace's relief, she felt the touch of the woman's hand, stroking Grace's head, then touching her forehead, so soft, and then wrapping her big arms around Grace's shoulders so she could smell Hannah's minty breath. Hannah held her for a long, long time, and it was easy to start crying then, even if she didn't even know what she was crying about.

Grace slept most of the way home. When she woke up, the ladies were in Callie's driveway, hugging each other. Grace rolled the back window down and tried to listen to what they were saying.

"Be well, take care of yourself," Callie said, but then she thought she heard Hannah say keep in touch. What did that mean? Where was she going? Why didn't people tell her things?

Grace was mad at herself for falling asleep like a baby and missing the part where they were saying goodbye. She wished she had gotten out of the car with them, so she'd know what they were talking about. If Callie were her real mother, she would have walked right out there with them, or if Hannah were her grandmother. But they were grownups, and she was just a kid. She hated being a make-believe daughter in a make-believe family.

The women kept talking, a long time it seemed, and now they were hugging again. Timothy was rolling his stupid car along the back of the front seat. Grace closed her eyes, slumped down in her seat and tried as hard as she could to disappear.

32.

THE KIDS SHOULD have been back by now, but when Robin drove up to Hannah's to pick them up, there wasn't a soul around. Had she said something about taking them out to dinner? He couldn't remember. He couldn't remember if he mailed in the boat company's employment application. He better have, because it wasn't on the kitchen table where he'd left it, wasn't in with the kids' stuff. He couldn't remember if he visited his father yesterday or the day before. No, it was yesterday, the little mint candies from the front desk still clean in his pocket.

He had lied to Grace this morning, telling her he was going to see her grandfather when he was rushing to get them over to Hannah's.

Truth is he spent six glorious hours fly-fishing over at Fordyce Lake. Best day he'd had for as far back as he could remember. Fuck it. He deserved it.

But where were they? Hannah must have taken them out to dinner. She'd been doing so much for them, he couldn't be mad if she was late. That new children's playhouse in Grass Valley, and then the Peach Festival. She had actually suggested taking them all the way to Roseville to see her other house but he wouldn't allow them to go that distance. The time she took them to Downieville without asking, drove them over the mountain pass for ice cream, he'd gotten pretty upset when he found out.

The mountain turns going out that way were treacherous. But she'd waved him away with a flick of her hand.

"We made it back, didn't we?" she scolded him, growing bolder by the week. "These kids need some getting out. They've been cooped up too long." He knew she was right.

Now he remembered. Hannah had mentioned they'd be going to the flea market again, this time with Callie. It seemed they were doing more and more things together. Grace couldn't stop talking about how much fun it was, getting to take care of the baby this, the baby that. He couldn't bear listening to Grace go on about how much she loved Callie.

"Could we spend the night at her house ever, please Daddy, she said it was up to you, please Daddy?" He put a quick stop to that.

Hannah had made a point of asking him if he'd mind if Callie and the baby joined her. Why did she think he would mind? Had Callie said something about their little fling? He was always aware of Hannah's eyes on him when he worked. Felt her questions digging into him like pinpricks, enough to make him wince a little but never bleed.

"I haven't seen Callie around here lately, have you? She never did get around to planting those iris bulbs." Like she was fishing for something. He just responded with an evasive grunt. Callie must have said something. Isn't that what women talked about?

It didn't help that his kids took to Callie like they did. Not that he blamed them. He was too short with Grace, impatient with her when she couldn't stop talking about how well the baby listened to her, even when Robin said he didn't want to hear about it any more. Much as he hated to admit the harsh truth of it, he knew it was a good thing for her to be around Callie. A girl needed a woman's touch. She was growing up faster than he could manage. A few more years she'd be inching her way toward womanhood and what good would he be to her then?

Robin crossed the road, looked up and back, no sign of any of them. He found himself at the foot of Callie's driveway, gathering up courage to knock on her door. They hadn't been alone since the night his father fell. They hadn't talked, other than the quick hellos and goodbyes that came with dropping the kids off at her house on days that Hannah had her own chores to take care of. The two of them had managed to reach a convenient understanding without actually saying a word, the situation with his father trumping any awkward unraveling of their relationship, if that was the word for it. It was as though his father bailed him out of yet another fuck-up.

Their conversations consisted of practical things. He'd say "Don't let Timmy forget his ninja doll," and he'd hold up the doll and give her a wink, as though they had always been a couple of friendly neighbors doing this childcare stuff together.

"What are you working on today?" she asked every once in a while, and he'd give her an update of Hannah's kitchen cabinets, or the deck disaster over in Porterville. Just like that, he was amazed to discover, like nothing had ever happened.

But this time she wasn't happy to see him. With her front door opened only halfway, she gestured with her finger that the baby was asleep, but made no effort to welcome him in.

"I'm sorry to bother you Callie, but I don't know where the kids are. Thought maybe you could tell me."

She gave him nothing, not a smile, not the slightest opening, holding the door firm in her hand to prevent him from pushing it forward.

"The kids are usually back by now. I wondered if you spent the day with them today, or had any idea where Hannah took them."

"Did you check over at your place?" she stared back at him. Of course. His place. He hadn't bothered to check over there. Hannah had the keys and often took the kids home late in the afternoon to watch TV or get their dinner started if he was running late. For some reason he had gone over to Callie's instead, like it was the next most obvious place to look for them. Maybe he did want to see her, be alone with her, after all.

"Callie, you've been so great with the kids these past few months, and I've been caught up with my father, and it doesn't seem right that we haven't talked."

"Talked?" She opened the door a crack more, but still no invitation to enter.

"We've got nothing to talk about, Robin. You've got your kids to take care of. And I've been busy getting ready for the move."

"Move?"

"We lost the house Robin." Her voice was flat. When did this happen? Was he supposed to have known about it? His mouth felt dry, his words scraped the back of his throat when he tried to push them out.

"Callie. I'm so sorry. I didn't know."

"I figured Hannah told you. Ralph's got a job over near Folsom. He says houses are going cheap there."

"Isn't that where your mom lives?" he was starting to remember some of the stories she had told him, surprised she'd be wanting to move closer to her mother. The door opened a crack more, he could see she was wearing her faded Grateful Dead shirt with the holes in it. He could hear her baby crying from somewhere in the back of the house.

"Callie, I'm sorry." He put his hand out to reach for her, safer now to touch her with their future already written away. But she pulled her hand back, out of his reach, muttering that she had to go.

"Callie, wait." He tried to push the door open, forced one step across the threshold, "Can't we at least talk?"

"I have to go, really, please." She closed the door, so quickly he didn't so much as get a last look at her face.

"I'm so sorry, Callie," he whispered to the closed door. He looked into the barren window box, nothing but dried leaves and a dirty baby rattle. He dug his fingers down and pulled out a thick wad of mud-encrusted cardboard, Ralph's business card that he'd stuffed down there that time he first knocked on her door. He unfolded the card, put it in his back pocket. He had no idea why.

Robin walked back up the road to his house, and sure enough, Callie was right. Hannah's car was parked in his driveway. Why on earth hadn't he checked there first?

"Anyone here?" he called out, but no answer came.

"Hello?" louder this time.

Robin walked around to the back of the house, noticed the door to the tool shed wide open, and surprised them all.

"What in God's name are you doing in there?"

Hannah was sitting on the ground, positively filthy, having unloaded boxes of carved birds that were stored inside. Some of them were broken, others unfinished, most of them nothing more than useless bits of scrap wood. She appeared to be fondling one bird in her lap, using the side of her sleeve to rub away the dust that had collected between the indents on the wings.

"Your daughter was showing off your amazing collection of carved birds. You never told me you were so talented."

"For God's sake Grace, you know you are not allowed in here without my permission. Sorry, Hannah, but this area is off limits."

"But she asked, Dad. She saw an old owl carving at the flea market and she really liked it. I wanted to show her the rest of them."

Hannah was staring at him that way she did the first

time she asked him about the owl head on her porch. Staring right through him.

"Grace, Timothy, go play inside. I want to talk to your dad about something."

"Hannah, really, get up out of there." He reached for her hand to bring her upright but she wouldn't take it. Pushed herself up on her own, slapping the dust off her hands. He reached over to rub away the cobwebs that had stuck to her old sweater, caught in her hair, but she stepped back, pushed his hand aside.

Here it comes. Robin always knew it was just a matter of time, the way she snooped around, thinking he didn't know why she was so interested in the damned bird carvings. Here it comes.

"My brother Ray started carving birds just like this when he was a kid. He came up with the idea of three lines above the eyes, kind of gave the owls a worried look. Our father used to tease him but Ray ignored it. Those three lines were his trademark, his signature. He told me he put them there to make the birds look meaner, like they could reach out with their talons and grab you. The more our father teased him about those lines, the deeper and thicker he'd carve them."

Robin said nothing. She went on, rubbing the sides where he had taken such care to count the rounds of feathers, matching it to the pictures, as Ray had shown him.

"These birds of yours have those exact same lines above the eyes. Now how ever did you learn how to do that?"

Robin seated himself on the dirt, his back to the shed, hands over the top of his head as though that might help him think up something to say. But nothing came.

"My brother taught you this, didn't he. Didn't he?" her voice growing louder by the word. "Robin, tell me. I have a right to know."

"I was a kid Hannah. I was just a little kid."

"Last time I saw my brother he was a wild buck who didn't have the sense to say goodbye to his family, just walked away from his sister and parents and never looked back. He's been as good as dead to me since I was about your age and these bird carvings are the first bit of his life I have been able to lay my hands on since I came into his piece of land, which by the way I didn't even know he had. He's been one big mystery for most of my life and these here birds look an awful lot like something he had a hand in making. Now I can sit here and guess that he taught you how to carve these birds. Or I can think that maybe these are his birds and you stole them all. But you can't tell me he didn't have something to do with them. And that you don't know what that something is."

She stood up then, brushed herself off, and handed Robin the owl's head that now shined from the cloth of her sleeve, looking more lifelike than he remembered. One of his best pieces. "Who made this?"

"I really don't remember."

"I DON'T BELIEVE YOU!" the shout taking her as much by surprise as it did him, since she immediately sank back down to her knees on the ground next to him, her hands over her mouth as though they might be able to stifle the horrid cry that fell from her lips.

Robin stood up then, and turned his back to her.

"It was a long time ago."

She waited. She waited some more. And then asked.

"How old were you?"

"It was when my mother was sick. I was twelve, thirteen, she was sick for a couple of years and I used to wander off to get out of Dad's way. That's how I met him, wandering down the road. He took me in, kind of, said I looked like I had nowhere to go."

"So did he live there a long time?"

"On and off. I can't tell you the exact years. Sometimes he'd be there for months at a time, then the place would be quiet again. By the time I was in high school I'd see his motorcycle from time to time but didn't want to go over any more."

Hannah motioned to him to sit back down next to her, right there in the dirt, and he did.

"I know that during the time my mother was dying, he was there a lot. That's the only time I'm sure about, because I would spend hours over there. He taught me how to whittle wood and it kept me busy, kept me out of the house. That's all I remember."

"You remember what he looked like don't you?"

"I was a kid. To me he looked huge. He had a beard that was always shaved neat, perfectly round under his chin, and a moustache that was just long enough he could twirl the edges with his fingers when he talked to me. His beard was a lot neater than the rest of him. I once asked him if he went to a barber to get his moustache so fancy and he said no, he said he did it himself. I remember being really impressed."

Robin fell silent for a minute, memories starting to rush in but he had to sort them quickly, some could be spoken and some best forgotten. He could feel her waiting for his next words. Her breath even, she didn't need to say a thing, begging him to continue.

"I don't know what it is that you want me to tell you."

"The truth. That's what I want. I want to know why you lied to me when I asked you about the owl head on my porch. I want to know why Pete hasn't said two words to me about my brother when he lived there all the time Ray was his neighbor. Ray is dead. You can't do him any harm by telling me the truth. You are the only link I have to him. Why are you hiding him from me?"

Robin looked down at the owl in his hand, tracing his fingers along the deep grooves carved above the eyes. Ray's work. Robin knew how to make the carvings look like birds, but Ray's carvings looked like they could fly away if you let them out of your hand. The eyes on this one seemed to follow you when you moved it from side to side. Ray tried to show Robin but it never came out as good. "Watch that knife," he'd warn him, "it's going to carve you if you're not careful." Robin remembered Ray guiding his hand, holding it so gently, always reminding him that it was better to go slowly and take longer. Once a cut was too deep it could not be undone.

Robin pictured Ray, like he was sitting right there on the dirt with them, that sweet musky smell that permeated his shirt, his breath. "Watch me," Ray would say, and he'd demonstrate the smallest curve of knife. Robin remembered the black tufts of hair on Ray's knuckles, the light filtering through his fingers, remembered the blackened edges of his fingernails that could never wash clean.

"I remember how he smelled," Robin finally offered. "Some kind of spicy cologne. My dad never wore that kind of stuff so it surprised me on a man. Especially one like him."

"What did it smell like?" she asked.

Like marijuana, Robin remembered, and a touch of bourbon mixed with those boxes of Red Hots he always carried in his pockets. Robin got to eat as many as he could stomach.

"Kind of like cinnamon. Its hard to describe."

"And he was good to you?"

"Very."

"How?"

And so he began telling her how Ray spent hours teaching him how to hold the different tools, how making indentations along the grain or against the grain brought out different qualities. Ray taught him that birds of prey, nesting birds, birds in flight, all had different expressions. He could carve each of them so you'd feel the difference. He told her how Ray had encouraged him to try new things, bringing him picture books of birds so he could study the different angles and textures of wings. He showed him the horizontal lines on the yellow warbler, the crescent ridges on the goldfinch's wing. And the heart-shaped face of the barn owl, the jagged edges of the sharp-shinned hawk, Robin memorized them all.

"And why would you keep this from me all this time?"

"What's past is past" came the weak response.

"I was sure he caused you harm, why else would you not tell me all this."

"It was a long time ago. I'm sorry. Sometimes people like to forget the past. I didn't really know how to talk about your brother, not knowing what you thought of him. I was just a kid."

"Did you know where he went after he left here?"

She was pushing again, but he wasn't about to tell her how Pete's big mouth finally got Ray busted, though Pete always swore he hadn't said a word to anyone about anything. In the end it would have been Ray who took the heat either way, since the stuff was all grown on his property.

And Pete was her neighbor now, even turning into friends, according to what the kids had been telling him, as impossible as that was to figure out. Maybe when it came to men and women, older folks were just as stupid as his generation.

"No I sure don't know where he went. Your brother kept to himself, came and went for months at a time. And like I keep telling you, I was just a kid."

"So are these birds yours or his?"

"I think maybe the one you just handed me is his. See the eyes? I knew how to make them look like bird carvings. Ray made them look like birds."

Robin leaned down and rooted around in the box, it had been ages since he looked at them. He held up a stellar jay, one of the wings broken off.

"This one's mine. I preferred the smaller birds, the jays and woodpeckers. Your brother liked the birds of prey. I keep meaning to get back to it but you know how that goes. There may be more of Ray's birds on your property, unless Pete got them all. For sure the one on your porch railing is his."

She got quiet then, stood up, brushing the dust and cobwebs from her pants, and he got up too, shut the shed door, as if that might finally shut down this conversation. Whatever else he knew about Ray wouldn't do her a bit of good. He had said enough.

And now Robin became aware that the kids had been alone in the house for some time, probably needing attention. Hannah followed behind him, clutching the bird, Ray's bird, then paused by the gate. Her hands were shaking and he reached out and touched them.

"I was just a dumb kid with a dying mom. Your brother was some guy who came in and out on a motorcycle and for a while when my life was hard, he gave me something to hold on to. Maybe I should have told you back when we first met, but it was all so long ago. I'm sorry."

"Well I'm glad you finally opened your mouth. And its time I shut mine. I think I'll go home now and try to shine this thing up a bit, maybe varnish it."

"Linseed oil does the best job. Doesn't discolor or streak. I'll get you a bottle and leave it on your deck."

"While you're at it, bring some of your other birds over. It'll give me something to do. You really need to take better care of the things you make. They're valuable."

"Daddy what's for dinner?" came the shouts, just in time. Like he expected, the kids were way past hungry.

"Can she stay for dinner?" Timothy asked.

"Go on ahead" Hannah waved, "maybe next time." Robin leaned down and picked them both up at once, something he hadn't done in a very long time, and ran them up the porch steps, leaving Hannah to head back across the road.

"What's for dinner?" Timmy repeated, as Robin bounced them both on the sofa, somersaulting over the both of them, burying them in tickles and chortles and threats of pickle soup.

He heard the gate latch. He should have insisted she stay for dinner, with all she'd been doing helping with the kids. Robin tried to wrestle Timothy off but the boy was sitting square on his dad's stomach and Grace had his feet locked down, getting ready for a tickle torture fest.

Maybe next time, he thought, yeah, next time.

33

CALLIE WAS LATE. At least five weeks, maybe more. It was hard to keep track with the nursing throwing everything off, but her last period had been a while back, she couldn't even remember exactly.

She looked at her calendar, started counting back, July 18, July 11, July 4, June 27, that was Ralph's birthday. Screw the condoms, he had said, tossing the package across the blankets, but its ok, she told herself, nursing is supposed to provide natural birth control. That would have been four weeks ago. For sure she didn't have her period that night. So when was her last period? Early May, she figured, so she probably missed June, or did she have a period in June? Shit, she couldn't remember.

The last time with Robin was back in April. Or did they get together again in May? That's the one thing she absolutely had to remember, but everything that had happened between her and Robin had become one big blur. When he dropped off his kids, he never even stopped long enough to make eye contact, like nothing had ever happened between them, like he was just the guy up the road that needed some childcare help. And she was more than happy to oblige.

Tiptoeing past the sleeping Daphne, and Ralph who had crashed out on the sofa, TV remote still in hand, (she would wake him up later and carefully guide him into bed)

Callie sat down on the rocking chair, glad to be alone with her thoughts. She felt a small cramp pass, a period cramp for sure, it had to be. Wasn't nursing supposed to provide natural birth control? Ralph hated using condoms, he said it cramped his style. "Let's see what God has in store for us this time" he loved to say right at the last second, like he was doing her some kind of holy favor.

No, if she was only two months late it had to be Ralph's. And anyway Robin always used condoms. Except for that one time the unopened packet somehow caught on a nail or something, the whole thing ruined. It hadn't stopped them, they went ahead and did it anyway. It was just that one time, but still. When was that?

Callie tried to imagine having another baby. Maybe it wasn't such a terrible idea. One kid, two kids, it was all the same. She could handle it. She was a good enough mother, wasn't she?

Maybe missing a period was nothing but a sign of stress. She certainly had her fair share of it lately. Just thinking about moving closer to her mother made her insides clench. That would stop anybody's blood from flowing.

For the first time in maybe the whole time she and Ralph had moved to this stupid house, she was starting to grow fond of the place, and she knew exactly why: Hannah. Callie had already concluded that Hannah must really have disliked her after their first meeting, since she never returned any of her messages, when there came a surprise knock on her door.

"It's me again, remember? Your neighbor who was supposed to hire you but didn't ever get around to it?"

Funny kind of greeting but it immediately reminded Callie why she had liked the woman so much that first time they'd met. Not too many older people made her laugh out loud. The woman made being old seem like it could be fun.

As it turned out, Hannah was going to be spending the whole summer across the way, in that filthy run down shack of hers, helping Robin take care of his kids while he worked on her place. And would Callie like to join them from time to time on outings, seeing as how his children seemed to really enjoy being with her.

It wasn't easy for Callie to take in this weird development. At first she felt a burst of anger. Wasn't she taking good enough care of Robin's kids? At first when Robin asked for her help, she took it as an invitation to maybe, well, get started again. Even though Callie had already decided that wasn't going to happen. But still, what if he might be interested?

He wasn't interested in anything other than dropping the kids off, racing off to see his father. He barely talked to her, just rushed through his perfunctory 'thank you's,' and off he went, like she was some kind of hired help.

She'd started resenting Robin, wondering why on earth she kept helping him out with his kids. Its not like she owed him anything. Truth was she loved having Grace and Timothy over. The baby loved them, and they were starting to grow on her too, make her feel more like a mother.

Now that Hannah had stepped in to take over child-care duties, Callie could rid herself of her resentment. It would be fun to join Hannah and the kids on outings, get her the hell out of the house more. Callie could say for the first time since Daphne was born that she was starting to have something to look forward to on that old stretch of funky road.

And then just a couple of weeks after she and Hannah started going on those 'adventures' as Hannah liked to call them, Ralph dropped the bomb on her: their house got foreclosed by the bank.

"For how long?" she screamed at him, while he tried to explain that the bank was screwing them. "For how long have you stopped making the mortgage payments?" she had to ask again, more specific this time because he refused to give her a straight answer. Just kept turning the whole disaster around, making it sound like it was everybody else's fault—the mortgage broker's—the Realtor's—the fucking government's fault that he stopped making payments after his ridiculously low adjustable mortgage exploded into double digits, like some kind of crazy magic trick gone bad.

Callie felt a cramp in her side. Maybe its coming, maybe that's my period, she thought, sitting down at the edge of the sofa, leaning into the pain, hoping it would get worse. Please, please, be my period, she talked to the cramp like it was somebody that could solve all her problems at once. She waited for the cramping to pass, went to the bathroom to check but no. No blood. Please, she whispered, please don't let this be Robin's.

She had been rude to him when he came by earlier this evening, asking about where the kids and Hannah were. How the hell was she supposed to know? Try your own house, she had said, practically closing the door on him. She could hear him on the other side of her door, he hadn't left right away but stood on the porch for what felt like a long time. Why did he have to do that? What was he waiting for?

She stood on her side of the door, frozen, afraid he might hear her. He was fiddling with the flower box, she heard him pick up Daphne's rattle and put it back down again. She listened hard until she heard his footsteps moving back down her porch step, until she heard him close her gate, until she was absolutely sure he had gone.

Maybe Ralph's new plan was for the best. Maybe it was time she made peace with her mom. That's what Ralph kept trying to convince her, as though losing the house was part of some grand plan to reunite the two of them. When she argued, he just insisted they were moving to where the jobs are, like he was some kind of financial wizard instead of the guy who fucked up big time.

"Sure, Ralph, I'd love to move closer to Mom, that sounds like a swell plan," Callie had answered him with that phony sappy voice she knew he hated. He either didn't hear or pretended not to, walking into the farthest part of the house he could find, which wasn't nearly far enough.

But now Callie moved over to the sofa where Ralph was sleeping, gentle as a baby. She leaned over, took in a sweet breath of that cologne of his. When she first met him it drove her crazy and it still did. She leaned over and kissed his ear at the very tip, in that place where a little fuzz of hair grew, soft like the tip top of Daphne's head. She loved to tickle it back and forth with her pinkie, a little trick she learned a long time ago that always got him going.

Maybe this move wasn't going to be such a bad idea after all. Ralph didn't object when she brought up the subject of looking for a part time job. There were day care centers in town (she had looked this up). She also found out about a bunch of garden supply stores and nurseries around Folsom, even made a few phone calls. One of the big chain nurseries was hiring, as long as you had some prior experience. She had lots of experience with plants, even though she just guessed at most of the plant names, but she wouldn't tell them that. Hadn't she improved that weed field across the road? Delphinium and iris and callibrachoa and phlox were blooming like crazy and she wasn't even sure if they liked sun or shade.

"You can do whatever you want honey," Ralph had assured her. This foreclosure business had humbled him a bit, and he didn't want to give her more cause for upset than he already had. He was actually the one who gave her the list of nurseries in the area.

"It would be good for you to take some time away from Daphne," he had suggested, sneaking up from behind her while she was washing some dishes, "take some time for yourself." He planted the lightest of kisses on her ear, as though his words weren't sweet enough by themselves. She turned toward him and for the first time since this foreclosure news, it felt like they were going to get through this mess.

And hadn't she racked up her own pile of mistakes? Wasn't this the 'for better or for worse' part they had promised each other? Callie put her hand on her belly, hoping suddenly, excited even, about what might be growing inside her.

34.

WHAT WAS THAT CHILL moving across his cheeks? Maybe an open window? He had always been so careful to lock all the windows. And now a slice of sun crossed the blanket, carrying with it a flash of hot air that momentarily warmed his eyes. Or was that a stray bit of leftover light from the dream. The same dream as always. Just him and Vera, digging up the bulbs out back, him cautioning her not to smash them, she kneeling on the ground, waiting for him to find the long trowel. "I don't have all day," she yelled after him, while he rooted around in the dirt, searching for something buried beneath that he really needed to find. What was it? He couldn't remember in the dream and he couldn't remember now, fully awake, the sun pouring in from the window that was definitely left open, someone must have opened it for him. He was sure he had closed it.

Where was he?

Winston noticed the shifting threads of cold and warm crossing his face, then moving over his feet. Even through the blankets he could feel the air move, a slow heavy movement making him think late summer, August, yes, he was sure of it, the way the air, though still comfortable, carried with it a foreboding of stifling heat about to descend.

August. Good. Now he felt better. Except for the

cracks in his feet. A frayed blanket rubbed thin from over-use had gathered up tight around his toes and he wanted to reach down to pull it away but where to start? His feet felt itchy and cold where holes had frayed into the fabric. This blanket was of no use to him, but he was helpless against its weight.

He rubbed his hands together, felt their thickness where the skin had hardened. Between the thumb and forefinger new fissures and crevices had formed, leaving light bloody trails along the bed covers. And at the wrist, the skin's surface all but worn away, veins zigzagged up and around the arm, settling in just below the lizard-like skin of his elbow. Is that me, he wondered?

Winston struggled and finally succeeded in reaching down below the covers, managing to unhook the rip of satin edge that had caught around his big toe, and then began his slow ascent to an upright position, though all those annoying pillows made it impossible to navigate. He wanted so badly to stand up and walk right out of there. But at least now he had freed himself from that horrible scratchy fabric. He squeezed his toes out and splayed them wide, wiggling them eagerly back to life, aware and grateful for this small bit of control. His lips formed an audible 'ahhh' because this new awareness of blood pumping through his legs reminded him in no small way that he was still alive. Rejoicing in that awareness, he swung both feet around to meet the harsh floor. His old familiar furry slippers, (how wonderful that someone had laid them on the side of his bed so he didn't even have to reach for them) caressed the soles of his feet. He winced and tried to stand.

Something felt wrong. His big toe pushed against an impenetrable shape, something lodged inside the left slipper, a knot of some kind, maybe a pebble and he sat back down, discouraged, one slipper on, the other in his hand. Inside the slipper's seams, sure enough, there it was, a small rock had lodged itself deep inside the furry folds.

"Get out of there" he barked at the thing, shaking the slipper hard, and then did the same with its mate, in case the two were in cahoots.

The pebble, once removed, was itself quite perfect. Smooth and round, opalescent when held up to the window, he rolled it around in both of his hands, held it to his cheek and even licked it, as though the taste of it might inform him of its identity. There was a time he would have gone to great trouble to look up its mineral components, but it was enough now to appreciate its flawless nature. What forces, he wondered, led to this pebble's perfect roundness?

Suddenly Winston became aware of a distant hum, maybe a refrigerator, or some kind of engine running on the other side of the wall. He looked around the room and recognized nothing. When he attempted to take in deep breaths, he felt a stinging sensation inside of his nostrils. This wasn't home, that much he was sure of.

But he felt safe here, somehow, certain there was nothing to fear. Safe and cold. Cold under the weight of his own stillness.

"Where is everybody?" he yelled, but no one answered. The shrill of his voice must have disturbed the wrens who were now fluttering haphazardly about the ground outside his window. Now a distant, unfamiliar dog bark echoed off in the distance. Sounds of doors opening and closing but not his.

The pebble had grown warm in his hand. He thought to store it in his pocket, a kind of rosary, but he had no pocket, or set it on the sill, but the sill was beyond his reach. Frustrated, Winston tossed the pebble across the room, watched it bounce then roll and finally land behind the door in the far corner of the room, what would be its final resting place.

He lay his head back down on the pillow. What else was there to do? He closed his eyes.

"Someone has visitors!" he heard a voice say, that same cheery voice that brought his food trays to him, a voice he could not silence, as hard as he tried.

And then the little girl, sweet thing, he couldn't recall her name just now and anyway, she was crying, standing at the side of his bed. He didn't dare reach out to take her hand, as badly as he wanted to.

"Don't cry," he said and then he heard his son yelling at the little boy, "leave those window blinds alone!"

"Go away," Winston wanted to say to all of them and then the girl started crying harder. "Shhh," he said to her but his words seemed to be locked inside so she could not hear him. Still, her crying seemed to stop. He was glad of that.

Vera should be back soon, probably still on her morning walk. She said the man across the road was giving her something to help her nausea. She seemed to enjoy those little outings, every few days, whenever her energy returned, in between doctor visits, she'd say, "stay home, Winston, you don't need to come with me. I best go alone."

And when she returned from her visits with the man across the road, she seemed different. He couldn't say how. Quieter. She told him that the man gave her something to help her feel better and sure enough, Winston would fix her a bowl of soup and she'd swallow it all up, finish the crackers, even ask for seconds.

"Vera?" he yelled and then remembered, no, she's not here. Shouldn't she be back by now?

"Mr. Till, are you feeling comfortable?" That woman was rearranging his pillows again. She carried with her an infusion of that bleachy perfume designed to kill sickness but the smell just made him feel sicker.

"You're lucky to have such nice visitors."

"Go away!" he said in a voice he barely recognized as his own. When was he ever rude like that? Once, when Vera stayed out until dark on one of her walks down the road he had paced around frantic, not knowing where to look. In truth, he did know where to look, but he was afraid of what he'd find—only now can he say this to himself, and even so, only in a whisper. He'd worried himself sick but she came back, sure enough, her face pinker than usual, smelling funny, too happy, if that was possible, and then kissed him on the forehead, which she didn't do very often.

"Where were you?" he had yelled, but how dare he yell at this poor woman, his dying wife, who despite being in the throes of death, seemed unreasonably cheerful in that late hour.

"I'm feeling so much better today, dear," she had said. "Just took a longer walk than usual."

It was that man up the road with the motorcycle. He suspected his son spent time over there too. There was something going on over there that drew them both. Something Winston didn't want to know about, but knew about just the same.

"Vera?" he said aloud, but not so loud this time that it might attract the nurse's attention. He knew Vera would never spend time in such a cold unfamiliar room as this. She would rather die. But why was it that he could hear her voice so clearly.

"It's me, Dad. I brought Grace and Timothy to visit you. They've been asking about you, Dad."

"Shhh, dear." Vera's voice again. "He just wants to say goodbye."

"Veeera," he called out again, the sound of her voice lulling him back to that old dream, digging up bulbs again, digging for something buried down in the dirt, something important he was sure of it, something he was just holding in his hand just a moment ago, that now was gone.

332

35.

PETE HATED TO ADMIT to himself how much he had enjoyed that lively afternoon with Hannah on Ray's porch. He had hardly expected her to take him up on his invitation to visit him at the flea market, but there she was the very next Saturday, as if on cue, sniffing around his display tables, just as a couple of teenagers had knocked over a china plate.

Hot summer weekends drew the largest crowds, people sniffing around for bargains, curious summertime tourists and bored locals alike, enjoying the flea market because it was free entertainment. Lots of dirty little hands picking away at his treasures. His 'You Break It You Buy It' sign led to one of the only sales he had so far that weekend. A couple of boys knocked over a ceramic plate (real Spode) reaching for a Ray Orbison LP that was leaning up next to it. The LP's were all pretty much useless, warped and cracked and sometimes missing from their album jackets altogether, but the photo covers managed to hold their value. Kids these days didn't have album jackets to hold and flip over and study, didn't even know what the singers looked like half the time.

The plate they broke was priced at $15, a steal, and he managed to wrestle $12.27 out of them, all the change they had between them. Other than that, there hadn't been a single sale so far that day. People weren't falling for frayed lace curtains from the 1860's anymore. They could care less about Buffalo Heads. Maybe they'd already seen it all, or maybe they didn't have a nickel to spare. With the land next door all but tapped out of treasures, and not really his anymore for the taking, Pete hated to think how else he could make a living if this flea market business didn't start to pick up.

He couldn't forget Hannah's first comment when she approached his booth that first time.

"Not too smart putting records next to something fragile. People like to rifle through record albums. If you keep all the albums together in one place, stacked upright, they're much more likely to sell."

He should have stopped her right there. What did she know about the junk business? It was the element of surprise that caused people to buy his stuff. The magic of picking up an old pillow cover and discovering an antique wooden train car underneath, that's what made people reach for their wallets. "Honey, look" they'd call out, thrilled at finding some long lost treasure. This wasn't Montgomery Ward, with all the shirts stacked by size and color on one floor, toy department somewhere else altogether.

He should have stopped her but for some reason, he gave the woman room, fascinated by the sight of her muttering away at his display tables, picking things up, moving them around, even chatting up perspective buyers.

After the teenagers had paid up, a young couple strolled by, eyeing a lace tablecloth. Hannah had them pegged correctly as newlyweds.

"My grandmother had a tablecloth just like that" she offered the young couple. "It's practically impossible to find that weave anymore. That's hand-made for sure. You can pass this on to your children." The wife hung wide-eyed on Hannah's every word. She kept looking over at her husband who was digging around in Pete's collection of drill bits. "Can we honey?" she asked, squeezing his arm close and he said sure, didn't even ask the price.

After the couple moved on, Pete had asked Hannah if her grandmother really did have a tablecloth like that. "Wouldn't you like to know?" she answered, then turned back to fussing with something or other on a different display table.

Sure enough she returned the following weekend, this time bringing with her an old plastic milk crate, perfect size, it turned out, to store his record collection, everything from Beethoven to Zeppelin. That might have been the same week she brought a clothes drying rack, looked like something she'd picked up at another flea market booth, and took it upon herself without so much as asking, to hang up the leather jackets, the moth-eaten sweaters and old painters pants that were scattered in heaps all around his tables.

"See, people know what you have now," she said leaning against his newly created record department, like she knew the business better than he did.

It turned out she was right about the records. Not too long after she set all the LP's upright in the milk crate, he sold a couple of Elvis Costello's, mint condition, for $10 apiece, and then an unopened Mario Lanza with the plastic cover still intact. The guy handed him a $20, walked away before Pete could hand him any change.

Why she found his claptrap collection worthy of such interest he couldn't say, but there was no doubt that her presence brought him business. Maybe the place could use a lady's touch, though thinking of her as a lady was a bit of a stretch.

And then one Saturday she showed up with a bunch of kids in tow, Winston's grandkids and that baby from across the road. Sniffing around like a bloodhound, she really had grown comfortable in his booth, acting like the place was hers. That's how she discovered one of Ray's carved birds, tucked away in a box underneath one of his fold-out tables, probably the last carving left from that batch he'd found under Ray's porch. Pete had forgotten all about it being there and for a few seconds, when she held the carved owl head up, he wondered if all hell was about to break lose.

But then Robin's little girl piped up that it was her dad's bird. And maybe it was, with all that carving those two did together, it was impossible to know which one of them did what.

So the next week when she came knocking at his house, holding some other owl head in her hand, he wasn't sure whether to offer her something to drink, or make a run for it.

"Do you remember that owl head I found at your

booth?"

How could he forget?

"What about it?" he said, as nonchalantly as he could muster.

"There's a whole lot more where they came from. Seems like my brother carved them. But I don't suppose you know anything about that."

Pete knew enough to say nothing. Let her go on, which mercifully, she did.

"So I've got a proposition for you. I've been shining them up, Robin showed me how, and I think they'd bring a good price. I haven't seen anything like them anywhere, no one around here has them, you'd be the only one. Word gets around you'd be known as the guy with the owl heads. Believe me, I know what I'm talking about."

Pete tried not to look surprised at what was the last thing he expected to be hearing. A good price sounded pretty appealing, along with relief that she didn't seem as interested in Ray as she was in his carvings.

Ray and those damned birds. Pete was sure he'd gotten them all off the property. The one she found in the box had to be the last of the lot, as far as he knew. The police had busted the place open, cleaned out every bit of evidence they could find to put Ray away, even took the carving knives and whittling tools, even though they had nothing to do with his farming enterprise. Pete remembered going back after all the dust settled, the last cop gone for good. He thought for sure he had removed all the bird carvings that were scattered under the deck. Pete was glad the police hadn't bothered with them, figuring they'd bring in a decent amount of change. But that was years ago. He really thought he had sold them all.

"Where did you find the one you've got there?" he asked her, since it did seem to be his turn to say something. Not sure he wanted to know the answer.

"Turns out Robin had quite a few bird carvings of his own, and some he told me my brother had made and given to him. I've been cleaning them up, putting some shine on the wood. I know a couple of stores in the town I live in that might like to carry them.

Of course. Robin. Winston's boy had spent a fair amount of time hanging out with Ray, not so much when Pete was around, but he'd hear the two of them talking in the afternoons, laughter coming through the manzanita hedge, along with the sweet smell of pot. He was corrupting the boy, that was for sure, but it wasn't any of Pete's business, then or now.

Pete kept his distance whenever the boy came around.

The last thing Pete wanted to do was be seen on Ray's land. The men had worked out a very tight business agreement: Ray did the growing and Pete moved the stuff. When anyone came to visit, Pete made himself scarce. The two men acted like they didn't know each other, like a lot of neighbors around those parts. As long as no one could link them, one of them had a chance if the other got caught. That was the plan and it had worked to the letter.

Pete had been over in Lake County at a coin convention the day Ray was busted. It took a few days for the police to come by and question him but he was a genius at acting dumb. He fooled himself half the time. The more Pete thought about it, he actually saved Ray, keeping up his end of the bargain. During the year and a half that Ray was locked up, Pete continued to wire money into an account Ray opened for just that contingency, until the last of the stuff was moved. Come to think of it, it was Pete's generosity that helped Ray pay his defense lawyer. That Harley, the one he crashed, most likely part Pete's money too. Hell, those monthly bank deposits most likely saved the land from going into foreclosure. No, Pete had nothing to be ashamed of.

"So what's your proposition?"

She turned away and started to head back through the hedges to her place. "I'll tell you over dinner," was all she said. Damned if he knew what to make of that woman.

When he arrived, the door stood wide open, and Hannah was fussing over the stove. The smell of onions frying made him crazy with hunger. A thick-crusted bread lay sliced open on a plate with a couple of jars of jam nearby.

"Don't be shy, come on in" she called out. It appeared as though she had attempted to groom herself, the thick clump that was her hair tied up in back, some kind of leather gismo that looked more like a harness than something pretty, but the hair pulled back off her face changed something. He hadn't noticed her cheeks before, the squareness of them, dead on like her brother's, barely more feminine. And now a clump of hair fell loose over her ear. She spread her fingers in a slow, generous scratch from forehead on through to nape of neck, trying to tame it, but instead causing a few more strands to unravel. And now some white flakes dislodged from her scalp into the grooves of her sweater. They lay sprinkled like sugar across the back of her collar and it was all he could do to stop himself from reaching over to brush them aside.

"What are you drinking?"

"What have you got?"

She didn't look back, still at the stove stirring the on-ions, leaning over slightly so he could see where her socks ended and a thin white slip of skin poked through below her pant leg. Hairless.

"Just some old brandy, mixed with tea if you prefer it that way. And now she turned to face him, a smile stuck to her face and she didn't bother to wipe it off.

"Sure." There seemed to be no getting around the tea part. "I'll have some of your famous spiked tea."

He watched as she tipped the brandy bottle gener-ously into the teacup, like she knew exactly how much he wanted. After a decent amount had been poured, she wiped a bead of sweat from her forehead, and he was relieved to see that the skin under her arms hadn't as yet begun to flap over itself like most of the women who sat near him at The Nugget, or who spilled themselves over his display tables, reaching for God knows what.

This one didn't seem like the type who ever spent time

prettying herself, but underneath all those rough patches, Pete was coming to recognize the remains of what must have been a fine looking woman, back in her day. Some kind of smell came off her skin, he was getting a hint of it now, breaking through the cooking onions. He brushed off his shoulder, needing to find something useful to do with his hands. What was he doing there anyway?

Oh yes, her business proposition.

Pete could feel a new spring in his step as he walked into George Lundale's office. Having just dropped off some owl heads at the post office, (she had in fact received a couple of orders from a store over in Marysville) he'd decided to stop in for an impromptu visit, "just to catch up," he told Lundale. But really, now that he knew he wasn't going to lose his precious gully, he couldn't wait to rub it in: there would be no sale on Blind Shady any time soon, at least not at Ray's place.

Pete strolled to the back of the realty office, past George's desk as though he weren't sitting right there, and helped himself to an ice cold Fanta out of the cooler.

"Any news about that parcel on Blind Shady?" he asked.

"Help yourself," Lundale answered, turning his back to Pete and picking up the phone, though Pete was certain he didn't have anyone to call.

"Here," Pete set the can in front of Lundale, "have one of yours." It was clear by now that no one was on the other end of Lundale's telephone on this humid August afternoon. Nor was anyone waiting in the fly-infested office looking to buy property anywhere near San Juan Ridge.

George took a long slow swig of soda, put the can down hard on his desk so a drop of soda spilled out. He wiped it away with the edge of his sleeve. "If you have something to tell me, spit it out."

Pete took his time, the stage being his, and pulled out one of the grey metal folding chairs that passed for décor in George's office. Sat himself right down in front of George's desk, cleared his throat, a dramatic gesture, that didn't have the desired effect. "Since you asked, it would seem like the woman who inherited Blackwell's property has invited me to join her in a business deal."

"And exactly why would she have done that?" Lundale's Fanta already chugged down, he crushed the aluminum can in his hand and tossed it across the room. It landed square in the wastebasket.

"My charm I suppose."

"Don't forget talents," Lundale added, then got up to use the bathroom, slamming the door shut behind him, the clearest goodbye he could think of.

But that put him right where Pete wanted him. No escaping now. Pete positioned himself just outside the bathroom door, he could hear the sound of Lundale pissing and spoke over the noise. "Nope, no sale on Blind Shady any time soon, looks like she and I will be needing every square inch of both our properties for our new little business venture."

"What's that you said?" Pete asked, after Lundale let out a particularly loud expulsion of gas, probably on purpose. But rather than sending Pete away, the noise revved him up all the more, sending him off into exquisite exposition about Lundale's lost chances for a sale.

George finally exited the bathroom, resigned to hearing Pete relay the practically instant success of this new owl head business. He got to hear how Hannah had convinced Robin to start carving again, and Pete was moving those birds at the flea market faster than Robin could bring him new ones. Blind Shady Birds, she called the business, and her marketing skills were yet another surprise in the woman's seemingly endless storehouse of surprises. George even got to hear the detailed account of how Hannah got Pete to clean out his garage to store the inventory, and then he was treated to the tale of how Pete and Hannah together had found an old desk at one of his competitor's booths, which they turned into a more-or-less adequate office to handle the shipping and tracking of orders. So no, George was made to understand, there wouldn't be any For Sale signs going up on Blackwell's place any time soon.

Pete was on his feet, having tired himself out from his own long-winded story. But it was a good story, even George had to admit it. Besides, he had long ago given up on selling that parcel. He didn't need to. A meditation retreat center had recently shown some interest in Winston's property that would be coming up on the market soon enough, along with the foreclosure the next parcel over. So no, he wasn't anything but amused by this new development. Ralph's foreclosure was one of many that were happening as fast as he could open the files. Even with the small commission they afforded, George was looking at a brisk year of sales ahead.

"Well, good for you," he finally granted Pete, tapping him lightly on the back, a bit patronizing Pete thought, but the thrill of talking about his new found success had worn itself flat in the laziness of this hot afternoon. Pete didn't need to play one-ups with George or anyone else for that matter. Not anymore. Pete was a changed man. Having the likes of Hannah Blackwell in his life wasn't something he needed to share with anybody. It was good enough to keep this unlikely treasure all to himself.

36.

TIMMY'S GIANT STONE SNAKE starts at the gully, then meanders around and through the madrones, ending up alongside the front porch. What began as a jagged line of rocks has somehow grown to resemble an impressive garter snake. Grace looked it up in the snake book I bought her, and confirmed it was the longest snake ever found in this area. Timmy discovered the snake's 'head,' just another dull grey piece of granite at first glance. But on careful inspection, he noticed it had two smudges of black on its rounded top edge, making it appear to have a pair of frightening eyes that seemed to squint up at us. When the moon shone above it, even I had to gasp at its fierce expression.

And then yesterday morning when I was searching for the level I'd left outside, a jagged-edged stone appeared out of nowhere, square in front of the tip of my boot, like it had been looking for me. It was definitely not serpentine, more of an orange cast to it. I hadn't seen its like around here before. My first thought was that this shape might form a perfect tongue for our snake. Finding it seemed like an omen, but everything seems like an omen to me these days and I don't take any of it too seriously.

But this morning, I took the jagged stone up to set it at the front of the sculpture, only to find that the entire head of the snake had been kicked loose. Probably some animal roaming around at night. The children have made a home for themselves in my dirt-filled paradise. What's going to happen to these magnificent rock sculptures after they move away? Who's going to make sure the snake's head stays in place?

We've spent so many hours together shaping this landscape. It was a joyful thing for me to teach them things I know, like how to identify sandstone, how it can be used as chalk, how to recognize serpentine, with its turquoise stripes. Sometimes, in the evening, long after Robin picked the children up, I would retrace their steps, finding telltale signs of whatever stories they scratched into the dirt earlier in the day. Stick figures, broken dinosaur bodies decapitated in the sun, handprints decorated with pebbles, scattered everywhere.

This morning I was around back when Robin dropped them off. "Who's there?" I called out, as if I didn't know, and saw them scoot down from the back seat of their truck, then scatter like squirrels, attempting to hide and surprise all at once.

"Who's there?" I yelled out again, pretending to search, turning my head every which way but toward them.

"Bet you can't find us," came Grace's voice but Timothy unraveled the mystery of their whereabouts by running breathlessly toward me, unable to contain his excitement about the thing he held in his hands.

"What do you have there Timmy?"

"Look, its got blue in it," he said, and so it did. Timothy always managed to notice the remarkable in even the dullest of things. The species of salamander that he had brought me this time featured an exquisite turquoise line down the middle of its underbelly. But before I could point out what might have also have been a glint of pink behind its ears, the slimy thing slid away, Timothy's hold too soft to contain it. Together we watched the salamander trace a dusty line along the dirt and disappear, somewhere underneath the deck.

Earlier in the summer Timothy had captured a salamander completely on his own for the first time. It had been sunning itself on the back porch step, and he made a quick solid pick, grabbed before the critter was aware of the grab. He'd stuffed the thing into his pocket, a present for his dad. But later on, when Robin arrived to collect them, the salamander was gone. Timothy couldn't stop crying and I had no resources to console him.

But this time it was Timmy consoling me. "Don't worry, Hannah," he said, sounding so grown up I barely recognized that little boy I had scared in the bushes so many months ago. "It's going away to find a new home. Just like we're going to do."

Much as I'm dreading their leaving, from what he describes, Robin's new job seems like a good situation. School starts September 7 and Robin got them enrolled in a school just three blocks from the boat company. The rental house he found even has a workshop out back, a space where he can keep carving his birds. It's become a real family enterprise. Robin has taught Grace how to use the linseed oil, very carefully, so as not to spill any or breathe in too closely. She has risen to the seriousness of the task and seems more like a young woman these days than the little girl I met just a few short months ago. And then Grace herself came up with the idea of having Timmy cut out squares of paper to make price tags. He's practicing writing his numbers and has taken to the job with great pride.

Robin's dealings over here will continue for some time, particularly cleaning up his father's house and finishing off the odds and ends of his estate, what there is of it. The dear old man finally passed away, peacefully in his sleep, Robin reported, sounding more relieved than anything else. And then there will be more birds to drop off, hopefully well into the future. So we're not going to have too big a goodbye. For the time being at least.

I took it for a sign that Robin's luck is on the upswing when some Buddhist outfit came along and swooped up his father's place before he even put it on the market. Along with Ralph's place next door it makes up a parcel of almost eight perfectly flat acres backing onto Bureau of Land Management acreage. Apparently the Buddhists are intending to open some kind of retreat offering workshops, yoga classes, meditation classes, what have you. This news all came from Pete, who is appreciating me more and more these days. I guess compared to a bunch of monks in orange jumpsuits, I'm looking like a pretty good neighbor.

I like to think I've played a part in this turn in Robin's

fortunes. From the moment I figured out the connection between Robin and those birds and my brother Ray I've had a bee in my bonnet. I started going over to Robin's in the evenings, helping him put the kids to sleep. I'd stay for a while, sit and watch him, intent and quiet, just watching him hold pieces of madrone and magnolia and cedar up to the light, like he expected to make them fly.

I watched him slowly move his hands along the rough edges, sanding down a wing, digging out the beginning shape of a feather. I saw a seriousness about the boy I had not seen before. Without my asking, he offered to coach me on some tricks he had learned from my brother, like rubbing the wood counter-clockwise against the grain to form deeper textures. He even trusted me with a knife, let me add Ray's signature three lines above the eyes. I must say it gave me a strange pleasure using that knife to carry on the work my brother had started.

During all those quiet hours, I managed to pry little bits of history out of Robin. His shyness seemed to fall away a little bit with each chip of wood. He got so comfortable with me he even lost his temper when I didn't come up to his standards. "Don't castrate the damned thing!" he yelled out once, though he quickly apologized, said that was one of the warnings Ray used to shout out at him when he was teaching him the fine points of wood-carving. The funny thing is, his voice even sounded like Ray's, as much as I could remember of it, gruffness and humor mixed up all together.

"Ray didn't teach me everything," Robin barked at

me another time when I asked one too many questions, and that quieted me down again. I knew there must have been a lot more to Ray's story, and certainly to their relationship, but some things are best left in the past. My life is surely a testament to that. Besides, watching Robin breathing life into those dry pieces of wood, told me everything I needed to know about my long lost brother. In the end, I came to the conclusion that he wasn't such a bad man after all.

When I first brought up the subject of selling his birds, Robin was stone silent. He glanced up at me from time to time, putting down a chisel, not saying anything at all. I kept bringing it up, badgering him was more like it. "Its about time that you started to take your talents seriously," I scolded him, like he was my own.

And then, without asking permission, I took the liberty of bringing a couple of his woodpeckers and a hawk over to the flea market. Damned if they didn't sell the same day, not priced cheaply either. Robin had to give me credit after that, allowed me to post some signs around town, "Blind Shady Birds" with directions to my property. I got him to admit there was nothing to lose in trying. And sure enough, a couple of weekenders made their way up the twisted dusty path and handed over $75 for a pair of swallows, carved from ponderosa pine.

I'd been mulling it over for so long, I had it all figured out by the time I presented my plan to Pete. Of course he started to fuss when I told him that 80% of all sales would go straight to Robin, but I hushed him up.

"Let's talk about it next week," I said. I had a pretty good feeling about those birds, and sure enough, he sold a couple of owls for $50 apiece, and a falcon for $125, netting him more than he often made in an entire weekend. He actually drew quite a little crowd over to his booth to look at the carvings, holding them up to the light, considering them. Pete figured out pretty fast what he had there. I heard him wheedling one young woman with a starling in her hand. "You can hang that on your Christmas tree, make a great little ornament," he told her, knowing full well that the season of spending was just around the corner. The man is not as dense as he pretends to be.

"And what exactly do you intend to get out of this whole bird business?" Pete asked me, after finally agreeing to a 20% cut of sales.

"Fun!" was all I answered.

"Fun?" Pete never seemed to understand me the first time, made me repeat everything I said at least twice.

"Yes, fun. I find that I really enjoy getting in your way and bossing you around."

Truth is, I can't remember having such a good time with anybody. What it is about the man I can't say. It makes no sense at all, certainly not to me.

"We'll have to have a place to store the birds," I insisted, having already wormed my way over to his side of the hedge, out of curiosity one afternoon. I'd never seen so many old magazines. Not anything he ever read, just whatever he could get his hands on thinking they might bring in money.

"Mildewed Better Homes and Gardens magazines. That should bring in a good price!" I teased him, holding up a stack of weather beaten papers that had appeared to be keeping the back of his garage from falling down. I tossed heaps of them into the back of his pickup without waiting for his approval.

When we were finally able to see the corners of his garage, it turned out to be a pretty decent workspace. I discovered a small window that actually opened (surprised him more than it did me). Once I swept away the thicket of cobwebs, the possibilities started pouring in faster than the freshly added afternoon sun. A couple of perfectly fine metal filing cabinets emerged from beneath a pile of rusted tools, and I was able to clean them up enough to store whatever paperwork we might need to keep track of sales.

I was getting ahead of myself. Robin only has about a dozen birds stocked up and he really can't commit to any kind of steady inventory while he's getting started up in his new job. But when I get an idea in my head I can't be reasoned with. I've already begun to talk to some of the owners of gift shops over on Main Street and one of them has shown some interest. And that's not even counting all the stores back at Pa's place I haven't hit yet.

I call the Roseville house Pa's place now. It just doesn't feel like mine anymore. Pete got a good price on a U-Haul rental, drove me down there to pack up what things I still needed. We lugged out the big easy chair, my bed, a couple of nightstands, just a few doo dads, nothing much.

When Pete saw old Dotty parked in the garage I thought he was going to have a heart attack. "It's not for sale," I announced, before he even asked, because I could practically hear the wheels churning in his head at the thought of what that beauty might bring. Truth is, if I thought he could make that old car run again, I'd give it to him.

I could feel the neighbors' eyes peering at us through slanted window blinds as we trudged up and down the driveway balancing table lamps and suitcases and my old stationary bike that I never used. Pete will get a couple of bucks out of it.

"Why don't you take pictures?" I yelled out at Mrs. What's-Her-Name across the street. She had finally finished painting her house a sickening mint green. Glad I won't have to look at that any more.

Pa's house is all but emptied out. I left the African Violets. See if Harry has better luck with them. I ran into him at Darlene's when I went back over to say goodbye, assuring her I hadn't gone entirely off the deep end. I brought her one of the smaller birds, one I'd polished myself, set it down on her shelf, right between the bottles of hair gel. Turned out Harry was there, big surprise, getting his four strands of hair trimmed. And looking for a place to live since his wife finally kicked him out. It didn't take me long to offer him Pa's place, on a month-to-month basis, at least for the time being. Darlene assures me he'll be good for the rent, making me wonder just how close those two are to each other. The things I don't know about people could fill a book.

Harry's rent check will give me the extra money I need to pay off the back taxes and attorney's fees, little by little, with some left over to pay Robin for some finishing touches around the house. I'd really like to get some new shelving in the tool shed, nothing fancy. Those flowery Mexican tiles in the bathroom would be nice. I'm sick of that hideous brown.

As for Callie, I took her out to lunch the day before they moved. Even met her husband, finally. Not such a bad guy from what I could see. He was holding the baby when I came to the door, reached out and shook my hand real hard, thanking me.

"For what?" I asked.

"For being such a good friend to Callie."

Callie kept her head down for most of the lunch. We picked up sandwiches at Rainbow's End and took them over to the river and sat down close so our feet could dangle in the frothy water. She was working hard to hold back her tears but we still managed to laugh, when I asked about those hair clips I found underneath the old mattress.

"So you knew about me and Robin?" she looked up at me, streaks of tears running down her cheeks.

"I know you two were up to something but that's none of my business, now is it?"

"You ever been married?" she asked, and it was nice to be able to finally tell her all about Ned and me, what fun we had once upon a time when we were about her age.

"Don't be sad for me," I scolded, because my story got her tears working overtime. "Life is full of surprises. Some of them good ones, others not so much."

"I have a surprise," she perked up. "I think I might be pregnant."

I'd had a sense of it for a while now. She'd been dragging that last weekend when we all went to the County Fairgrounds. Looking flushed. A woman knows these things.

"When will you find out for sure?" I asked, wondering why I was so certain of it while she seemed content not to believe it yet.

"I'm going to wait until after we move. Ralph's got so much going on right now, finding a new place for us, getting started up with a new job, some guy he knew from back in high school owns a company that sells motorcycle parts. 'Something there will always be a need for,' he assured me."

"It does seem like he wants what's best for you and Daphne," I said to her, hoping it was true.

"Ralph's a good husband. He really does love me. I just got bored, I guess. I made a big mistake," she started to explain.

"Shhh," I interrupted. I was not interested in confessions on our last outing together. "Here, have some more fruit salad," I offered, handing her a clump of grapes. "And honey, don't ever regret the things you've done. It's a whole lot worse to regret what you haven't done."

Callie put her sandwich down, slid across the rock

she'd been sitting on over to where I had precariously placed juice cups and potato salad, practically knocking the entire picnic into the river. She leaned over and wrapped her arms around me.

"I'm going to miss you Hannah."

Now it was me fighting back the tears.

"Who says I won't come visit you?" I answered her, knowing that probably wasn't going to happen.

"For sure," she answered, her voice trailing off like she had already moved away.

On my way to bed, just a few minutes ago, I took one last look around the porch, like I usually do before heading in, and noticed something sticking out from behind a log. I stepped back down the porch steps and sure enough, just what it looked like, a rubber boot. However had I missed that? I had to wiggle down on my belly to pry it loose from where it had gotten wedged deep underneath the rock. Could this have been Ray's boot? I started to scrape off the mud then stopped. Even in the dark, I could see that the boot had sprouted seedlings. I took it back up onto the porch, set it on a ledge where it would get the first rays of morning sun, just in case the seedlings might decide to grow into something.

I read somewhere, or more likely its one of those little jewels Darlene used to throw at me back when I let her paint my hair with that awful blue dye, that if you open yourself up to new possibilities, the world responds. Hoo haw is what I think of that kind of talk. There's Darlene, clipping purple curls off old ladies' heads, a lot of good opening up to possibilities did for her.

But here I am, a month away from my 70th birthday, and it feels like I'm coming back to life again, for the first time since back when I lost my sweet Ned. Every day I come up with a dozen new ideas for places to peddle Robin's birds. Last week I took a side road for no reason whatsoever and discovered a bakery connected to an organic farm where I can buy orange raisin scones and fresh made fig jam. Who knows what I'll find next week? I figure at the rate I'm moving these days, it'll take me to the end of my life to finish exploring this new life that Ray handed me. What I'd give to be able to thank him. I suppose keeping those birds of his alive is one way to do it.

And Amos! I packed him up as soon as I had made the decision to help out with the kids. I was hoping that they'd play with him, but he's got a field of priorities here that take up all his attention. Mice, gophers, God knows what else, not to mention five acres of litter box all to himself. He's taken to this land like he was born here. He fairly reeks of Kit-kit-dizze now. The twigs stick to his paws, and the smell sticks to my sheets since it's impossible to pry him out from under the covers at the end of a long day of hunting. I brought along his favorite pillow with those awful dangly beads. We lie together at night, curled up in each other's warmth, imagining all the wonderful trouble we might discover when morning comes.

Special thanks to my editor and friend Laura Wine Paster, who helped me breathe life into these characters, insisting that I treat them with respect, even when I felt like abandoning them. Without her guidance, insistence, and insights, this novel would not have come to light.

And to my husband Brooks, whose eye for detail and commitment to integrity helped smooth out the finest wrinkles. Thank you for keeping my creative spirit warm.

About the Author

Adina Sara is the author of *100 Words Per Minute: Tales From Behind Law Office Doors* (Regent Press 2006) and *The Imperfect Garden, A Memoir* (Regent Press 2009). She was the feature garden columnist for *The MacArthur Metro*, a Bay Area newspaper, and her poetry and essays have appeared in various publications including *East Bay Express*, *Oxygen*, *Green Prints* and *Peregrine Press*. She resides in Oakland, California.

Visit her web site at www.adinasara.com.